ACCLAIM FOR JAMES PATTERSON'S HOTTEST SERIES!

PRIVATE L.A.

"*PRIVATE L.A.* IS ONE OF THE MORE CINEMATIC OF PATTERSON'S BOOKS—FITTINGLY SO, GIVEN AT LEAST PART OF ITS SUBJECT MATTER—AND, AS A RESULT, THE STORY IS AN EASY AND COMPELLING ONE-SIT READ... There is plenty to enjoy here, with no question that Patterson's regular and occasional readers, as well as those reading his work for the first time, will be fully satisfied." —BookReporter.com

"A GREAT READ DEVOURED IN ONE SITTING... [I'M] LOOKING FORWARD TO SEE WHAT HAPPENS NEXT FOR JACK MORGAN AND HIS TEAM(S)." —RandomActsofReviewing.com

PRIVATE BERLIN

"PATTERSON HAS ALWAYS BEEN AN EXPERT AT CONCEIVING CHILLING VILLAINS OF HIS MANY PIECES, AND WITH SULLIVAN, HE ACHIEVES NEW HEIGHTS (OR WOULD THAT BE DEPTHS?) OF TERROR WITH THE INVISIBLE MAN. AND WHILE THE STORY PROCEEDS AT BREAKNECK

SPEED…PATTERSON AND SULLIVAN CREATE PLENTY OF SCENES THAT READERS WILL NOT SOON FORGET…*PRIVATE BERLIN* will make you a fan of this wide-ranging and marvelously conceived series, if you are not one already." —BookReporter.com

"FAST-PACED ACTION AND UNFORGETTABLE CHARACTERS WITH PLOT TWISTS AND DECEPTIONS WORTHY OF ANY JAMES PATTERSON NOVEL." —Examiner.com

"ONE OF THE BEST AND MOST ENTHRALLING NOVELS PATTERSON HAS WRITTEN."
—Quick-book-review.blogspot.com

"THIS COMPLEX AND LAYERED EUROPEAN THRILLER GRABS YOU FROM THE START, AND COMPELS YOU TO READ." —TheMysterySite.com

PRIVATE LONDON

"THERE ARE THE USUAL TWISTS AND TURNS AND EVERY TIME YOU THINK YOU HAVE IT FIGURED OUT, ANOTHER WRENCH IS THROWN IN. I WAS CAPTIVATED WITH THE STORY AND READ IT IN ONE SITTING." —AlwayswithaBook.blogspot.com

"REGARDLESS OF PLACEMENT IN THE PRIVATE CANON, *PRIVATE LONDON* MEETS THE HIGH STANDARD ESTABLISHED BY THE OTHER

VOLUMES, AS IT IS LOADED WITH ACTION, TWISTS, TURNS, AND SURPRISES...CERTAINLY ONE OF PATTERSON'S MORE COMPLEX WORKS OF LATE...If you haven't read anything by Patterson for a while, you should give *PRIVATE LONDON* and the Private series a try and acquire a healthy addiction."

—BookReporter.com

"THE STORY CONTINUES ALONG QUITE QUICKLY WITH THE TWO-PAGE CHAPTERS FLYING PAST FASTER THAN YOU CAN IMAGINE. I READ THIS BOOK IN ONLY AN EVENING. If you are a Patterson fan then you will probably enjoy this one as well."

—TheFringeMagazine.blogspot.com

PRIVATE GAMES

"EVEN IF YOU ARE NOT INTERESTED IN THE SUMMER GAMES, YOU WILL WANT TO READ THE BOOK, NOT ONLY FOR ITS THRILL-A-PAGE PLOTTING BUT ALSO FOR THE OPENING DAY SPECTACLE THAT'S ON DISPLAY...*PRIVATE GAMES* SHOWS BOTH PATTERSON AND SULLIVAN TO BE AT THE TOP OF THEIRS."   —BookReporter.com

"ANOTHER FAST-PACED, ACTION-PACKED THRILLER THAT WILL HAVE YOU NOT WANTING TO PUT IT DOWN UNTIL THE VERY LAST PAGE."

—ThePhantomParagrapher.blogspot.com

"[AN] EXCELLENT READ...THE WRITING IS BETTER, THE CHARACTERS MORE DEVELOPED, AND THE STORY MORE SUSPENSEFUL THAN MOST OF THE RECENT JAMES PATTERSON NOVELS...LOOK FOR *PRIVATE BERLIN*."   —TheMysteryReader.com

"PATTERSON, HE OF SIX DOZEN NOVELS AND COUNTING, HAS AN UNCANNY KNACK FOR THE TIMELY THRILLER, AND THIS ONE IS NO EXCEPTION...A PLEASANT ROMP."

—*Kirkus Reviews*

"THIS ONE IS SET UP WITH SHORT CHAPTERS THAT YOU CAN'T HELP [BUT] FLY THROUGH...I REALLY HAVE COME TO ENJOY THE PRIVATE SERIES AND HOPE THIS SERIES CONTINUES FOR A LONG TIME."   —AlwayswithaBook.blogspot.com

PRIVATE: #1 SUSPECT

"BETWEEN THE COVERS OF THE FIRST TWO BOOKS (*PRIVATE* AND *#1 SUSPECT*) IS SOME OF JAMES PATTERSON'S BEST WORK...A PLOT THAT CONTAINS SUBSTANCE WITHOUT SACRIFICING READABILITY AND IS INHABITED BY CHARACTERS WHO ARE SYMPATHETIC AND MULTI-DIMENSIONAL. [THE] CONCEPT AND EXECUTION ARE FLAWLESS... And if someone doesn't latch on to these novels for a television drama, they should find employment in another industry. Jump on now."   —BookReporter.com

"[THEY] MAKE ONE HECK OF A GREAT WRITING TEAM AND PROVE IT ONCE AGAIN WITH [THIS] CLASSY THRILLER, THE LATEST IN A PRIVATE INVESTIGATION SERIES THAT'S SURE TO BLOW THE LID OFF A POPULAR GENRE... If you want to be entertained to the max, you can't go wrong when you pick up a thriller by Patterson and Paetro."

—NightsandWeekends.com

"AN AMAZING STORY FROM A FABULOUS STORY-TELLER."   —MaryGramlich.blogspot.com

"I READ ON THE TREADMILL, AND TOWARD THE END I ALMOST FELL FROM ALL THE CLIFF-HANGERS AND REVELATIONS... CHOCK-FULL OF INTRIGUE, MYSTERY, AND EDGE-OF-YOUR-SEAT TWISTS AND TURNS! I CANNOT *WAIT* FOR THE SEQUEL!"   —ReadingWritingBreathing.com

"*PRIVATE: #1 SUSPECT* STARTED OUT WITH A BANG... LITERALLY. I WAS CAUGHT UP IN THE ACTION FROM PAGE ONE."

—MeMyBookandtheCouch.blogspot.com

PRIVATE

"A QUICK READ WITH SHORT CHAPTERS AND LOADS OF ACTION... DESTINED TO BECOME ANOTHER SUCCESSFUL SERIES IN THE JAMES PATTERSON ARSENAL... If you are a Patterson fan, you will not be disappointed...Jack Morgan is a great protagonist...Bring on even more PRIVATE."

—TheMysteryReader.com

"A FUN AND ENJOYABLE READ...PATTERSON LETS THE READER FEEL LIKE THEY ARE RIGHT THERE IN THE ACTION...It's such a treat knowing there is so much more to explore about [these] characters...He certainly set things up for some explosive action in future novels." —CurlingUpbytheFire.blogspot.com

"*PRIVATE* MIXES ACTION, MYSTERY, AND PERSONAL DRAMA TO CREATE A HIGHLY READABLE AND ENTERTAINING EXPERIENCE. If this first volume is any indication, Patterson and Paetro may well be on their way to rivaling—and possibly surpassing—the popularity of their Women's Murder Club series."

—BookReporter.com

"SLICK AND SUSPENSEFUL IN THE USUAL WELL-RECEIVED PATTERSON STYLE (SUCCINCT AND SIMPLE CHAPTERS, LARGER-THAN-LIFE CHARACTERS, AND A PLETHORA OF SURPRISES)."

—BookLoons.com

"A GREAT READ...FAST-PACED...If you like James Patterson you will be more than happy to add this one to your 'To Be Read' pile." —LuxuryReading.com

"*PRIVATE* WILL HAVE YOU ON THE EDGE OF YOUR SEAT...WITH TWISTS AND TURNS THAT MAKE YOU WANT TO KEEP TURNING THE PAGES."

—ChickwithBooks.blogspot.com

"EXCITING...A GREAT WAY TO SPEND THE AFTERNOON...COMPLEX AND INTERESTING CHARACTERS."

—BibliophilicBookBlog.com

"*PRIVATE* WILL GRAB YOU FROM PAGE ONE AND FORCE YOU TO SIT THERE UNTIL YOU TURN THE VERY LAST PAGE...A GREAT START TO A NEW SERIES FROM THE MASTER OF FAST-PACED THRILL RIDES."

—LorisReadingCorner.com

"THE PACING IS FRENETIC...I REALLY LIKED JACK MORGAN...THE SECOND-TIER CHARACTERS WERE GREAT...an impressive array of detectives and specialists."

—BookHound.wordpress.com

"PATTERSON ALWAYS DELIVERS A GOOD READ, BUT IN THIS CASE IT WAS SO MUCH MORE...YOU ARE ENTERTAINED WITH MULTIPLE STORIES. Somehow Patterson blends them all seamlessly together, never letting the novel skip or jump, always keeping the reader flawlessly on track and riveted. I LOVED THIS BOOK. A FANTASTIC READ!"

—DemonLoversBooksandMore.com

Private Down Under

THE PRIVATE NOVELS

A complete list of books by James Patterson is at the back of this book. For previews of upcoming books and more information about James Patterson, please visit his website or find him on Facebook or at your app store.

Private
Down Under

James Patterson
AND
Michael White

GRAND CENTRAL
PUBLISHING

New York Boston

Copyright © 2014 by James Patterson
Excerpt from *Burn* copyright © 2014 by James Patterson
All rights reserved. In accordance with the U.S. Copyright Act of 1976, the scanning, uploading, and electronic sharing of any part of this book without the permission of the publisher constitute unlawful piracy and theft of the author's intellectual property. If you would like to use material from the book (other than for review purposes), prior written permission must be obtained by contacting the publisher at permissions@hbgusa.com. Thank you for your support of the author's rights.

Grand Central Publishing
Hachette Book Group
237 Park Avenue
New York, NY 10017
www.HachetteBookGroup.com

Printed in the United States of America

RRD-C (split)

Different versions of this book were published as *Private Down Under* by Century, a division of Random House, in the UK in 2013 and *Private Oz* by Random House Australia in 2012.
First Grand Central Publishing edition: August 2014
10 9 8 7 6 5 4 3 2 1

Grand Central Publishing is a division of Hachette Book Group, Inc.
The Grand Central Publishing name and logo is a trademark of Hachette Book Group, Inc.

PRIVATE is a trademark of JBP Business, LLC.

The Hachette Speakers Bureau provides a wide range of authors for speaking events. To find out more, go to www.hachettespeakersbureau.com or call (866) 376-6591.

The publisher is not responsible for websites (or their content) that are not owned by the publisher.

Library of Congress Cataloging-in-Publication Data
Patterson, James.
  Private down under / James Patterson and Michael White. — First Grand Central Publishing edition.
     pages cm
  ISBN 978-1-4555-2976-6 (hardcover, library edition only) /
978-1-4555-2978-0 (trade pbk.) / 978-1-4555-8221-1 (large print trade pbk.) /
978-1-4555-8585-4 (trade pbk., Target stores edition)
1. Private investigators—Australia—Fiction. 2. Murder—Investigation—Fiction. I. White, Michael, 1959– II. Title.
  PS3566.A822P764 2014
   813'.54—dc23   2014002851

Private Down Under

PROLOGUE

I HAD GOOGLED plenty of info on Justine Smith before I met her. Funny thing, though: even the most serious, businesslike websites couldn't resist slipping in how great-looking she was.

Justine Smith, the stunning second-in-command to Jack Morgan at Private L.A. . . .

Justine Smith, well known to the L.A. underworld for her unsurpassed police smarts, is also known to the L.A. paparazzi for her unsurpassed figure and face . . .

I couldn't resist: I pressed the Google Images button and took a tour of some mighty impressive photos. Justine posing with fifteen police officers after a major blow-and-smack bust in Venice Beach; Justine, all businesslike at her desk, with Mayor Garcetti on the other side; Justine in a very snug gray Versace gown at the Oscars.

I was mentally reviewing these images as I waited for her at the Sydney airport Customs arrival. Jack Morgan, perhaps the most important private investigator in the world, was sending her to help me launch Private Sydney, his latest addition to what is probably the most important investigative bureau in the world. Once described by Jack himself as "what Interpol tried to be, what the FBI wants to be, and what the CIA should be."

Private was located in major cities throughout the globe. Now Sydney would house headquarters for the Asia-Pac branch. And Jack Morgan had chosen me, Craig Gisto, to oversee this newest jewel in the Private crown.

Jack Morgan had the resources—both personal and financial—to do it. He installed scientific police and laboratory equipment that went beyond state of the art. He paid university researchers to bring their findings to him first. And Jack Morgan had something else . . .

He had the brains to hire the best people. Yeah, I know that sounds easy, but it doesn't happen much. A lot of CEOs say they *want* the best people, but what they really mean is "I want someone *almost* as good as me" or "someone who's really good . . . at *taking my shit*." Not Jack. He wanted the best. And in his mind, that meant equal amounts of brainpower and guts.

It was a select group, all right, and I was excited, ecstatic, and frankly terrified that Jack Morgan had put me in it. Having Justine help me was another wise move. She knew Private; she knew Jack Morgan. And, watching her—the first passenger out of Customs—I immediately knew one thing: the Google image search had not done her justice.

I held back and let her family greet her first. There was her sister, Greta, and Greta's husband, Brett Thorogood, my new best bud. Brett was the deputy commissioner of New South Wales Police and was nothing but happy to have Private Sydney opening in his town. Brett and Greta's kids—Nikki, eight, and Serge, ten—ran to their aunt Justine. Hugs and kisses all around. Then I stepped forward. I shook Justine's hand. This was going to be one fine partnership.

I'd parked my Maserati GranCabrio in the pickup zone. The Thorogoods headed off after we'd all synchronized watches for the launch party that evening, and we were off, pulling out of the airport and onto the sun-drenched freeway.

Neither of us knew then that we were in the fast lane—the *very* fast lane—headed toward a great big pile of shit.

CHAPTER 1

THAT SAME NIGHT

HE RUNS LIKE a crazy man, a horribly injured crazy man. The stumbling and falling, long strides of a man overwhelmed with pain and fear.

He runs, gasping, then he hits a hard object—face-first. His nose shatters, sending a cascade of blood and snot down his face, agony through his head and down his spine. The man falls back, slams to the floor. His head cracks as he hits the concrete.

He has been deaf since birth. He can sense his frantic heartbeat. The rumbling of his stomach. He feels the blood on his stomach and hips. The blood feels more like a thick syrup than a thin liquid.

He is blind. They have tied a leather sack around his head, fastened it at the neck with wiring and rope. The leather sack is tight and painful and totally immovable from his neck.

He vomits. The vomit starts to fill the leather bag that covers his head. The sack begins to fill with the chunky, nauseating upchuck. He is about to drown in his own hideous diving mask.

The man hits a wall. Literally. He clings to it and suddenly feels a searing pain, a slash in his right thigh. Now two deep wounds shoot into his back. He thinks, *Kidneys.* He also thinks he cannot collapse. If there is salvation it will be entirely due to his own willpower.

He feels the vibration of feet, people running after him. A burst of terrible agony in his back. Two thumps propel him to the wall. He smells fresh blood. He smells tire rubber. Another crunch, his thigh exploding. He keeps to the wall; blood drips from his nose, his leg, his back. He feels wet all over.

I'm not really awake. I'm not really asleep. I am afraid that the pain is so great that something will explode. Like in a mad cartoon, the top of my head will shoot right up and off. The pain will burst out of me like the fire spitting out of a volcano. My eyes have disappeared. They have been replaced by swirling pools of agony. How will I see the long white tunnel of death when it comes to take me away?

He keeps trying to feel his way along the rough cement wall. He moves left. He wills his knees to hold him up. And that works. For a moment. A bullet stings his right earlobe. He keeps moving. Sharp flying pieces of the wall bomb his hands and bare arms. Then another bullet. Now the pain is so encompassing that he is not certain where he's been hit. A new source of burning pain erupts. It is the back of his neck. The new blood and the old vomit mingle.

A doorway. He feels an iron handle. The door opens. He can no longer move from the waist down. The man falls through the open door. He falls headfirst onto a concrete floor. The pain eases. Maybe it's a dream. Maybe they've slipped a painkiller into him. *Maybe*, he thinks. *Maybe*.

He lies there.

Blind. Bloody. Deaf. Dead.

CHAPTER 2

PLEASE EXCUSE MY raging ego, but I think most police types would say that I'm a good private investigator. (After all, Jack Morgan chose me to open and operate Private Sydney.)

Now, please excuse my *really* raging ego, but I think quite a few women would say that I'm a pretty good romancer. (After all, I've sported more than a few fine lady types around the hot pubs of Sydney.)

What can Craig Gisto *not* do? Well, high on the list is *throw a party.* The best I'm capable of is bringing in a few cases of Tooheys Extra Dry, setting out a few bowls of crisps, and hoping for the best.

Well, the kind of party—excuse me... *reception*—I had to give for the official opening of Private Sydney was not the kind of party I usually threw.

So I asked Mary Clarke, my second-in-command,

how I should handle the situation. Mary looked at me as if I'd been born last Tuesday and said, "Hire a caterer and forget about it." Then she added her favorite phrase: "Now why didn't you think of that?"

As is often the case, Mary had the correct solution. Wild Thyme Catering filled the huge atrium reception area of Private Sydney with tables full of cold prawns and rock lobster, skewers of tenderloin chunks, huge bunches of sunflowers. The bar had good Australian Shiraz and even a few tins of ice-cold Tooheys.

As soon as I felt certain that everything was going smoothly, I was hit by a problem. Suddenly a tremendous crashing sound filled the room. At first I thought one of my fancy caterers had dropped a tray of fancy crystal glasses.

I watched as Mary Clarke spun around on her heels in the direction of the crash. Mary's very tall, muscular—a big-boned woman—but she has the reaction speed of an Olympic gold-medal sprinter.

A nanosecond later I turned to see what had happened. I didn't have to look far. A few feet from where I'd been standing was a human figure, facedown on the floor. Blood was pooling around the body. Mary crouched beside him. I knelt, and as the people in the room gasped and turned dead quiet, Mary and I turned the corpse over to reveal a vision of horror: a male with some sort of hood tied over his face. I had seen a few seconds earlier that he had both stab wounds and bullet wounds in his back. Now that he was lying on his back, his right thigh looked like a piece of ragged, jagged, bloody meat.

I looked over for a moment and saw Justine Smith and her brother-in-law, Deputy Commissioner Thorogood, standing over me and the dead man.

"Jesus H. Christ," Thorogood said as I tried in vain to undo the wires and ropes that held the leather hood in place.

"Let me," I heard someone say. It was Private's techno and lab genius, Darlene. My usual picture of Darlene was of a skinny woman in a drab gray lab coat, protective goggles, and a thick, white hairnet. Tonight she was dressed in a snug red silk dress, and "skinny" had turned to "curvy."

She slipped on a pair of latex gloves that she happened to have in her pocketbook, and then—I shouldn't have been surprised—she dug into her bag a little deeper and produced a multifaceted knife. One of those facets was a wire cutter. She cut through the wires and rope quickly, and then Thorogood and I eased the sack from the victim's head.

"Holy fuck!" Justine said. She was speaking for all of us.

The victim's eyes had been gouged out. The sockets were red craters. A gray and beige bundle of nerves oozed from the left one. Nerves stuck to the dry skin. The blood around his neck mixed with—I wasn't sure what it was: a disgusting-smelling brownish-yellow-pink liquid.

As if she could read my mind, Darlene said, "It's vomit."

It was tough to guess the guy's age, but what little amount of skin was left intact was smooth and lightly tanned. He was a young kid, maybe in his late teens. At the most he was twenty years old.

I saw Johnito Ishmah, the youngest guy on my team, standing behind Mary.

"Johnny, get everyone out of here. Everyone." Then I looked at Mary and said, "Come with me." We both stood up as I watched Deputy Commissioner Thorogood pull out his phone. I heard him say, "Inspector..." And I knew his boys would be here in a few minutes.

"Well, not your average gate-crasher," I heard Darlene mumble as Mary and I headed toward the blood-stained service door.

CHAPTER 3

WE OPENED THE door and followed the trail of blood down three flights of stairs.

"How'd he manage to get so far when he had to be so weak from blood loss?" I asked.

"Probably had some people helping him along," Mary said. *Yeah,* I thought, *why didn't I think of that?*

As we approached the first floor, Mary said, "Passage ahead leads to the garage."

Holy shit. The concrete garage walls looked like someone had thrown buckets of red paint on them, almost like a macabre kind of modern art. As we picked our way round the puddles, I leaned on the second door, and we were out, onto garage level 1. Plenty of blood still, oval droplets on the rough concrete. The sort of splashes someone makes when they are running and bleeding at the same time.

The poor kid had stopped here; blood had pooled into a patch about two feet wide that was rippling away toward a drain in the floor. The trail led off to the left. Three cars stood there: a Merc, a Prius, and my black Mas. Tire marks close to the bend, more blood.

I bent down and picked up a shell casing, holding it in the tissue still in my hand.

".357 Sig," Mary said. She was ex–military police, knew a thing or two.

"Pros."

Mary surveyed the ceiling. "They've got cameras everywhere," she said.

"The guard at the gate has the security-camera monitors." I led the way to the guard booth, and I found exactly what I was afraid of. The place had been hit.

Glass everywhere, the guard slumped unconscious but not dead, a row of monitors an inch from his head. The cable to a hard drive was dangling. Standard system—record the garage for twelve-hour rotations on a terabyte hard drive. Wipe it, start again.

"They took the hard drive," Mary said, nodding at the lead.

I crouched down beside the guard and lifted his head gently. He stirred, pulled back, and went for his gun. Of course, the gun was gone too.

"Whoa, buddy!" Mary exclaimed, palms up.

The guy recognized me. "Mr. Gisto." He ran a hand over his badly bruised forehead.

"Easy, pal." I placed a hand on his shoulder. "Do you remember anything?"

He sighed. "Couple of guys in hoodies. It happened so bloody fast..."

"All right," I said, turning to Mary.

There was a sudden movement beyond the booth window. I looked up to see a cop in a power stance, finger poised on the trigger.

A moment later Deputy Commissioner Thorogood appeared in the doorway. Thorogood touched the officer's arm. "Put it down, Constable."

It was then that I saw a third guy. He was standing next to Thorogood. Average build, five ten, with a cold, lived-in face. I recognized him immediately and felt a hard jolt of painful memories. I was absolutely sure the guy recognized me also. But he stood motionless, expressionless.

Yep, he was still the same devious son of a bitch.

CHAPTER 4

A COP CAR screeched to the entrance gate. Right behind it was a van with the word FORENSICS on its side.

Outside, Thorogood made the introductions. He was
oblivious to the animosity that was starting to fill the air.
"This is Craig Gisto and Mary Clarke, Private Sydney—
a new investigative agency started by a friend of mine,
Jack Morgan, in L.A. These guys head up the Sydney
branch. Craig, Mary, this is Inspector Mark Talbot, Sydney Local Area Command."

Mary extended her hand. Talbot didn't shake it.

"And what exactly are they doing here?" Talbot
looked straight at me as he spoke. I half smiled back.

"We have an arrangement . . . ," Thorogood responded.

"Arrangement, sir?"

"I sent an e-mail, for God's sake. We help Private, Private helps us. Understand?" Thorogood didn't wait to

hear if Talbot understood. Instead he turned to me and said, "So, what do we have here, Craig?"

"Lotta blood. Your forensics guys'll have fun. The hard drive for the security cameras in the booth walked." I motioned with my thumb toward the booth. "And I found this." I pulled the tissue from my jacket pocket and handed the bullet casing to Thorogood.

"That should have been left where you found it," Talbot said.

Thorogood ignored the inspector. He looked hard at the casing and said, ".357 Sig. Okay, so what do you and Mary want from us?"

"Give Darlene access to the crime scene and ten minutes with the body before it's taken to the morgue," Mary said.

Thorogood nodded. "Fine."

"That's bullshit!" Talbot exclaimed, and glared at us. Then he saw Thorogood's expression—icy and pissed off.

Talbot shut up. But I knew it wouldn't be for long.

CHAPTER 5

DARLENE'S LAB STOOD just off the atrium corridor where Private Sydney's launch party had been. It was Darlene's own little kingdom. In spite of the grim work she often dealt with, in here she felt relaxed, isolated from the troubles of the outside world.

She had designed the lab herself and been given carte blanche to install the best equipment available. Better still, through her contacts, she had some technology no one beyond Private would see for years to come. Frankly, there was no one in Australia—perhaps even in the States—who was as superb at this job as Darlene.

She was completely revved up to deal with the grotesque, uninvited corpse from the party. Police Forensics had worked through the night and cataloged everything before passing on the samples to Darlene an hour ago. A courier had delivered a case of test tubes and a USB at six a.m. She'd already been at Private for an hour.

She opened the clasps of the sample box and looked inside. Each test tube was labeled and itemized by date, location, and type. They contained samples of the corpse's blood, scrapings from beneath his fingernails, individual hairs from his jacket. She had put together a collection of her own photographs and a file from the police photographer.

There was no ID on the body. The victim was male, Asian, between eighteen and twenty-one years old. Both eyes had been hacked out with a sharp instrument. It was clearly not a professional job. By the condition of the wound, it was done at least thirty-six hours before death. The sockets were infected. His clothes were thick with filth. They stank of sweat, urine, and excrement. He'd probably been wearing them for days, held captive someplace. But the jacket he'd worn was expensive — Prada. His hair had been well cut, maybe two weeks ago. This was a rich kid.

So it seemed likely they were looking at kidnapping, Darlene thought. Maybe the kid had escaped his captors. Maybe he'd stopped being useful. Maybe the family had refused...No way of knowing—yet.

She removed seven test tubes from the case and walked over to a row of machines on an adjacent bench, each device glistening, new. She slotted the test tubes into a metal rack, pulled up a stool, switched on the machines, and listened to the whir of computers booting up and electron microscopes coming on line.

The first test tube was labeled "Nail Scraping. Left *digitus secundus manus*." With the tweezers, she slid out the piece of material. It was a couple of millimeters square, a blob of blue and pink. She placed it on a slide, lowered a second rectangular piece of glass over it, and positioned it in the crosshairs of the microscope.

The image was a yellowish white. Set to a magnification level of x1,000, human flesh looked like a blanched moonscape. She tracked the microscope to the right and refocused. It looked almost the same; only the details were different. She set the tracking going again, back left, past the starting position. Refocused. Paused. Sat back for a second, then peered into the eyepiece once more. "Now, that's just weird," she said.

CHAPTER 6

AS I PULLED into the parking lot of Private, I wiped away a trickle of sweat running down my cheek. My car's thermometer read ninety-two degrees. Then, as I eased into my parking spot, my cell phone rang. I guessed that it was Darlene. I guessed right.

"Hey, Darlene. What did you find out?"

"The police have ID'd the victim. His name's Ho Chang, nineteen, left Shore School last year. His father is Ho Meng, a very well-known and very wealthy importer-exporter. The boy was reported missing more than two days ago."

"Well, that's something."

"I found out some other stuff too."

"Great...what?"

"I'd rather show you—in the lab."

"See you in a minute."

I got to Reception and was surprised to find Mary and Johnny waiting for me. It was only eight a.m. I was even more surprised to see a tall man in a finely tailored silk suit standing with them. Beside him stood a guy in a gray suit. A bodyguard, I guessed. He had that certain boneheaded look about him. And his suit was neither silk nor finely tailored.

Johnny nodded to me and exited. Then Mary said, "Craig, this is Mr. Ho Meng. Mr. Ho, my boss, Craig Gisto."

We shook hands.

"I just heard the sad news," I said. "Please accept my..."

He raised a hand, shaking his head slowly.

I stopped talking. Then I said that we should go to my office.

Mary and Ho sat on opposite ends of my sofa, and I pulled round a chair. Meanwhile the bonehead stood by the door, arms folded.

"Mr. Ho and I have met before," Mary began. She was wearing cargo pants and a tight, short-sleeved black T-shirt that accentuated the girth of her arms. "Mr. Ho was a commissioner in the Hong Kong Police Force. I met him when he delivered a special lecture at the Military Police College a few years back."

"I would like you to find my son's killer," Ho responded. His voice was remarkably refined. I guessed Oxford or Cambridge.

"I assume the police are—"

"I do not trust the Australian police, Mr. Gisto."

I watched him. He'd drifted off into grief for a second, but then his expression hardened, and he spoke again.

"My son was reported missing more than two days ago. His death was preventable. The police did nothing."

"I'm sure they tried."

"Please do not make excuses for them, Mr. Gisto." He held his hand up again. "They're either incompetent, lazy, or lacking resources. Whatever it is, I won't work with them."

Mary, of course, realized that I didn't want to get into a debate on this subject.

"Mr. Ho, what can you tell us about your son? Any clues how he got into this trouble?" Mary asked.

He sighed. "Chang was a wonderful boy. Headstrong, for sure. Like his father. He was profoundly deaf but struggled for independence. He was a highly accomplished reader of lips. Insisted he have his own apartment as soon as he left school."

"He was deaf?" I said, surprised.

Ho nodded. "From birth." He glanced at Mary. "Listen. I would be the first to admit that I've not always been a model father. Chang's mother died twelve years ago. I've been obsessed with my business. I could never find the time. I shouldn't have let him leave home so young."

"When did you last see your son?" I asked.

"Thursday night. A family dinner—rare—at Rockpool." I knew Rockpool, the most expensive restaurant in Sydney.

"So that would be three days ago?"

"Yes. I went to his apartment on Friday morning. He wasn't there. I tried to SMS him, e-mailed him. Nothing. I reported him missing by late afternoon."

Another glance toward the window.

"The police called me just after midnight, when they'd identified Chang's body. I went to the morgue at six this morning." His voice was brittle. "I saw what they did to him." He looked at Mary, then at me, his face like a mannequin's. "You have to find the killer, Mr. Gisto. I am a very wealthy man. It matters little to me what it costs."

CHAPTER 7

DEPUTY COMMISSIONER THOROGOOD was coming into Reception just as I was escorting Ho Meng and his bodyguard to the elevators.

Thorogood and I then walked silently back to my office.

"That was the father of the murdered kid," I said as we sat down. "He's mighty pissed with your people."

Thorogood's face creased into a frown.

"He can't understand why you didn't save his boy."

"So he's come to you?"

I nodded. I could tell that Thorogood was trying to remain calm.

"Well, you know our agreement, Craig. We share intel."

"He doesn't want to talk to the police."

The deputy commissioner blanched, anger in his

eyes. "Well, it's not up to him, is it?" he snapped. "If he's withholding evidence..."

I let it go, went to change the subject. There was a knock on the door. Darlene poked her head round. "Bad time? You said you'd——"

"Sorry, Darlene," I said quickly. "Come in."

"Deputy Commissioner, you've met Darlene Cooper, haven't you?"

He stood up, extended a hand. "We...ah...met last night at the..."

Darlene gave the man a brief smile. The girl was a cool paradox, beautiful *and* brilliant—a nerd who would also look great in a *Sports Illustrated* swimsuit edition. She'd done the whole modeling shtick for a year after finishing her degree in forensics at Monash, became a disciple of Sci, Jack Morgan's resident lab genius at Private L.A. Then she'd come back to Oz and helped us establish Private Sydney.

"You wanted to know the latest," she began, before flashing her baby blues at the deputy commissioner.

"Absolutely," I said.

She handed me a couple of sheets of paper. They were covered with graphs and numbers. I turned them sideways, then back again.

"Analysis of skin samples and DNA," she explained.

"Oh, great."

"That was bloody quick!" Thorogood said.

"So, what're your conclusions?" I asked.

"I took a range of samples from the body. Unfortunately I haven't been able to get any prints, but I found three distinct DNA profiles. One of these is certainly the victim's."

"No luck finding a match for the other two?" Thorogood asked.

Darlene shook her head. "Nothing close on any database."

"Anything else?" I asked.

"Well, yeah, actually. I took a sample of material from under Ho Chang's fingernails." She handed me a photograph. I stared at it for several moments, passed it to Thorogood. He sat back, held the photo up to the light.

"It's human skin. I suspect there was a serious struggle. Ho must have taken a chunk out of the other guy."

"But what's the blue?" Thorogood asked, studying the image. It showed a highly magnified, ragged rectangle of skin. One corner was dark blue.

"Stumped me," Darlene replied, "for a few seconds. Then I realized it was probably a bit of a tattoo."

Thorogood looked at Darlene, back at the picture.

"Very clever," I said.

"Oh, I'm even cleverer than that."

I shot a glance at Thorogood, who was now giving Darlene a skeptical look.

"I took a sample and ran it through a gas chromatograph that separates out the constituents of a blend. Tattoo ink is a cocktail of many different ingredients. The gas chromatograph pulls these away from each other and gives a readout to show everything that makes up the blend. This is what I got."

I took another sheet of paper from my science whiz.

It showed a graph with different-colored bars lined up across the paper.

"There were forty-seven different elements in the ink—vegetable dyes, traces of solvent, zinc, copper. But one thing stood out."

I handed the sheet to Thorogood.

"An unusual level of antimony," she said.

We both looked at Darlene blankly.

"Only Chinese tattooists use that type of ink."

She paused, then said: "It's commonly found in the tattoos of members of the..."

Darlene paused again, perhaps for dramatic effect. But I always predict the worst. So I finished the sentence for her.

"The Triad gang," I said. It was a good guess. Unfortunately.

Darlene nodded. Thorogood said, "Oh, shit." And suddenly my mind was racing as if it were on fire.

I was suddenly dealing with a ritual murder *and* the most notorious gang on the continent of Australia.

As if I didn't have enough chaos on my hands, Thorogood unknowingly brought up another problem.

"Darlene, please text this info ASAP to Inspector Talbot," he said.

Inspector Talbot. Inspector Mark Talbot. I had forgotten for a while that he was my assigned municipal police contact on the case.

He was also my cousin. He was also in love with the woman I married.

CHAPTER 8

IT WAS A perfect Sydney morning. Pristine blue sky, not a cloud in sight, a crispness to the air that made you kid yourself that everything was right with the world. Even the traffic was light, for seven a.m. I had the roof down on the old Porsche convertible I'd bought fifth-hand ten years before.

We were en route to the airport. Becky, my wife of nine years, our three-year-old son, Cal, and I. Becky looked amazing. She was wearing a diaphanous dress and a thick rope of fake pearls. She was tanned from the spring sunshine. When she moved her hands, the collection of bangles on her wrists jangled. She'd put on a bit of weight and looked better for it. We'd made love that morning while Cal was asleep, and I could still visualize her.

I was ever grateful that I'd ended up with Becky as my wife. It was a tale that started with tragedy and turned into joy.

You see, when I was an eight-year-old lad in London, my crackhead mum died on the streets of Hackney. The grown-ups bundled me off to my uncle Ben Talbot in Australia. From the dreariest place in the world to the sweetest land on earth. It might have been heaven except for Uncle Ben's devil of a ten-year-old son, Mark. He hated me from the start; I was an unwelcome intruder, and Mark showed it by using my head as a human speed bag.

I was set free at eighteen, when I went to college to study law. In my second year I joined an exchange program with UCLA, spent a year in the States. It was the best year of my life.

When I returned home to Oz at Easter, Mark and a sweet chick named Becky were having an engagement party. Mark seemed a bit nicer, a bit friendlier. And his wife-to-be seemed—well, she seemed too good for him. When Becky and I began to talk, the old Mark came out of hiding. He accused me of trying to seduce his fiancée, and Becky accused him of being crazy, and so we ended up tearing into each other. Becky, who now saw Mark in the fullness of his madness, ended up calling off the engagement.

I never saw Becky again. Well, not *never*. Nine years after Mark's engagement party Becky, Cal, and I were on our way to holiday. Sweet Jesus, I was a lucky man.

I glanced around and saw her long auburn hair blown back by the warm breeze. She was excited about our trip to Bali. We all were—our first holiday in two years. I'd been working hard to build up my PI agency, Solutions, Inc., and I was only now able to take a week off, splash some cash on a fancy resort.

I'd woken up that morning feeling more relaxed than I had in years. I'd had nice dreams too. I was back on our wedding day. Nine years before. It was a bittersweet occasion. I'd bumped into Becky by chance one morning at Darling Harbour. The old spark was there; we were both single. It just happened. We were meant for each other. Within a year we were married.

Mark must've heard I was with Becky, but, seeing as I hadn't spoken to him since my second year in college, I had no idea what he'd thought about it. Though it was his craziness that brought it on, he would never forgive me for what happened at his party. But, hell, it was such a long time ago.

Cal was strapped in the back, a suitcase next to him. On top of that was the brightly colored Kung Fu Panda carry-on bag he planned to wheel to the plane and put in the overhead locker. He'd not flown before, but I'd told him all about it the previous night in lieu of a bedtime story. Cal had the same auburn hair as his mother, the same eyes. In fact, there wasn't much immediately obvious about his looks that confirmed he was mine. But he definitely had my temperament—patient and calm but vicious when riled.

"So, you looking forward to the trip, little man?" I called to Cal over the noise of the road and the wind and the powerful engine. "I know I am."

He nodded. I saw him in the rearview mirror, a big smile across his face, baby teeth gleaming.

"What you looking forward to most, Cal?"

He thought for a moment, forehead wrinkled. Then hollered: "Catching fish!"

I glanced over at Becky, and we both laughed. I turned back and saw the pickup truck on the wrong side of the road, coming straight for us. And I knew immediately that this was the end. I could feel Becky freeze beside me, watched as the ugly, great vehicle covered the distance between us. With each vanishing yard, I felt my life—our lives together—drain away.

CHAPTER 9

I DON'T REMEMBER the impact—no one ever does, do they? The horror began when I started to open my eyes. But at first, everything was blurred, and I was stone-deaf. I just saw colored shapes. Then my hearing came back—but I couldn't make out a single human sound. Instead, a loud, shrill whine, the engine freewheeling in neutral.

I felt a *drip, drip, drip* on my face.

My car had rolled and ended up driver's side to the tarmac. I could see a shape close to—almost on top of—me. Gradually my vision cleared enough to make it out. Becky's face. Her dead eyes open, staring at me...droplets of her blood falling onto my cheek.

I tried to scream, but nothing came out. I couldn't speak, just produced animal noises in my throat. Tried to pull away, horrified. I turned my head slowly. A pain shot down my spine. I could just see Cal in the back. He'd slumped to the side, body contorted.

I managed to twist in the seat and had the presence of mind to feel for Becky's pulse. Then I saw the cut in her neck. She was almost decapitated.

I felt vomit rise up, and I spewed down my front. I thought I'd choke, and a part of me wished I would. I could visualize the new life if I were to survive. A life alone, my family gone... *just like that.*

I turned back to Cal, unbuckled my seat belt, gained enough leverage to slither into the rear of the car.

"Cal? Cal?" My voice broke. "Aggghhh!" I screamed again. Another stream of vomit welled up and out. I started to cry.

"Cal?" I pulled him up. His head lolled, blood trickling from the side of his mouth.

I thought I saw his eyelids flicker. "Cal?" I shouted again. I got his wrist, pulled it up, tried to find a pulse. His arm wet with blood. My fingers wet with blood. No pulse.

"CAL... CAL." I shook him.

I reached for my cell, pulled it from my jacket, but it fell to pieces in my hand.

There's a gap in my memory after that. Next thing I knew I was clambering through the passenger window. The buckled window frame and remnants of glass were cutting me open, but I didn't care. I landed on the road, guts churning, blood in my eyes diluted by tears flowing down my cheeks. I groaned—a primordial sound.

There was a revolting smell—gas, rubber...I managed to get to my knees, leaned on the car and pulled myself into a hunched, twisted figure, feeling like an octogenarian suddenly. The front of the pickup truck stood ten feet away, hood crumpled, windshield smashed. I could see the top of the driver's head above the steering wheel.

I shuffled over. From far off came the sound of sirens.

The door of the truck fell away as I yanked on the handle, and I just managed to step back before it landed at my feet. It was an old, screwed-up wagon. The driver hadn't been wearing a belt. His face was smashed in, spine snapped. A vertebra protruded from his shirt back.

I leaned in, caught the smell of alcohol. Then I saw the can of beer on the floor of the passenger side. It lay in a puddle of foaming liquid.

Fury hit me in a way I'd never experienced before or since. It was pure, all consuming. I grabbed the guy's hair, yanked his head back. His features were just recognizable. He was maybe twenty-five, blond, little goatee.

I felt the vomit rise again, but this time I held it down, lifted my fist, smashed it into the dead driver's face. I hit him again and again. "BASTARD! AAGGGHH! MOTHERFUCKER!"

I kept hitting him and hitting him, the dead man's shattered head lifelessly falling back and forth.

Then I felt a hand on my shoulder.

"Stop it, Craig," a man said.

I was in so much pain. I was so exhausted. I

stopped on command. My vision was blurred. I could tell that it was a cop talking, but I couldn't make out the features.

"You're lucky to be alive, mate," the cop said.

I heard the words, but they didn't really register. I managed to turn my head a little to the left, then the right.

I looked at the face, focused. *Shit, man!* It was my cousin Mark. Mark fucking Talbot.

Strangely, I didn't care. Mark didn't matter. Nothing mattered. Becky and Cal were dead. Mark shouted toward the ambulance.

"Let's get a gurney over here. One victim's still alive!" Mark yelled. Then, with a smirk, he looked down at me and spoke very softly.

"You smashed that driver's face to a pulp," Talbot went on.

I didn't care what he said. It was not worth the pain to try to respond.

He spoke again. "But you've always been lucky, Craig. A lucky man you are. Sure, you smashed the lorry driver's face up. But . . ." He lifted a thin, beige folder into view. "Forensics preliminary report. The driver died on impact."

I didn't care. I was alive, but I wanted to be dead. Three emergency medics eased me onto the rolling stretcher. They carefully wheeled me toward the ambulance.

Mark started to walk away. Suddenly he stopped. He walked back to me and leaned in close to my ear.

"You got what you deserved, you fucker. And you'll go to hell."

Then he was gone.

And I didn't care.

CHAPTER 10

THE VIEW OF Darling Harbour from the top floor of the Citadel Hotel was breathtaking. When Justine Smith walked into the room, her beauty totally dwarfed the beauty of the view. Luxurious room, shimmering evening sun. A fabulous woman in a fabulous room. Sliding doors opened onto a walled deck, a Jacuzzi sunk into the balcony.

She'd naively hoped that the opening of the Sydney branch of Private would offer some welcome relief from the usual death and destruction back home in L.A. Fat chance!

She kicked off her shoes and walked into the bedroom. The air-con was set to the perfect temperature, the bedding turned back, an Adora chocolate truffle placed on the pillow. The room smelled faintly of orange.

Unbuttoning her blouse, she turned and caught her

reflection in a wall of mirrors. Slipping off her skirt, bra, and panties, she stood naked and considered her body.

"Not bad, baby," she said. Did a half turn to her left. She had a narrow waist, a flat tummy, firm breasts. "Gotta be some benefits from eating nothing and having no bambini, I guess." She did a pirouette and headed for the bathroom.

Then she changed her mind. Pulling on a robe, she went back into the main room, slid open the doors, and felt the crisp heat. A refreshing breeze came in over the harbor. She strode to the chest-high wall, admired the view.

Two minutes later, Justine was naked and immersed in bubbles, a glass of Krug on the side of the Jacuzzi. "God! This is the life!" she said aloud, and rested her head against the soft cushioning behind her neck. With her eyes closed, she reached for the champagne flute, brought it over, and let the bubbles tickle the inside of her mouth.

Her cell rang.

She groaned, and a voice in her head said *Ignore it*. But that wasn't in her nature. She lifted herself from the Jacuzzi, padded over to the phone wet and naked.

She saw the name on the screen—GRETA. Stabbed the green button.

The first thing she heard was sobs.

"Greta! What is it?"

Something unintelligible.

"Hey, sis—slow down."

More sobs. Finally, a sentence. "Oh, Justine. One of my friends has just been murdered."

CHAPTER 11

JOHNNY ISHMAH AND I were in my office, reviewing the police report on the Ho kid.

Johnny was only twenty-three, not much older than the victim. He was born in Lebanon and came over here with poor immigrant parents when he was three. Johnny could have ended up a criminal or dead, but he was smart and got out of the ghettos of Sydney's western suburbs. Fridays, Saturdays, and Sundays, he worked as a bungee-jump instructor. At night he was working on a psychology degree. And, in case the bungee-jumping job wasn't dangerous enough, all his other time was spent at Private Sydney. I trusted Johnny, and trust is always top of my list when it comes to the job.

"There are two Ho boys, right. Dai and Chang. Chang's the younger by three years," Johnny said. "The mum died when he was seven. Rich businessman father, probably never home."

I nodded. "Severely disturbed by his mother's death?"

"Definitely. His deafness made him determined to prove to his father he's every bit as good as the older brother."

The phone rang.

"Justine—" I began, and she cut over me. Johnny could see my expression darken. He raised a questioning eyebrow.

"What!" I exclaimed. "How long ago? All right, we'll go to the Thorogoods' place together. I'll pick you up in five. The Citadel Hotel, right?"

"What's up?" Johnny asked as soon as I clicked off.

I was already out of my chair. "A woman named Stacy. She was a really good friend of Justine's sister, Greta."

"Christ!"

"The cops are all over the street."

"What's the neighborhood?"

"Bellevue Hill. A very convenient location."

"Whaddaya mean?"

"The slaughter took place on a fancy, quiet street, just across from Deputy Commissioner Thorogood's house."

CHAPTER 12

I SPED OUT of the garage and pulled onto George Street. I checked my watch: 6:57 p.m. The city was packed with shoppers, bargain hunting in the January sales.

The heavy traffic threw me slightly off schedule. It took me eight minutes, not five, to pick up Justine, who was waiting in the drive-through outside the hotel. It was impossible not to register how amazing she looked: white linen pants, a tight beige top, her slightly damp hair flowing over her shoulders.

We merged with the highway traffic. "Did your sister offer any details?" I asked, and I tried to put out of my mind the intoxicating smell of Givenchy Dahlia Noir perfume that wafted toward me.

"She was a mess. She could barely speak."

I drove east down Park Street and onto William Street, and we fell silent. I could hear a siren far off.

Bellevue Hill is mostly old money, with a sprinkling of nouveau business gurus and gangsters. The Thorogoods' house was an ultramodern place that backed onto the Royal Sydney Golf Club. Its wide, glass-balustraded balconies offered views east, toward the ocean.

I followed Justine up the granite path.

Greta, eyes moist, mascara totally messed up, opened the door before we reached it and beckoned us in.

"Tell us what happened," Justine said as her sister fell into her arms. We walked into a vast living room and sat in a horseshoe of low-slung white leather sofas.

"It was about six o'clock. Brett telephoned me. He was on his way home. He said there was a 'problem' in the neighborhood and I should stay in the house. I had heard sirens, and then I saw the blue and red police lights. Then squad cars pulled up...just over there." Greta pointed through the window. "Brett asked me if I knew what was happening, and, of course, I didn't. And then he said again that it was probably better if I stayed inside. I agreed, but then...I thought... *The kids are both on sleepovers. What the hell?* I snuck out."

Her face froze for a second. She looked at us, her eyes watering. "I wish I hadn't." She swallowed hard. "Stacy's got three kids...There was blood everywhere." She broke down, and Justine encircled her in her arms, letting her younger sister sob into her shoulder.

"Greta," I said, as sympathetically as I could, "is there anything at all unusual about Stacy? Anything that could suggest she would be targeted?"

She looked lost. "No. Stace was just a regular mum.

We got to know each other through the school. Her eldest son's the same age as Serge."

"Okay, Greta, I know this might sound insensitive, but were Stacy and her husband happy?"

She shook her head. "Craig, please! I'm upset, but I'm not stupid! My husband *is* the deputy commissioner!"

"Yeah . . . sorry."

"As far as I know, Stacy and David are—*were* happy. You never can tell, though, right?"

I glanced at Justine. "I'm going to . . ." Flicked my head toward the street. Justine nodded and turned back to her sister.

As I walked down the front path, I kept thinking of Greta's question: "You never can tell, though, right?"

CHAPTER 13

IT WAS EARLY evening, but the summer sun, along with the glow of headlights and police floodlights, made it look like midday. I jogged down a side alleyway.

The end of the lane was cordoned off with crime-scene tape. A cop was standing just to my side of it. I showed him my ID. He glanced at it, then asked me to wait a moment. Two minutes later, he was back with a young guy I'd seen with Thorogood last night.

"Is the deputy commissioner around?" I asked.

"He just left for HQ, Mr. Gisto. Inspector Talbot's given you the green light, though." He offered little more than a nod, lifting the tape to indicate I should follow him.

I could see the back of a car in the alley. It was a new Lexus SUV, an LX 570. All the car doors were opened. The intense white of the floodlights lit up the number plate: STACE. Forensics was already there—blue-suited figures picking and poking around.

I walked toward the driver's side. The dead woman was strapped into the front seat. The seat had been lowered back, almost to a completely horizontal position.

Mark Talbot saw me and came over. "I'm only agreeing to you being here because Thorogood insisted," he said woodenly, and lifted his cell to indicate that he'd just spoken to his boss.

I wanted to say, "Who gives a fuck about your opinion?" but I held my tongue, ignored him, and walked over to the body. The woman's face was disfigured with fifty or more cigarette burns, all over her cheeks and down her neck.

She was, I guessed, early forties, with a blondish bob, a well-preserved figure, smooth skin. All that moisturizing and sunscreen had helped, I guessed. She wore an expensive watch. There was a big diamond—my guess? four carats—next to a simple gold wedding band. She was dressed in a flimsy pink cotton dress. Someone had placed a green sheet over her from the abdomen down. I still wasn't sure of the cause of death.

"Tortured and then stabbed repeatedly in the back," Mark Talbot said, and pulled the woman forward. A mess of congealed blood, three—no, four long, black gashes.

"What's with the sheet?" I asked.

"Look for yourself."

I pulled aside the fabric—and took a step back.

CHAPTER 14

"WELL, YOU ALL know the basic story," I said as I walked into the conference room. "A close friend of Greta Thorogood was tortured and killed a few yards from Brett and Greta's front door. Bizarre MO."

I looked around the table. I'd called in the entire team, plus Justine.

Yeah, they already knew the basics of the homicide. Bad news travels fast.

"Let's see if anything I have brings something to the party—you should excuse my choice of words."

I flicked a remote, and the blinds closed. A second touch on the rubber pad, and a flat-screen lit up at the far end of the room. "I shot this on my phone."

My homemade video was a jumbled mess at first, but then it settled down as I steadied my hand and set the phone to Stabilize Video.

The inside of the victim's car.

"Stacy Fleetwood," I said flatly, as the horrific image of the dead woman appeared. "She was murdered sometime around five thirty yesterday evening in the car alley next to her house in Bellevue Hill. Facially disfigured and stabbed four times in the back as she got out of her vehicle. She was then returned to the car...postmortem." The camera moved to show the dead woman straight on. I had panned down, zoomed in.

"Get ready for some terrible shit," I said.

The camera revealed that the victim's lower garments had been removed, her legs spread wide. A bunch of money had been inserted into her vagina. You could see the golden yellow of Australian fifty-dollar bills.

The video ended. The blinds came up. No one spoke.

I looked round the room. Darlene was staring straight at me. Justine studied the table. Mary was still glaring at where the image had been a few seconds ago. Johnny was counting his shoes.

"Not nice, I know, but there you have it."

"Pretty fucking sick, actually," Mary said with a steely look.

"Yep. Certainly is," I said. "Pretty fucking sick."

"What've the police found out?" Darlene asked.

"Not a lot. Their forensics people have promised to get a complete set of crime-scene samples over to you by midmorning. Thorogood is being very cooperative. I guess Greta is putting pressure on him to keep us fully involved."

"So am I, Craig," Justine remarked. "Brett's subscribing to the idea that two heads are better than one. He knew Stacy too. He's genuinely upset."

"So what now?" said Mary.

"Darlene, you go to work on the samples soon as they arrive," I said.

She nodded.

"Justine, you and I should take a trip to the police morgue. Find out anything we can."

"Can I say something?" Johnny asked.

"Of course," I answered.

"I've got a very nasty feeling that the unfortunate Stacy Fleetwood is only the first victim."

"What makes you think that?" I asked, swiveling my chair.

"Because—and Justine will verify this," Johnny began, glancing over to where she sat, "the murder was ritualistic."

Justine nodded solemnly.

"So?" I persisted. And Justine elaborated.

"One-off murders are a type—the most common sort. Someone dies in a violent crime—a bank raid, a gang killing, domestic violence: collateral damage. Or people are slaughtered clinically: revenge, jealousy. But this one, a woman who's tortured, killed, dumped in her car, and has her vagina stuffed with banknotes, is not the victim of a spontaneous act. It was planned, and everything about it has meaning. I hope it's not the case, but I think Johnny's right—Stacy Fleetwood is just the first."

CHAPTER 15

I CALLED MARY over as the rest of the team filed out.

"What's up?"

"The Ho murder. You gotta stay on that too. Darlene's found some interesting stuff."

"Yeah, I heard…the Triad gang. You're thinking drugs?"

"Possibly, but from what Ho Meng said, his son was hardly the sort."

"And Darlene found no evidence he was a user—totally clean."

"Maybe the kid was dealing."

"Well, yeah. Maybe, but it might not be drugs; the Triads are involved in all sorts of shit."

"Maybe it wasn't the son," Mary replied. "What about the father? Could've been something to do with him. I'd be surprised, but we have to consider it."

"It crossed my mind. I don't think Mr. Ho gave us everything he had yesterday."

"I agree."

I looked at Mary. I'd known her for years, and I knew she had a soft side, but I think only a handful of people had ever seen it.

"You know the guy a little. Reach out to him," I suggested. "Find out if he has connections with the Triads."

"He must. But he won't like us asking about it."

"No, he won't," I replied. "But that's too goddamn bad. He needs reminding that if he wants us to find his son's killer, we have to have every single thing he can give us—not just about Chang, but about himself too."

She nodded and looked straight into my eyes.

"You okay with that, Mary? The Triads are not nice."

"Oh, please! I'm a big girl, and I thrive on not nice."

CHAPTER 16

I KNOW THIS from way too much experience: all morgues smell the same.

The scent of the New South Wales police morgue in Surry Hills, a couple of miles from the central business district, was no different. A mixture of chemicals, blood, and heartbreak.

A tall, fiftyish-looking man with a gray beard and round tortoiseshell eyeglasses met us in the small, overlit anteroom. A pass was clipped to his lapel—photo and name, Dr. Hugh Gravely. Yeah, I know. Very appropriate name.

Dr. Gravely was friendly enough and showed Justine and me into the main part of the morgue. The ceiling and the room were lit brightly by fluorescent strips. The stink was much more intense here.

Stacy Fleetwood lay on the slab. Gray skin, wet hair

pulled back, a red, crudely restitched Y-shaped incision on her upper torso. She would have been a very handsome woman yesterday.

I suddenly felt like I needed to sneeze. A horrible pain exploded in my chest. I almost let it show, but I reined it in. I knew exactly what this was. I had been to a very similar morgue... after the crash. I'd had to identify Becky's and Cal's bodies.

"The victim was thirty-nine," Dr. Gravely said, his voice emotionless. "Died from multiple stab wounds. Two distinct thrusts to the thoracic spine, two more to the lumbar. Each one approximately two inches deep. The knife had a serrated blade approximately eight inches in length. It punctured her liver and right kidney. The lumbar penetrations perforated the large intestine. The victim almost certainly died from heart failure precipitated by shock."

Justine stepped forward and inspected Stacy's lower half. "You've removed the banknotes."

"They've gone to Police Forensics, along with the woman's clothing, jewelry—everything on her person."

Justine nodded.

"I did examine them first, of course. But you'll know about them from the police, right?"

"No," Justine and I said in unison. "What about them?" I added slowly.

"Well, the money... They're fake notes—photocopies."

CHAPTER 17

EVERYTHING ABOUT THE bar of the Blue Sydney hotel in Woolloomooloo was ultramodern and be-yond—oversized concrete buffet counters, exposed brushed-chrome pipes, metal grills.

Mary sat at the huge steel bar, drinking her third espresso of the morning.

"Good morning," Ho said as he walked toward her and extended his hand.

"Thanks for agreeing to meet with me," Mary said.

Ho ordered a glass of Evian "with no ice, no lime, no lemon. And please open the bottle in front of me."

After he got that all straightened out, Ho turned to me.

"I wasn't being entirely forthcoming with you and Mr. Gisto yesterday. I don't know Mr. Gisto. But I've done some checking, and he seems like a worthy man.

And besides," he added with a small smile, "you obviously trust him, and that is good enough for me."

Mary stayed stony faced. She didn't care about Ho's opinion of Gisto.

"The fact is: I believe my son was kidnapped and killed by the Triads."

"I know."

"How do *you* know?"

"Our forensics experts have found compelling evidence to support that idea."

"I see. Well, I have a lot of experience with the gangs, going back years. I know how these animals operate."

"From your time in the Hong Kong Police Force?"

"Before I met you at the Police Training Academy, I had already been one of the senior officers in Hong Kong involved with breaking up the Huang gang in 'ninety-four. Then I headed up the task force who smashed two other big Triad teams, in Kowloon and Macau."

"You told me you immigrated to Australia because it was so beautiful here."

He smiled slightly and said, "It was beautiful . . . beautiful to get away from the Triads."

"And you think this attack on your family was some sort of revenge?"

"I'm convinced of it."

"Why?"

Ho was silent for a few moments, gazing around the almost-empty bar. "I received a ransom note."

Mary raised an eyebrow. "Maybe we should start at the beginning, Meng."

"Yesterday I told you that the last time I saw my son was on Thursday. I reported him missing the following day. That night, Friday, I received a package. The note demanded that I cooperate with a gang that's planning to smuggle heroin from Hong Kong. The note was delivered in a box...along with one of my son's eyes."

"And you didn't go to the police when this happened?"

Ho shook his head. "No, as I've told you—"

"You don't trust the cops. Why?"

"I'd rather not say."

Mary rested an elbow on the table and rubbed her forehead. "Okay," she said. "What happened next?"

"Saturday night I received a call from the man who called himself Big Gang Leader. He said I had twenty-four hours to agree to their 'request,' or my son would be killed."

"That would give you until Sunday night. And they *did* murder him." Mary shook her head slowly.

"I've concluded that they were going to kill Chang and dump his body in a public space—a building lobby, a church, a parking lot."

"But why?" Mary asked. "Surely they would have been more discreet."

"Quite the opposite. They would have wanted to advertise it. I'm not the only Asian businessman in this city. If I kept refusing, they could go elsewhere. They wanted to broadcast the murder, as a warning to others—that's how they operate: fear and arrogance."

"But you did refuse them," Mary said.

"I *could not* agree to their demands. They are targeting me because of my past. Helping them smuggle heroin would go against everything I believe in."

Mary looked away from him.

"You may seem outraged, Mary. But I had to do it for the greater good of the public."

His eyes filled with tears. Ho Meng banged down on the bar with his fist and growled, "And, yes, my heart will break every day for the rest of my wretched life!"

CHAPTER 18

I'D JUST WALKED into the lab at Private. Darlene was tapping at a computer. She used only her thumbs to tap, like a teenager urgently text-messaging on a cell phone. I had made certain that the police had sent over absolutely everything from the Stacy Fleetwood murder scene for her to study.

"Find anything?" I asked.

"Not a lot more than the Police Forensics guys have found, I'm afraid. The banknotes are photocopies... high quality—about the grade of a top-end domestic printer."

"Fingerprints?"

"I wish! No...zip. Actually, to be honest, I didn't expect anything. The killer wore latex gloves. I found traces of the cornstarch powder that coats standard gloves."

"And nothing special about that?"

"Nope. These gloves could have come from any one of a hundred outlets, a thousand—Coles, Woolworths, any drugstore."

"Okay. Anything else?"

"Biological matter from the woman's vagina. I could tell you where she was in her menstrual cycle and whether or not she'd had sex during the past twenty-four hours. But I can't give you anything practical about what was put into her."

"She wasn't raped?"

"Definitely not."

I looked round the lab. Benches on both sides. On top of these benches stood impressive-looking machines with elaborate control panels and flashing lights. I recognized a powerful microscope and a centrifuge, but that was about it. The rest might as well have been Venusian technology.

"The cops gave you all the material you need?"

"Yeah, personal effects, plus a file containing several hundred photographs of the crime scene. I've analyzed Stacy Fleetwood's jacket. I can confirm the police pathologist's assessment of the attack—the number of stab wounds, the angle of entry, the type of knife. Although, of course, the weapon hasn't been found. I wish I could have been at the crime scene. It's hard, working secondhand like this. I might have caught something the cops missed."

"I understand," I replied. "And you found nothing unusual with anything Police Forensics handed over?"

"No, Craig. I'm sorry. Hate to admit it—but right now I'm drawing a complete blank."

CHAPTER 19

LOVE WAS IN the air-conditioned air. At least, love was in the small space of air-conditioned air that existed between our ridiculously hip receptionist, Cookie, and our ridiculously love-struck assistant, Johnny. Johnny was leaning over Cookie's desk so far that he looked like he might have been bodysurfing.

"Don't fall over," I said. I was on my way back from Darlene's lab.

"I just stopped to say good morning to Cookie," he said as he brought his feet back to the floor and headed toward his cubicle.

Then another voice, Justine's: "Am I just stupid? I never knew that the city of Sydney is so hot. This heat'll take the hop out of your kangaroos."

Justine was dressed for the weather, her hair pulled back in a yellow scrunchie. A good, old-fashioned ponytail. The white linen sundress she wore would fit in just fine on a tennis court.

"Well," I said, "the Internet said it was thirty-nine degrees at six o'clock this morning."

"Jesus! That's almost a hundred and three Fahrenheit," Justine said.

"Now, that's impressive. An American who doesn't need a thermometer translation."

We both laughed.

"If you're willing to go back outside and brave the heat for a few more minutes, I can show you something that you'll really like," I said.

Justine pulled her iPad from her big, white canvas bag, tapped quickly at the screen, and declared that she was "yours for a half hour."

Moments later we were walking down Macquarie Street, looking out at Circular Quay. If it weren't for the fact that she was the sharpest woman investigator in the world, if it weren't for the fact that two hideous murders were nowhere near a solution, if it weren't for the fact that I was launching the most prestigious investigative firm in Asia-Pac, and if it weren't for the fact that Justine was intimately involved with my boss...well, then we were just an ordinary couple strolling along Sydney Cove.

Straight ahead of us stood the opera house, the tiers of wide steps leading to its massive windows just a couple dozen yards away. People were sitting on the steps, drinking Slurpees and Cokes and bottled water.

"Bottled water," she said. "I never got it. Why not just take it from the tap?"

"I think we agree on that," I said.

We turned onto the quay and walked in the shade, an arcade of shops to our left. An Aboriginal man was playing a didgeridoo over a hip-hop beat spilling from an iPod plugged into a big speaker.

"Very postmodern!" Justine observed. "So, where exactly are you taking me?"

"I've decided it's going to be a surprise."

We came to a bar, with tables and umbrellas outside, a few people eating a late breakfast. A big flat-screen TV on the wall inside was showing a soccer game from the English Premier League, Chelsea versus Tottenham. I led the way through the bar and up a flight of stairs. On the wall was a sign that read: ICE BAR.

"What's this?" Justine asked.

"In a minute," I said.

I stepped up to the counter. A few other customers milled about. Sixty seconds later, I had two tickets in my hand and guided Justine around a corner. A perfectly tanned blond woman was waiting for us by a rack of fur coats.

Justine turned to me again.

"Okay, this is the deal," I said. "You want to cool down? The ice bar is set to minus twenty—Fahrenheit. Everything is made from ice, including the cocktail glasses. We stay in for a drink—twenty minutes. You'll feel a lot cooler by the end of it."

"I'm ready," she said, and the blond babe helped her into a totally unfashionable brown, fur-lined anorak and mittens. She seemed to be loving it all.

We went into the antechamber to acclimatize. Here

I told her that it was just eighteen degrees Fahrenheit. From there we went into the prep room.

"Here we're down to five degrees Fahrenheit."

"I get it, Craig. You're talking Fahrenheit English," she said.

Then the door to the bar swished open, and we were inside. The digital thermometer on the wall told us it was minus twenty degrees Celsius—and it felt it, even through the fur-lined boots, the fur-lined anorak, and the fur-lined mittens.

The floor was covered with ice. The chairs around the walls were made of ice, the bar was ice. Everything was backlit electric blue.

"This is fantastic, Craig!" Justine beamed, her breath steamy and fragrant. I told her to drink her sour-cherry daiquiri quickly...before it froze.

"Since we're here, and since we're cool, do you mind if I take this opportunity to have a small meeting?" I asked.

"It's never the wrong time for a meeting," she said.

I brought her up to date on where we were on the Chang murder. I also brought her up to date on the obstacles ahead of us and the limitations that Darlene had come up against.

"If it can be solved, Darlene can solve it," Justine said.

We discussed Stacy Fleetwood's gruesome murder.

"Do you think there are any connections in these things?" she asked.

"If there are, I haven't found them."

There was a pause, and then Justine said, "I know what you're thinking."

"You do?"

"You're thinking Jack is going to be disappointed in you. Let me tell you something, Craig. Jack doesn't expect miracles right away. He expects hard work, out-of-the-box thinking. *Then* he expects miracles."

"I'll try not to disappoint him."

"And I'll help you. But Craig, listen. Before my butt freezes permanently, I need to tell you something."

Uh-oh. Watch out. Some load of manure is about to fall on me.

"I know that Mark Talbot is the cousin you lived with when you came over here as a kid from England."

"You did a background on him?"

"I do a background on every person I come in contact with."

"This is the one time I skipped it. I figured they were Thorogood's boys."

"I'd have assumed that too. And nothing serious showed up, just the info that you and Talbot have some bad blood between you."

"I'll tell you about it someday," I said.

"You don't have to," she said. She smiled.

Then, with deadly seriousness, she said, "There's one more thing I've got to tell you, Craig."

What the hell was coming now?

"My goddamn daiquiri froze."

CHAPTER 20

THE HO MANSION was in Mosman, a few hundred yards from Taronga Zoo. It was an easy house to spot. Most houses in the area were elegant Victorian mansions, meticulously preserved. The Ho house was a total McMansion—an ornamental mess of marble, flagstone, and vulgarity.

Buzzed in through an electrically operated gate, Mary and I strode up a gravel path that passed over a pond filled with koi. A Malaysian maid met us at the front door and showed us in to a grandiose, circular hall. A young Chinese guy in a perfectly tailored blue suit appeared in an archway to the right of the hall. He had an earpiece in place, a wire disappearing into his shirt collar. It was hard to miss the bulge of a firearm under his jacket.

I was about to show him my ID when he said, "That's

unnecessary. You've been ID'd and cleared, and you're four minutes early."

Mary and I followed him down a corridor. We hung a right, then a left. We passed huge rooms—a gym, a home theater, a couple of living areas, each with the floor space of your average basketball court.

We reached a door on the right. Another guard— identical blue suit, identical earpiece, identical jacket bulge. He stiffened as we came around the corner.

The first guy walked off without a word. The second guard opened the door and nodded us in.

"Wait here," he said. Then he left the room.

I could have, by now, predicted the look of the room: a four-meter-high ceiling, gaudy red-silk sofas, a mahogany carved desk that could easily have served as a banquet table. Ancient framed prints, potted palms, thronelike chairs. Everything but Ho himself.

I heard a faint sound from the far corner. There was a door into another room. I noticed a flickering light coming from beyond the doorway but couldn't make out the sound.

I turned to Mary and put a finger to my lips. Stopping a yard from the door, I pulled up close to the wall, peered in. Mary was right next to me.

There was a wide flat-screen on the far wall.

I looked at the screen. The film was beautifully shot: a small Chinese boy, perhaps five years old, playing with a toy train. The boy lifted his head and looked directly at the camera, a beatific smile on his face. Then the film cut to another scene. The boy was a little older here. He was flying a kite on the beach. The camera shot widened, and I saw the Bathers' Pavilion, the landmark café on Balmoral Beach, a mile from here.

Ho Meng sat in half profile on a sofa. He stared at the screen. A line of tears ran down his cheek. His body shook.

I felt a hand on my shoulder. Now both hands were gripping my shoulders. Whoever was touching me now turned me gently from the sight of the weeping Ho Meng.

When I looked around at the person who was touching me I couldn't help but blurt out: "Holy fucking shit!"

CHAPTER 21

"NO, MR. GISTO. I am not a ghost. I am Dai, Chang's brother," the young man said. Dai then led us on the long journey halfway across the room and indicated that we should sit on a sofa. He pulled up a chair and leaned forward.

"I'm sorry you had to see that."

I started to reply, but he lifted a hand.

"Please. I'm sorry because my father would have been so ashamed if he knew you were there. I'm sorry for him, for me."

I nodded.

"We didn't mean to intrude," Mary said.

"What is it you want?"

"We had a meeting set up to talk to your father about your brother's murder."

Dai shook his head.

"You don't have to be discreet with me. My father has told me all about the Triads. I grew up with them as a dark presence in our lives."

There was a sound from the doorway. Ho Meng was standing there. He quickly walked toward us as Mary and I stood up. He gripped my hand and then kissed Mary on both cheeks. He had transformed from the grief-stricken father we had just seen in the home theater and was once again the upright businessman.

"Please, everyone, sit," he said. "I heard what my son told you, and it is absolutely true. The Triads have hung over our lives like a black shadow, and they still do. In fact, their shadow has grown even darker."

I had to say what I had to say.

"Meng, this morning we knew that you were holding back."

Mary spoke. "If you want us to work with you in hunting down your son's killers, you have to tell us everything."

"You are right. Let me tell you what I know *and* what I think. First of all, I am certain that my wife, Jiao, was murdered by the Triads twelve years ago, soon after we came to Australia. She was last seen in Chinatown, in the middle of the day. Next morning her headless body was discovered in Roseville. The police were convinced it was the work of a psycho killer. They connected it with two similar unsolved murders from three years before. But they never found the killer."

"And *that* is why you don't trust the cops," I said.

Ho merely nodded. "They have consistently let me

down. First Jiao, then Chang. I reported him missing. They did nothing. Then he died."

I felt like saying that the police could not be everywhere all the time but thought better of it.

Then Mary said, "But, Meng, I know you and I have been over this, but . . . what I don't understand is this: if you are convinced the Triads killed your wife, then surely when Chang was kidnapped, you knew they would be serious about killing him if you didn't agree to work with them?"

Dai was about to speak, but his father silenced him with a look. "You're missing the point, Mary. The members of the Triads are not honorable men. They would have killed Chang either way. They would have kept him until I fulfilled my side of the bargain, then they would have slit his throat—he knew too much about them to live. Now perhaps you begin to understand why I don't trust the police."

His lip curled just a bit. A sneer enveloped the rest of his mouth. His eyes filled with tears.

"Do you have a son, Mr. Gisto?"

Only Mary understood the piercing pain of Ho Meng's question.

"No, I do not."

"Then you cannot understand how awful the loss can be."

CHAPTER 22

JOHNNY AND I were in my office. We huddled over a laptop that mapped out various undercover positions in the Bellevue Hill neighborhood, the area where Greta's friend Stacy had been murdered.

"We're placing too many fake gardeners," Johnny said. He was right. I pressed a few buttons, tapped a few arrows, and replaced one gardener with an au pair girl and another with a pool-maintenance worker.

"Much better," Johnny said. He pointed to the screen and continued. "This way you can position one gardener near this patio and—"

Suddenly Johnny froze. I mean really froze. His right arm in the air. His left hand near the screen. Then he spoke.

"That voice. I'd know it anywhere," he said.

I listened. "I don't hear anything."

"Over here," Johnny said softly, and we both walked to my open office door.

"There. Listen," he said.

I listened and could hear the faint sound of a rough Australian voice coming from the reception area.

"Don't fret me, sweetheart. Mr. G. will be happy to see me. It'll be a bloody fine surprise."

"All right," Cookie said. There was an unusual dreaminess to her voice. "Mr. Gisto's the first office on the right."

And within seconds Johnny and I were face-to-face with Mickey Spencer.

If Mickey Spencer was not the most famous rock star in the world, he was certainly the most famous *Australian* rock star in the world. This guy spent his nights singing in eight-thousand-seat arenas, and he spent his days fighting with the paparazzi.

"Sorry to barge in," he said. He even sounded as if he meant what he said.

"Oh, no. That's perfectly fine," said Johnny, clearly stunned that he was talking to the most important entertainer on the continent.

"No, it's not perfectly fine," I said. "But since you've already barged in, come on inside, and bring your... um...friend with you."

His "friend" was apparently his bodyguard, a massive, bald Maori in a tight-fitting suit. He easily weighed 140 kilos or more.

As for Mickey Spencer, he was quite a bit shorter

than I'd have guessed. Fame seems to make celebs *look* taller. He wore black leather pants, a brown T-shirt, and a black suit jacket. His hair was carefully gelled and carefully messy. A few days' growth and far more wrinkles on his face than any guy in his twenties should have.

"You must be Craig Gisto," Mickey Spencer said as he took a step into my office. He had a light, jaunty voice, and I could hear one of his songs in my head as he spoke.

"How did you work that out?"

"Got the biggest office," he said, and he glanced around. "You're obviously top dog here."

Johnny was now staring at the bodyguard.

"Oh, I'd best introduce you. This little guy here is Hemi," Mickey said. "He watches out for me. Looks really mean, yeah? But only with the enemy—otherwise, he's a pussycat. Aren't you, Hemi?" No response.

"What can we do for you?" I asked.

He spun on his heel, lowered his voice. "Can we go...somewhere?"

We walked into Reception. The pop star gave Cookie a brief, professionally flirtatious smile. She'd been chewing the end of a pen and staring at him with a lost expression.

I took Mickey and Hemi along the hall and indicated to Johnny that he should come with us. "We've a comfortable lounge through here," I said.

"Coffee?" I asked as I closed the door to the room.

"Hemi'll have water—sparkling, if you have it. I'll

have something a wee bit stronger—bourbon, if you have it."

I had a bottle of Blanton's Private Reserve bourbon in the small bar against the far wall.

"Great choice, man!" Mickey said as I poured him a very generous measure.

I waited for him to take a sip, but he downed it in one gulp. Meanwhile, Johnny had found a bottle of San Pellegrino and a glass. He handed them to Hemi.

"Now I'm feeling better," Mickey said.

I decided to wait for him to start talking, but he seemed a bit confused. "Not used to this sorta thing," he began. "Feels like we're in a Raymond Chandler novel!"

I was a bit surprised by that and must have shown it.

"I'm a big reader. Hated it at school, of course, but on tour there's only so much drinking, snorting, and screwing you can take...gets boring." He produced a megawatt smile. "Anyway." His face straightened, and he looked quickly at Hemi, then back at me. Then he continued.

"I'm here about Ricky Holt."

Both Johnny and I looked at him blankly.

"Ricky Holt is my manager. He's quite well known, dudes!"

"Sorry," I said. "You may have noticed—I'm not a teenage girl. So I haven't really followed your career."

My sarcasm obviously whizzed right past Mr. Spencer's enormous ego.

"No prob," Mickey said as he held up his hands. "You

got another little taste for me?" He flicked a nod at the bourbon.

"Sure." I refilled his glass. "So what is it about Mr. Holt?"

Mickey knocked back his second big glassful, wiped his mouth, and said, "Well, you see, it's like this. It's sorta like . . . Well . . . How can I put it? Oh, fuck it all. Why don't I just say it outright: *Ricky Holt is trying to kill me.*"

CHAPTER 23

WHATEVER ELSE MICKEY Spencer had already drunk, smoked, or inhaled before he showed up at Private and drank a few pints of bourbon, only God—and possibly Hemi—knew. Miraculously, besides a slight shaking in his hands and some seriously bloodshot eyes, he seemed completely compos mentis.

"Okay, Mickey. What makes you think your manager is trying to kill you?" I asked.

"Simple equation. I'm worth more to him dead than I am alive."

"That doesn't mean—"

"Listen, Mr. G., the bastard's bent. I've been with him for three years. He picked me up when I was at my lowest point, right after I left my old band. He's a ruthless mother. You need that in a manager, but I know he wants me snuffed out." Mickey clicked his fingers in front of his face.

"If you really think that, why don't you just leave him?" Johnny asked, and glanced at me for affirmation.

Mickey laughed. "Wish I could! How I wish I could. But I'm bound by a watertight contract. I've spoken to every lawyer from here to New York City. Holt has me by the balls."

"There must be—" I began.

"Listen, Craig, you've got to understand. Forget it— there's no way out of the contract." He drew a deep breath. "Look, man, it's all about Club Twenty-Seven."

I flicked a glance at Johnny. He stared back, shrugged.

"What is Club Twenty-Seven?" I asked.

"Christ! You don't know?"

"Sorry. The teenage-girl thing again."

"Almost every dead pop star checked out when they were twenty-seven."

"Really?" I turned to Johnny, who seemed suddenly animated.

"Actually, yeah, that's right," Johnny said.

"Kurt, Hendrix, Janis, Morrison, Amy Winehouse... It's a mighty long list, man," Mickey added.

"So?" I said.

"Dude... I'm twenty-six."

CHAPTER 24

"WELL, WHAT DO you make of that?" I asked Johnny as the doors of the elevator closed on Mickey Spencer and the ever-talkative Hemi.

"Seems genuinely scared, boss."

We walked back into Reception and saw Cookie on the phone. She did a good job trying to disguise the fact that she was telling a friend about her celebrity encounter.

"Tell her you'll be selling autographs tonight," I said. Cookie rolled her eyes. But she did not look flustered.

Back in the meeting room, Johnny settled himself into the chair that only moments ago had held the butt of rock-and-roll royalty. Highly paranoiac royalty *or* highly endangered royalty.

"Refresh my memory," I said. "I was never a big fan. He was in Fun Park, right? Before he went solo and became a massive star?"

"Yeah, Granddad," Johnny replied with a grin.

"I'm more a Nirvana and Chili Peppers kinda guy."

"Yeah," Johnny said, "during the Sinatra era."

"Back to the question, sonny," I said.

Johnny turned serious. "Fun Park was big. Three number-one singles, a hit album. They just got together again—without Mickey, of course."

"But when Mickey left them, his solo career eclipsed his old band, right?"

"Definitely. He is—*was*—huge."

"Was?"

"Gone off a bit recently. Last hit was well over a year ago."

"Which is an eternity when most of your fans are seven-year-olds."

Johnny laughed. "A bit of an exaggeration. But not *that* big an exaggeration."

"Okay," I said. "Could he just be delusional? He obviously has issues."

"I guess we have to take him seriously," Johnny offered.

"We do? Why?" I paused a beat. "Look, okay. I get it. He's Mickey Spencer—megastar—and, I dunno, he seems like a pretty nice guy, actually. But do we believe him?"

"We obviously need to know a lot more about his manager."

"Okay. Let's take Mickey seriously—at least until we know otherwise."

Johnny seemed to be lost in thought.

"I reckon this one's for you, Johnny."

"Me? On my own?"

"Most definitely. Right up your alley."

"Me? Alone?"

"That's right. But I have one piece of advice. Only one." I paused.

"And that is?"

"Be sure to signal if you think you're drowning."

CHAPTER 25

SYMPATHY AND GRIEF can really get trampled on when a murder investigation has to move forward. Urgency and heartbreak are usually not good companions.

I had wanted to see David Fleetwood, husband of the late murder victim Stacy Fleetwood, as soon as possible, and Greta Thorogood had eased the way for me. So at six o'clock on the day after Stacy's funeral, I was shaking hands with the very recent widower in his smart office on the thirty-fifth floor of Citigroup Centre.

David Fleetwood was very tall, very handsome, and clearly very sleep deprived.

"You haven't taken compassionate leave, Mr. Fleetwood?"

"I was offered it, of course," he said, his voice a smooth baritone. "But I didn't see the point. Why would I want to kick around the house? My mum is there for a while to tend to the kids. If I'm working I can focus on something other than…" He stopped.

"Makes sense."

He gestured to a seat on the gray leather sofa and said, "I've given a full report to the police. Not sure what more I can…" He trailed off again.

"Look, Mr. Fleetwood, I know this is tough, but I have to ask some fairly personal questions. I need to get some background. I appreciate it's a raw time. I've been through it myself."

"You have?"

I looked around at the white walls, a Balinese wall hanging softening things a little. "I lost my wife and son three years ago."

He stared into my eyes; his expression was absolutely vacant.

"An accident," I added.

It felt so odd, speaking about it to a complete stranger, as if I were just meeting a brand-new grief counselor.

He shrugged. "Ask away."

I paused for a second. "Were you happily married, Mr. Fleetwood?"

"As far as I'm concerned, I was. I think Stace was also. And I'll save you asking, Mr. Gisto. I wasn't having an affair, and I'm pretty sure my wife wasn't either. I do realize this is your first port of call. It would make life easier if she had been…or if I was, I guess."

"Okay, sensitive question number two. Money. Everything all right?"

He waved a hand around the big modern corner of-
fice. "I'm third in line to the throne. Sort of the baby
Prince Georgie. There's the boss, Max Llewellyn, then
Max's son, then me. I pull down a seven-figure salary."

I knew that this didn't necessarily mean that everything was cool, but I moved on. "It may sound ridiculous, but can you think of anyone at all who may have
hated your wife?"

"Stace was a normal wife, a normal mum, Mr. Gisto.
She cared for the kids, had her book club, her Pilates
class. Who would hate her enough to murder her . . . ? It's
nuts."

"You're absolutely sure? Within your social circle?
Any grudges? Any big bust-ups recently? Or for that
matter . . . ever?"

He was shaking his head. "No. We are—we *were*
part of a big social circle: golf club, yacht club, neighbors, work colleagues." He stared straight at me. "But
nothing . . . We were . . . rather boring, actually."

"What about you, Mr. Fleetwood? Do you have any
enemies?"

His expression changed for the first time. A bleak
smile. "Me? Mr. Gisto, in my business I've acquired so
many enemies, if I lined them up, they'd stretch from
here to the Harbour Bridge."

CHAPTER 26

"WELL, IT COULD be a lead," Justine said.

She was at my apartment in Balmoral, sitting on one of my sofas. She was drinking a cup of coffee. By the way, I thought that she looked exquisite in a bright orange dress with a simple, ropelike belt around the waist.

Don't go getting any ideas. This was not a seduction setup on my part. I had called her while driving home after my meeting with David Fleetwood. I wanted her to know everything. I got her in her car. She was driving out to Bonnie Doon Golf Club to get in nine holes. My place seemed a logical meeting locale.

"I guess these money guys live close to the edge... Plenty of wars," I said.

"And there's also the symbolism of the money—the fake money."

"Of course. All a bit vague, though, right?" I said.

"Oh, totally. But we have to start somewhere, don't we?"

"You've talked to Greta. Did she have any insight? Anything?"

"Just confirmation of what we already know. My sister is part of the same social scene. There are always silly feuds between the moms, she says—the usual thing, rich women, bored, overindulged; husbands never there. The ladies crave excitement. So they invent problems between themselves. Same in L.A., London, anywhere."

"Yeah, but I can't get past the relationship angle. You said it—bored women, husbands never there. Perfect recipe."

"Sure. Look, Craig, Greta told me stuff. Half the women she knows are having affairs with their personal trainer or tennis coach or even the interior designer, if he's so inclined. But Greta reckons that Stacy and David were simply not like that."

"She's sure?"

For the first time since we'd met, Justine sounded impatient with me. "Would you like to give Greta a shot of amobarbital to be certain?"

I assured her that "truth serum" wouldn't be necessary, and I said I wasn't doubting the veracity of Greta's opinion.

"So, let's check out David Fleetwood's associates. See if any of his enemies hate him enough to kill his wife," I said.

"Find out if he's been a naughty boy, you mean?"

"Oh, don't even question that!" I said. "The guy lives

in a five-million-dollar mansion and earns a seven-figure salary. As he more or less told me himself, he's definitely been a naughty boy, if not with women, certainly with money."

Justine gazed out at the view across Middle Harbour, checked her watch. "I'd better go if I want to catch nine holes before dark."

As I was leading her to the door she turned suddenly. "Nearly forgot—would you like to come to my sister's fortieth birthday party?"

I was startled for a second. "Well...er...yeah."

"It's at a restaurant called Hurricane's Grill, at Bondi. Greta raves about it." She took a breath. "She almost called the whole thing off, but Brett and I talked her round. I told her that she couldn't let the bastard who murdered Stacy rule her life. That got her blood up. She can be quite fierce when she's riled!"

"When's the party?"

"Tomorrow night."

"Well, I'm honored."

Justine held my eyes and grinned mischievously. "Don't be. You and young Johnny are the only two men I know in Sydney."

Then she pecked me on the cheek and left.

CHAPTER 27

THE ONLY SPACE at Private Sydney smaller than Johnny's cubicle was the room that housed the brooms and mops and slop buckets. But Johnny's location did have two distinct advantages: number one, he could never fall asleep, because he had the constant, mind-numbing sound of the whirring, clanging photocopier machine next to his cubicle wall, and, number two, if he swung around in his chair, he had a direct view through the glass entry doors of the luscious-looking Cookie, the receptionist.

At the moment he had taken his eyes from Cookie and was staring intently at his computer screen. He'd been following a paper trail—well, a cyber trail—to find anything helpful about Mickey Spencer's manager, Ricky Holt. But the facts were scant.

Holt was fifty-six, American, born in Utah. Went to Brigham Young University, studied economics. He dropped out after two years and became a minor pop star himself. Played on the New York, CBGB scene in the late seventies, fronting a band called Venison. Then he became a manager for Toys and later Rough Cut, who were pretty successful. He left for Australia in 2010 (for no discernible reason), hooked up with Mickey Spencer as the singer was leaving his own boy band, Fun Park. Six months later Holt had turned Spencer into a big-deal solo star. (The fact that Spencer had a huge voice, played terrific guitar, and exuded sexiness helped Holt work that magic.)

Johnny tapped a few more keys. The screen showed sales figures for Mickey Spencer's three solo albums. Mickey had peaked with his first album, *Love Box,* which had made the U.S. Billboard top 10. But since then, his career had begun to falter. His latest CD, *Much 2 Much,* had bombed everywhere except in Australia. Yeah, Johnny realized that MP3s and pirated music and iTunes were changing everything, but he also knew that other artists were in the top 10 and Mickey wasn't even close anymore.

So, there's your motive, Johnny thought. *If Mickey is right and the manager is trying to have him snuffed out, it's because his career is on the ropes. Holt's going for the dead-pop-star revenue.* Johnny began typing as fast as he could.

The next ten minutes were a waste. He went through all the official sites linked to Spencer—

everything from *Metal Hammer* to *Rolling Stone* to the hundreds of personal teeny-bop blogs where young girls imagined some pretty randy exercises they could personally offer Mickey Spencer. Johnny kept searching the old material on the bands Holt had managed in the eighties. Nothing.

Well, whoa, wait one goddamn minute. Here was one of those websites where you could learn about the criminal record of anyone in the world. It was worth five Australian dollars on his Visa account to learn that...Holt had been a junkie, had served six months in L.A. Men's Central for possession (it didn't say possession of what) in 1979, spent time in rehab. Okay. That was something.

Johnny went back to some of the personal blogs about Mickey. Okay, this one looked, well, at least interesting—a blog called *Spencer Hate-On,* apparently a collaboration of people (mostly young men) who, as the title implied, detested Mickey so much that they wished him dead or, at the very least, castrated, with the severed organs then fed to Ricky Holt.

Most of it was inane garbage, and Johnny began to scroll down faster and faster, until a sentence jumped out: "Holt's bad times in the States were the best thing that ever happened to Mickey Spencer. What would the useless douche bag have done after Fun Park if Holt hadn't come to Australia to start over again?"

Johnny stopped scrolling and reread the two sentences. Then he checked the responses. There were no more comments.

Johnny leaned back in his chair. A tingle of excitement zipped right through him. It wasn't much, but it was interesting. And then again, Craig Gisto always said, "You've got to start somewhere."

CHAPTER 28

ELSPETH LOMBARD HAS put the kids to bed and is walking down the stairs when she realizes just how very much she needs a glass of Jamsheed Cabernet, her favorite. "Chewy." That's the word her husband, Alex, uses to describe the wine. "Red." That's the word Elspeth uses.

Alex is away on business in Frankfurt. He won't be back until next week. Elspeth is not exactly sad, certainly not depressed. She's just...lonely. Yes, that's the word—lonely.

She opens the temp-controlled wine-storage closet. Damn. The least expensive wine there is a Penfolds Shiraz. The Shiraz is "chewy" also, but it's also about three hundred dollars. Alex would not be a happy guy if he found one of his treasured wines had gone missing.

She'll just take a quick walk to the liquor store two streets away.

Five minutes later, she's thirty yards from her house with her Jamsheed Cabernet. Two bottles, actually. After all, there's tomorrow evening to plan for.

It's quiet, sticky, hot. Most of Elspeth's neighbors are indoors watching TV or lounging by their blue-lit pools with cocktails in hand.

She hears a clicking from behind. Some animal. Some bug. She ignores it. Then a shuffling sound. She turns. Nothing. Sidewalk clear. Elspeth spins back again.

The blow comes from behind.

She falls to her knees, as confused as she is hurt.

There's a blur of houses, concrete, darkening sky. She falls forward and hits the sidewalk hard. The wine bottles smash—red liquid everywhere. Pain shoots up her neck, then streaks across the left side of her face. She tries to turn, makes it halfway, and sees a figure in a cheap winter coat leaning over her. Elspeth can actually smell the pizza on her assailant's breath.

She has no chance, no time, no strength to get up. Her attacker is bigger, stronger. She feels herself being dragged into a narrow alleyway between two gardens— her own and the Pressmans', next door. She can see a huge cloud of yellow. She realizes she is being pulled past the yellow tea roses, the little bushes she so carefully nursed through the heat. She tries to scream, but as soon as she opens her mouth, a gloved hand comes over it, grips her lips, and pulls hard. The hand rips and crushes the flesh around her mouth. Elspeth feels a tooth snap inward. More pain. Terrible pain. It spreads out across her face and around her skull.

She's pushed up against the high fence that surrounds the swimming pool. A vile-smelling rag pushes up against her insanely bloody mouth. The attacker is leaning over her. Then the attacker is knotting a part of the rag behind her neck. She struggles, but she's drained, and the assailant is too strong. Elspeth feels a wire being wrapped about her wrists. Then her arms are pinned behind her back.

She can't resist anymore. Her vision is blurred. She sees a head appear in front of her. No details. The face is in shadow, hooded. She sees a match light, a cigarette lit. The flame illuminates part of the hooded face, but only the mouth—pale, thin lips.

Elspeth screams as the cigarette burns her face, but the sound is soaked up in the gag. She can smell her own burned flesh, and now she screams a muffled scream, helpless, as the cigarette is pushed into her again, just beneath her left eye. She starts to cry. The pain sears her insides. It feels as though her head is going to explode. She vomits into the cloth in her mouth and starts to choke on it.

The attacker grabs her, spins her over onto her front. Elspeth's disfigured face hits the sandy ground of the alleyway.

Next comes the knife. She just knows something has pierced her back. She feels a strange dislocation in her spine. In her confused state, submerged in agony, she imagines she's a puppet and her strings have been cut.

The knife goes in again, and Elspeth convulses and gasps. But now the pain has gone. She is now far beyond pain, beyond life.

CHAPTER 29

TONY MACKENZIE RAN the same route at the same time every day of the week. This morning he was coming to the end of his five-mile run. He always felt that runner's sense of euphoria at this point in his circuit. He had just turned onto Wentworth Avenue, the final stretch before the wind-down.

This morning he felt extra energized. The sun was coming up, but the oppressive heat hadn't shown up yet. He passed the end of an alleyway leading off the sidewalk. Tony just kept running. But then his energy began to flag. Something was wrong. He couldn't figure out what it was, but it nagged him. He tried to brush it aside, but the nagging would not let up.

He'd had this feeling before. It was an almost extrasensory talent. Tony would be running and feel that something grim was waiting around the block. Once that happened and he discovered dead koala roadkill; another time there was a woman standing naked at her front door, wildly throwing clothing onto the front lawn (her husband's clothing, presumably).

It was that small feeling of dread that ran through him now. The day was sunny. Bright. A coolish sort of breeze. Sprinkler systems in full swing, an occasional fellow runner.

"G'day."

"G'day."

And yet...

A few yards beyond the alley between the Lombards' property and the Pressmans' property, Tony Mackenzie decided to stop. He'd seen something. Something wasn't quite right.

He turned and jogged back toward the entrance to the alley. Looking down the narrow lane, hands on hips, he steadied his breathing. Ten yards ahead, to the side of the alley, lay a dark object. He might have guessed it for a pile of leaves, a delivery of gravel. It could have been a bundle of rags.

He walked toward the object. Sweat dripped into his eyes, leaving a salty kind of burning sensation.

As he drew closer he considered the "pile of rags" theory. Now he thought it might be a homeless person. He stepped forward cautiously, walking not too close to the pile of—

"Holy shit," he whispered. "It's a person." He half expected it to jump up and attack him. He moved back. Then forward again. Closer. He bent over. A few beads of sweat dropped from his own face onto the bloody, ragged figure on the ground. A woman. A blond woman. A woman he knew.

Tony Mackenzie gagged and clutched himself as if a very strong, cold wind had suddenly appeared. He felt a surge of terror in the pit of his stomach. The nerves all over his body seemed to fire simultaneously.

"Oh, fuck, man," he whispered. Then he stumbled back and leaned against the fence. Then he began to cry.

CHAPTER 30

I WAS JUST pulling onto the Harbour Bridge. Glanced at the dashboard clock. It was 6:59 a.m. I felt like shit— I'd hardly slept at all last night. In my nightmares and half sleep, I kept going over Stacy Fleetwood's murder. And the worst of the groggy nightmares was that she sometimes looked like my dead wife, Becky.

I'd gulped two strong coffees before leaving the house, and then I stopped for a Red Bull at my regular gas station in Mosman. Any more caffeine and I could make it to the office faster on foot than in the Maserati.

I moved my thumb to the remote on the steering wheel and switched on the ABC news. My cell rang. I pushed the Receive button and heard Justine's voice. "Craig?"

"That's me! Hi, Justine."

She got right to the point.

"We've got a second murder."

I glanced in the mirror, sped into a gap to my left. "Any details?"

"No. Brett's there now. It's a street away from his and Greta's house."

"No way!" I changed lanes and accelerated along the Cahill Expressway. The traffic was building. "Where's the body, exactly?"

"Wentworth Avenue. Runs parallel to Brett and Greta's street."

"Know it. How did you learn of the murder?"

"I'm *at* Greta and Brett's. Stayed over last night. Brett got the call just as he was leaving for HQ."

"Okay. I'll be there in fifteen . . . hopefully."

It was pretty much a straight run, and I was there in twelve. I stopped just beyond the police cordon and walked briskly toward the tape. A very self-important-looking constable was guarding the sidewalk. I showed him my ID, and I was relieved when he let me through without any arguments. *Maybe this liaison with the cops could actually work after all,* I thought as I ducked under the yellow tape and walked quickly to where the forensics team was poking around.

Brett Thorogood spotted me and waved me over. I saw Mark a few yards away, his back to me. He was talking to a man in Lycra running shorts.

"Runner found the body," Thorogood explained, his expression grim.

I followed the DC over to where the victim lay—another Stacy, really: a woman, about forty, shoulder-length blond hair. She was dressed in a blood-soaked dress that had been severely torn. The exposed label said DOLCE & GABBANA. The soil under her and around her was discolored—an ugly blackish purple. Blood. Her face had been mutilated—cigarette burns.

Her dress had been hitched up over her hips, legs splayed. The end of a roll of fifty-dollar bills could just be seen protruding from between her legs. Blood had dried on the insides of her thighs.

"Same MO," I said unnecessarily. Thorogood just stared at the dead woman.

I turned to see Justine at the tape. The cop who'd let me through was questioning her. I strode over, and just as I reached them, he let her under the barrier.

"Same thing as before," I told her as we walked along the alley. Thorogood had moved to one of the police cars on the street. Justine put a hand to her mouth, but as I went to turn her away, she shook me off. "It's okay, Craig!" she said. "Not very much shocks me anymore."

I saw Talbot finish up questioning the jogger and decided to leave Justine to it. I walked over to Mark just as another cop escorted the runner toward Wentworth Avenue.

"Oh...how nice!" he said.

"History repeating itself."

He nodded toward the dead woman. "Doesn't help that poor thing."

"Might help us, though. What do you have?" We weren't talking as if we hated each other; we were talking like two guys with a job to do.

He let out a heavy sigh. "Jogger found her about five forty-five. Jogger's name is Tony Mackenzie, some big-shot trader. The woman had been stabbed repeatedly in the back."

"Do we know who she is?"

"Name's Elspeth Lombard. Address: Forty-Four Wentworth Avenue."

"That's just two houses behind the deputy commissioner's house." I gestured back toward the main road. "Any idea how long she's been here?"

"Eight hours or so."

I nodded. "Makes sense. She'd probably have been spotted sooner if she'd been killed earlier. So after... what?...eight p.m.?"

Talbot didn't answer. Then we both caught sight of Darlene walking toward us with her forensics equipment.

Talbot smirked and spoke: "Here's the rest of your playgroup."

As Talbot began to walk away, he spoke again.

"Your turn to poke around."

CHAPTER 31

WHENEVER DARLENE CAME to a crime scene, I thought—for a split second, at least—that we'd contacted her while she was on her way to the airport. She was always pulling a large wheelie behind her. But, of course, Darlene's wheelie was packed with boxes of test tubes, piles of testing papers ready to be smeared with unpleasant body fluids, portable microscopes, scalpels, scissors, medical film. She was a takeaway laboratory.

Darlene headed straight for the victim. Justine met her, and I took out my iPhone and started walking in the direction of Wentworth Avenue.

I tapped the codes and double codes to get into Worldwide Private files. Then I tapped out "Elspeth Lombard" in Private Sydney's cryptic code. I pulled out my iPad to learn today's daily substitute code name for

"Australia." Today the word for "Australia" was "Nova Scotia." *Got it.*

Elspeth Victoria O'Mara Lombard was the daughter of Norman O'Mara, a wealthy mining entrepreneur in Western Australia. The lady had married well also. Her husband was CFO of Buttress Finance Group—a big, global player. Made a name for himself on the Australian stock exchange in the early nineties, spent time in London at a British bank. Elspeth and Alex met in London, dated in London, and married in London.

Other background: the Lombards had two boys, nine and eleven, both at Cranbrook School. I lifted my eyes from the screen of the iPhone as I passed the end of the alley. Now I was on Wentworth Avenue. I saw a policewoman a couple of houses down. She was walking toward a squad car with two young boys. The Lombard kids, I figured. Jesus Christ! In one second, life can change from supergood to supersucky.

Leaning against a low wall, I gazed back at the screen and processed what I knew so far: *So, a second victim who's linked to the financial sector is found dead with fake banknotes stuffed inside her.* I wondered if Elspeth knew the first victim, Stacy Fleetwood...or, indeed, David Fleetwood? Must have. He was a senior cog at Citigroup. Thorogood would have all these answers in no time.

What other links could there be? I started to think laterally. Called Greta.

"Hey," I said gently.

"Is that Craig? Hi."

"Look, I'm calling about the latest—"

"Yep," she said. She was clearly trying to keep herself together.

"The dead woman is Elspeth Lombard." I heard a sudden intake of breath. Paused for a second. "You know her?"

There was a delay. "Um...not that well, Craig. But, yeah, I knew her."

"I'm trying to find links, Greta. Links with..."

"Okay..." Another sharp inhalation. "Er...let me...let me think. Alex, her husband...he knows David well—David Fleetwood."

"Through work?"

"Yeah, and socially. They're neighbors. They play tennis together. Stace...she played there too. Same club as us...down the road. And...er...the gym. Yeah, Elspeth goes to my gym...and Stacy's..."

"Okay."

"You think this is some sex thing, don't you?" she asked.

"No, Greta. I don't."

Silence.

"I'm sorry," she said after a moment. "I'm just..."

I kept quiet for a few beats. Then: "Can you think of anything? Anything unusual? Anything going on? I don't mean merely tossing the keys into the bowl."

"What *do* you mean, then?"

"Elspeth's husband is in finance. So is David Fleetwood. They work for different companies, but could the husbands maybe be working together on something?"

"Craig. I have no idea." She paused for several

seconds. "All I know is that Stacy and Elspeth were just nice, normal women . . . right up until the times that somebody killed them."

"I understand, Greta. I understand," I said.

And then, in a manner totally uncharacteristic of her, she said, "Well, if you understand, then why the hell don't you and my husband try to *do* something about it?"

CHAPTER 32

FOUR KEY PLAYERS. The best and the brightest. Darlene and Mary and Johnny and Justine and four other folks sat waiting for a status meeting to begin in Private Sydney's conference room.

When I looked around the table, I saw four tired, drawn faces and eight, tired bloodshot eyes. These people were beyond the best and the brightest. They were passionate people. They cared deeply. They didn't need any hand-holding. I got to the point right away.

"All right. I know that everyone's up to his or her bum in work. And I know that we're not making a boatload of progress...yet. But, at the risk of sounding like some asshole of a coach, we're going to solve everything, every fucking thing. Take a deep breath. Let's get up to date, and then let's get to work."

A few nods, a few *okays*.

"First, the Ho murder. Darlene has isolated DNA samples, but they don't tally with any records. Ho Meng is convinced the police can't help, and he's certain the Triads want him to coordinate a smuggling operation."

"There's this," Mary said. "Ho Meng is sure the Triads are out for revenge. He firmly believes that's why they've targeted him, killed his son. He believes they murdered his wife soon after the family arrived in Australia, a dozen years ago. I'm inclined to go with his hunch. Mainly because it's a lot better than just a hunch."

"So, Mary." I turned in my chair. "You have to dig further, and you've got to get him to dig further. That's key. Ho thinks he knows the gang, we have some DNA, but that's it. We need names, background. We need to know where the gang hangs out. For the moment, Ho refuses to work with the cops, and frankly I don't feel comfortable with that."

"Can we force him to cooperate with the police?" Johnny asked.

"No, we can't." I scanned the faces around the table. "But perhaps the police themselves could exert some . . . oh . . . influence on Ho."

Johnny smiled slightly. He caught on quickly.

"I don't mean to make this a family affair, but, Justine, could you talk to your brother-in-law about approaching Ho?"

"I already have."

I said "Good," as if I really meant that I was glad she'd spoken to Brett before I asked her to talk to Brett.

Then I turned to Darlene.

"Okay, Darlene. What's your latest?"

She looked down at a short stack of papers. Cleared her throat. "Dead woman: Elspeth Lombard, forty-one. Multiple stab wounds, fatal one to the heart. Tortured, face disfigured. She must have died pretty quick. I've found no prints, no alien DNA other than background stuff. The lab says there's no sign of sexual assault per se. But that's a stupid, academic argument. I would certainly call photocopied banknotes in a vagina an absolute form of rape and sexual assault."

Darlene paused, as if daring someone to disagree. No one did, and Darlene continued.

"There are, though, some long hairs that don't match Elspeth Lombard's hair. I found those on her dress. Doesn't necessarily mean much. She could've picked them up walking along the road, or at a restaurant, even a hair-cutting salon—any number of places. And, of course, as I just said, the banknotes—just like the last time—are photocopies."

"The victim's husband, Alex Lombard, is CFO of Buttress Finance Group," I said. "So I'm wondering if there's a link with big-time corporate money." I looked at Justine and then Johnny.

"Obviously, our first touchstone has to be money, doesn't it?" Johnny replied. "Both husbands work in the financial sector. Banknotes placed ritualistically."

"But what about the elephant in the room? The fact that the money is fake?"

"In *both* murders," Mary added.

"But you don't have to be a genius to know it can't just be a coincidence the husbands are in finance *and* the two dead women were both abused the same way," Johnny insisted.

"Unless the killer is trying to trick us," Justine commented.

"Yeah, okay, anything is possible." I took a deep breath. "But money *is* the most obvious link we have at the moment, isn't it?"

"No," Justine said, and she said it quite emphatically.

"No?" We all looked to her.

"The most obvious link is…geography. The two women lived a street apart in Bellevue Hill. That's a stronger link than the financial one."

"You really think it has more to do with the fact that the victims lived in the same suburb?" I asked.

"Obviously I do," Justine said. "I just said that."

The room now held a bit of "who's the boss?" tension.

Justine continued. "If you're killing women in a neighborhood where most of the husbands are physicians or circus clowns, you're bound to conclude that their murders have to do with their husbands' being physicians or circus clowns. But I'm proposing that it's just the other way around. The killer is killing women who happen to live in an area where most of them are married to finance guys."

I had to admit: Justine's point was very well taken, and it would do me no good to debate it. The others on my team were waiting to hear what I thought. I spoke.

"So this asshole is actually killing women randomly,

except it doesn't seem random. They live within a few streets of each other...Bellevue Hill is teeming with banker types, stockbrokers. It's that sort of area."

"I've experienced this sort of thing in L.A.," Justine interjected, and swept her eyes around the table. "The guy could be going for women with the same hair color—Stacy Fleetwood and Elspeth Lombard were both blond. He could be targeting women of a particular age. Fleetwood was thirty-nine, Lombard forty-one. It could be someone at their gym, the tennis club, the local coffee shop."

"Okay. So, basically, what you two are saying is that we're next to nowhere, because the financial link could well be absolutely wrong," Johnny shot back.

"Guess we are," I said.

"I think we've got to pursue the financial angle, but I think we should give equal weight to the neighborhood theory," Justine said. "And any other smart theory that we hatch."

She was doing her best to make me look good, and I did my best to try to appreciate it. I was actually about to congratulate her on her helpfulness when my cell phone rang. Only five or six people had the code to override my phone's Off position, and apparently—I looked at the caller ID name—Mark Talbot was now one of them. His boss must have shared my code with the asshole.

"Gisto, do a download on the e-mail marked 'Confidential Outdoors.' "

"Wait a minute," I said. Then I turned to Johnny and said, "Mind if I borrow this?"

He didn't have time to say yes or no. I flipped his MacBook Pro open, signed on to my backup e-mail, the one entitled "Case Confidential Only," and began scanning down to find "Confidential Outdoors."

"What's this about, Talbot?" I asked as I waited for the pages to load.

"The security company for your fancy building, Matrix? They've some images of the guys who killed Chang."

"But the killers snatched the hard drive from the guard booth," I said.

"Turns out they had another camera just outside the exit gate of the garage. Separate system. You got it there yet?"

I told him that it was still loading, and I took a few seconds to give his info to the others in the room.

Mary seemed to speak for everyone when she said, "That's the best news we've had all week."

The page was now loaded. I found the e-mail. I pressed Download. A snowy, scratchy video of a car stopped at the garage exit started to roll.

"Stop it at twelve seconds," Talbot said.

I pressed Pause at twelve seconds. The camera held a nice medium close-up of the front windshield of the car. A driver's head. A passenger's head.

I played with a few video-control buttons to try to get better detail resolution. Finally I yelled into the phone.

"Talbot!" I screamed. "These faces are all blurred. They're blobs of gray. I can't even see a nose or an eye or a mouth. There's not a lab technique on earth that'll get us an ID on these guys."

I heard an unmistakable little chuckle from the other end. Then my cousin said, "It's the best we could do."

A moment later he hung up.

CHAPTER 33

THE PHONE IN Darlene's lab rang. She picked it up.

"This is Mickey Spencer. I'm stranded in your reception area, and it's lonely. The charming Cookie has disappeared. There are two VIP extensions here. Mr. Gisto's and yours. The choice was easy. Always call the girl."

"I'll be right out, Mr. Spencer," Darlene said, while she thought to herself: *Mickey Spencer. Mickey Spencer. I'm about to meet Mickey Spencer!* In that same split second she remembered her childhood bedroom and the two huge Mickey Spencer posters that hung next to her bed. She remem—

"Please. It's Mickey."

Cookie the receptionist must have stepped out for a moment, Darlene thought. Receptionists always had to "step out for a moment." A cig, a pee, a secret cell-phone chat with their man. So Darlene left her lab and walked the few yards to the reception area. There was Mickey Spencer, seated behind Cookie's desk. Right behind him was the massive, unsmiling Hemi.

"G'day, young lady. I've actually come to see Johnny." Mickey stood as he spoke.

"Right. I'm Darlene...as you already know. Johnny—ah, Johnny isn't here."

Why is the leading forensics expert on the continent of Australia feeling like a teenager? That was what Darlene was thinking.

But Darlene said, "Uh, Cookie stepped out, I guess. If you'd like to wait—" she said, pointing to the chic reception-room furniture.

"Perhaps someplace a bit less public," Mickey said. Then he added, "Funny how Johnny *and* Cookie are both MIA at the same time."

"Isn't it? Come on to my place," she said.

"So what do you do here, then?" Mickey asked as they walked toward the lab.

"Forensics." Now Darlene was acting as if she were quite used to finding people like Queen Elizabeth, Pope Francis, and even Mickey Spencer in Private's reception area. Fact was, now that the initial surprise was wearing off, Darlene was becoming a good deal calmer.

"Wow! This lab is so bloody cool. I love *CSI*. Do you watch that show?"

"No," Darlene replied. "I see enough bits and pieces of dead people during the day."

Mickey stared at her, then shook his head slowly and grinned. "That is just the most insane job, Darlene!"

"Really? I think being a rock star is pretty insane."

"If you say so."

Hemi stood next to Mickey. He only moved when it was absolutely necessary, and his blank expression never changed.

"Can I get you something? Coffee?" Darlene offered.

"No, thanks," he said. "And I'm sure Hemi is well hydrated." Another pause, then: "Tell you what, though. Show me some interesting lab stuff. The creepier the better."

For a moment Darlene looked surprised. "Yeah, sure."

"You know, my parents always wanted me to become a doctor or a scientist, something like that," he went on. "I got stung by the rock 'n' roll bug, but I always regret not going to college or anything. I love science...Don't know much...but..." He laughed.

Darlene wasn't certain if he was telling the truth or if this was merely a part of his "I'm just an ordinary guy" act.

"You could still do it. You're not dead yet," Darlene said. She immediately wondered if she should have used a different expression.

"You reckon?" Mickey chuckled. "Yeah, I can see it now." He put a hand up, indicating newspaper headlines. " 'Former Rock Star Now Leading Forensics Expert.' "

"What are you working on this very moment?" Mickey asked.

"Amusing you," Darlene said. Then she quickly added, "Sorry, couldn't resist."

"You are a cheeky one," Mickey said, but he was obviously quite enchanted by her.

"Okay. Truly. Right now I'm investigating a kidnapping and murder."

"Wow!"

"We have some security-camera images of the suspects, but they're really not good. I can't make anything out."

"So what can you do about it?"

Darlene led him over to a flat-screen. "I'm trying to enhance them with some new software I have."

Mickey gazed around the room. "Looks like pretty high-end stuff."

"Yeah, it is," she replied proudly. "State-of-the-art. But these stills are just too degraded."

"I can help," Mickey said.

Darlene lowered herself into a chair in front of the monitor. "You can?" She couldn't keep the skepticism from her voice.

"Well, not me personally. But I know a really great computer guy. A genius, in fact."

Before Darlene could reply, Mickey cut across her. "No, listen. The guy's amazing. This stuff "—he swept a hand around the room—"is cool, don't get me wrong, but in the recording studio, I use some really high-tech gear too. And my buddy—well, he works for me, actually—is *the biz*."

Darlene took a deep breath and put up her hands. "Well, great, Mickey. I'd appreciate any help I can get. What's your colleague's name?"

"Software Sam. I'll send him over."

"We pretty much know all the big-deal audio-video people here, and in Tokyo and Beijing. I appreciate it. However—"

Her sentence was interrupted by a muffled sound coming from the doorway where Hemi was standing, filling the space.

"Park it elsewhere, Hemi," Mickey said. Hemi moved left, and Johnny entered. He shook Mickey's hand.

"Good to see you again, dude. So, what's new?" Johnny said.

"I was worried for a moment that Ricky Holt might have eliminated you," Mickey said.

Johnny laughed, a bit too heartily, Darlene thought. Then he said, "Let's head to a conference room."

"Right on," said Mickey. Then he turned to Darlene. "Thanks for the tour, and thanks for listening to me babble."

"That's okay. Maybe next time I can show you some of the machinery in action."

"That'd be grand," Mickey said. And Darlene was slightly surprised when Mickey gave her a peck on both cheeks.

She was even more surprised when he said, "I'll give Software Sam a call and have him come by to see you."

"That won't be nec—" Darlene began.

Mickey interrupted and spoke to Hemi. "Make a mental note for me to call Sam," Mickey said. Then, with a laugh, he added, "Hemi makes a 'mental note.' That's a good one."

CHAPTER 34

"I WANT TO help you, Johnny," Mickey said. They were in the small conference room near Johnny's cubicle.

"Well, the best way to do that is to try to remember every detail," Johnny said.

"Such as . . . ?"

"Well, if Ricky Holt wants you killed because you're apparently worth more dead than alive, that means either he's absurdly greedy or has money problems."

"Well, course it's 'cause he's greedy, Johnny. He's a businessman. Only thinks about dollars and cents."

"Yeah, but we also discovered that he'd filed for bankruptcy in the States. Did you know that?" Johnny asked.

"Sure thing, I knew it. Didn't really think it was important."

Johnny gazed into Mickey's pinkish eyes and counted

silently to three before responding. "Not important— huh. Well, I hate to be condescending to a music legend, but around here, it's what we call 'motivation.'"

He glanced over at Hemi, who had sunk into a sofa at the back of the room, same fixed expression as always.

"God, this is all so fucked up!" Mickey exclaimed. Then he put his head down for a moment. "You got a drink, man?"

Johnny left the room for a few seconds and returned with a bottle of Johnnie Walker Double Black and a glass. He handed them to Mickey, who stared at the label.

"Is your last name Walker?" Mickey said with a laugh. Johnny just plowed ahead.

"Do you know anything about Ricky's finances, Mickey?" Johnny asked. "He must know all about yours. Does it only go one way?"

Mickey took a swig from the bottle, held it at arm's length. "Good shit."

"I'll take your word for it," Johnny said. "I don't drink."

"Lucky you."

Johnny raised an eyebrow.

"No, I mean it. Wish I didn't have to…"

"Holt's finances? Before my hair turns gray."

"I'm not an accountant, man. I don't know much about my own money, let alone my manager's money!"

Johnny rolled his eyes. Maybe he had overestimated this guy. Maybe Craig was right, and Mickey was drug addled. Or, put another way, maybe he was as dumb as his jokes.

"But he must have made a fortune," Johnny tried again. "How could he have ended up bankrupt?"

Mickey said nothing, just took another swig.

"Look, Mickey!" Johnny snapped. "How do you expect Private to help you if you don't tell us everything you know about the man?"

The rock star looked up and held Johnny's stare. "Yeah," he said finally. "You're right."

Of course I'm bloody right, Johnny thought, and he waited for the singer to sing.

"Ricky had a major problem. Blew fifteen mil...apparently."

"How?"

"Compulsive gambler, is what everyone said. But, look, dude, we all have our demons. I've never seen Ricky bet so much as a dime since I've known him. Got him drunk a few times, and he's told me straight that gambling is a mug's game. Says he put an end to the beast when he moved to Oz. Went into therapy, the lot. Gave up his old vices, doesn't even smoke weed now."

"And you believe him?"

Mickey considered the bottle again. "Well, I'll put it this way, Johnny." He lifted his eyes. "It's up to you to prove it if my manager has been lying, isn't it? And if he has been lying, then it will lead us to what we need— motivation!"

CHAPTER 35

THE GUY HAD described the car with absolute precision: 1971 Torino GT, bright lime, jacked-up rear wheels, avocado-and-red flame job along the sides. Mary recognized it immediately. How could she not? It was just like the anonymous writer had said in his e-mail to Craig.

He said he had important info about the murder of "that Chinese kid" but refused to come into Private's HQ. He'd meet someone from Private on the edge of Prince Alfred Park in Parramatta. Mary was that someone.

Mary crossed the hot gravel. She saw the guy in the driver's seat—bleached blond mullet, navy-blue baseball cap, shades, cigarette, a mountain range of acne on his cheeks. His e-mail didn't mention that he'd have a very big Rottweiler in the back.

The guy leaned over, pushed open the door. The dog growled.

"Shut up, Thor!"

Mary kept her eyes fixed on the dog and slipped into the passenger seat.

"He's cool," the guy said. "Knows who's boss. Don't you, Thor?"

Mary moved to the edge of her seat.

"Buckle up. We ain't staying here," the man said, and fired up the engine.

"Five nights ago—Friday. I saw a kid that fit the description of that Ho boy in the paper. I found out you guys are investigating. Didn't wanna go to the pigs—hate 'em, but I felt I ought to say something. Other thing is, I hate the Chink gangs even more than I hate the pigs. It's the Chinks, right?"

Mary kept silent.

"I saw a car pull up about eleven at night. I was with a chick." He gave Mary a wolfish grin and turned back to the road as they took a corner, past some ravaged tenement blocks.

She gave him a hard look. "You saw this from your window?"

"Yeah, the Chinks were staying in an apartment a few floors beneath mine. I'm on the ninth."

"Can you describe the car?"

He looked affronted. "Course I can, I'm a bloody mechanic. 'Ninety-six Toyota Corolla. Piece o' shit. Blue. Faded rear bumper had an I LOVE MACCA'S sticker on it. They dragged the kid from the back. His hands were tied behind him. He was gagged, but he was squirming like a sonuvabitch. So they kicked him in the balls. I heard him grunt, poor little bastard."

"What did the two Chinese men look like?"

"That's the thing. I only caught a glimpse." He spun the wheel hard, left. "It was dark, right? The council hasn't fixed the streetlights. Besides, those Chink dudes all look the same, don't they? Usual shit—short, skinny, long black hair. One was wearing a leather jacket. I thought that was odd, as it was about a million fucking degrees outside, even that late."

Mary pursed her lips, looked away at the sidewalk flashing by.

"You got the number plate?"

"Oh, yeah. I left it for a bit, then I went downstairs."

"You did?"

"Told you. I hate 'em. That's why I'm here."

"Okay."

"The plate number was GHT . . . ah . . . two three R."

"Sure?"

"Absolutely."

"Well, thanks," Mary responded. "Anything else?"

"Yeah. I'm pretty sure they were in apartment sixteen, third floor."

"*Were?*"

"They left a couple of nights ago," he said quickly, then pulled the car to the curb, turned in the road, and headed back to the park.

"How do you know that?"

"Saw 'em, didn't I?" He glanced over at Mary. She

caught a glimpse of the dog, dribble dangling from its chops. The guy accelerated down the street, screeched left, and the park lay directly ahead. "I checked with the block manager, Harry Griffin. I know 'im."

"You certain?"

"Of course I'm certain—Christ!"

"What's the full address?"

He paused for a beat, oddly reluctant. Then he pulled back into the lot. "Newbury House, Seventeen Canal Street. And that's all I got for you."

Then he said, "What have you got for me?"

Mary reached into her small leather duffel bag. She removed ten Australian hundred-dollar bills and handed them to him.

He took them, smiled, and made a loud kissing noise.

"Anything else for me?" he asked. He was looking directly at her breasts.

Mary said no way. She stepped out of the car, delighted that the 1971 Ford Torinos were built before the invention of driver-controlled door locks.

CHAPTER 36

AS SOON AS the scuzzball with the Rottweiler drove off, Mary called Darlene. She arranged to meet her an hour later at the address the guy had given her. Mary also told her to come prepared for forensic work. Then she called Parramatta Council. Within two minutes she had learned that Newbury House was serviced by a private cleaning company called R&M Cleaners.

Their address was barely a thousand yards from where she'd parked. Plus, the traffic was light.

The office was open, and as she approached the door to the left of an Aces Charcoal Chicken shop, a small group of Asian women in overalls were walking quickly down a flight of stairs. A van was parked at the curb. It had R&M CLEANERS written on the side.

Mary paused on the sidewalk to let the women pass. She glimpsed the plastic ID each of them wore attached to the straps of their overalls. That was all she needed. Twenty minutes and a trip to a passport photo booth in a stationery store later, she had a duplicate ID that she was sure would pass a cursory inspection. Then she drove on to Newbury House.

The block manager's office stank of cigarette smoke. The manager sat behind a small desk strewn with papers and an overflowing ashtray close to where he rested his left elbow. He was studying a racing paper.

"R and M Cleaners," Mary said confidently. He looked up from the paper, scrutinized her.

"Council sent me. Special clean for apartment sixteen," she said.

He looked puzzled for a moment. "You got ID?"

Mary pulled the fake from her pocket and held it out.

"Where're your overalls?"

She lifted her duffel bag and tapped it.

He shrugged and stood up, plucked the keys for the apartment from a rack on the wall behind him, and tossed them to her.

"When you're done, drop 'em in the box outside."

"Will do." Mary walked out, turned left, headed for the elevator. Emerging on the third floor, she saw Darlene waiting by the door to number sixteen, already prepped in plastic overalls and holding her metal box.

Mary unlocked the door to reveal a place where drunk college kids would feel right at home.

"Probably best if you leave me here for an hour, Mary," Darlene said as she began to pick through the trash lying everywhere.

"Leave you alone around here? You mad?"

"All right, but if you're going to nose around with me, at least put these on." She plucked a pair of latex gloves from her box of tricks.

Mary walked into the tiny kitchen as Darlene busied herself with a pile of rotting sandwiches and crumpled paper napkins on a cigarette-burned coffee table. The carpet stank of feet, cigarettes, and fried food.

The power had been cut off. In the kitchen the only light came from a tiny window over the sink. She heard a crunching sound underfoot and could make out dried noodles scattered on the cheap tiles.

She walked back into the living room. Darlene was bagging some cardboard cartons of the spoiled food and a few wooden chopsticks. She emptied two ashtrays into another bag and sealed it.

"Pretty bloody disgusting," Darlene remarked, looking up.

"Total arrogance," Mary replied. "Think they're above the law."

"In some places they are."

"Not in my city, they aren't!" Mary said, and turned to search the bedroom.

Moments later she called from the doorway. "Darlene?"

"Yep?" She stopped a foot inside the room. Mary had opened the curtains. The sheets were caked in dried blood. "I think we've found the operating room where they performed Ho Chang's eye surgery."

CHAPTER 37

JULIE O'CONNOR WAS a chubby little piece of flesh: flabby all around, with straggly blond hair, courtesy of a bottle of Nice 'N Easy lifted from the local 7-Eleven. People often say about fat people: "She'd be pretty if she'd only lose a little weight." Nobody ever said that about Julie O'Connor. The hair color didn't help. The thick layers of Maybelline didn't help. When she read in *People* magazine that David Bowie's ex-wife, Angie, had shaved off her eyebrows, Julie thought, *Hey, why not me?* So off came the eyebrows. And, of course, that sure as hell didn't help.

Bruce Frimmel was 265 pounds, with thick arms, vibrant red hair. He was one of those guys who had done everything to his face that a person could do: he had a Van Dyck beard, muttonchops, a haircut long on top and short on the sides, a diamond stud in his right ear.

A friend of theirs said that when big Bruce and fat Julie walked down the street together, they looked like the number ten.

The two of them lived in a public-housing apartment in Sandsville, in the western suburbs—no-man's land for any respectable Sydney-sider. It looked pretty much like a cheap motel room, just a little bigger. Two rooms: a cramped living area with badly stained green carpeting, a kitchen in the corner; next to that a bedroom, a bathroom with a cracked toilet, a cracked washbasin, and a shower curtain decorated with a pattern of hula dancers and palm trees. There were bars on the windows, bars on the front door.

Julie loved Bruce. Bruce tried to love Julie. But everything had gone wrong.

They wanted a kid, desperately. But nothing was working. So a month ago Julie had gone for an op, an op that, like their lives, also had gone spectacularly wrong. She developed an infection in her fallopian tubes, and within two weeks she was left infertile, completely barren. She would never have kids of her own.

Bruce had taken it badly. Very badly. Julie finally understood how badly one Tuesday at dusk, when she came home from the supermarket across town and heard Bruce slamming drawers in the bedroom.

"What ya doin', babe?" Julie asked. No answer.

When Julie walked into the bedroom, she saw Bruce bending over her own ratty, pink suitcase on the bed.

"Did we win the lottery?" She chuckled nervously.

Bruce ignored her.

"Tickets to Honolulu, Brucie?"

He turned, face hard.

She sank to the bed.

Bruce tossed some T-shirts into the case. They landed on top of his footie DVD and *Muscle Car* mag.

"I'm movin' out," he announced, hands on hips.

"Moving out... Why?" Julie's face was twisted. Then the inevitable question: "Someone else?"

Bruce nodded. He made to sit next to Julie on the bed but decided against it.

"Who? That slut from the video store?"

Bruce looked down between his trainers at the dirty carpet. Shook his head.

"Who, then?" Julie's voice was far too calm. Then she screamed...

"*WHO...?*"

Bruce was shocked for a second.

She pulled herself up from the bed, rushed toward him. He was a lot taller than Julie and a lot heavier. Still, he stepped back. He thought she was about to cry. He'd never seen her cry, and an odd thrill rattled through him. A strange moment of pride that even he was a little ashamed of. But she didn't cry. Not at all.

"You piece of shit!" Julie howled, and she went straight for his throat, digging her nails into his skin.

Before the huge hulk of a man could pull her off, she'd drawn blood—deep nail drags across his neck. Then she smacked him across the face. It stung, but it also knocked him back into reality. He hit her, made contact with something hard, Julie's jaw. He almost lost his balance but caught himself, straightened, and really went for her.

She stumbled, landing hard on her back. Her head hit the rough carpet. Bruce dived on her, swung his fist round, and smacked her in the face.

"Useless bitch!" he screamed. "Can't even do the business…Well, thank Christ! Who'd wanna have a kid with you?"

He smashed his fist into her face again, pulled himself up. Looked down at the red mess, blood streaming from Julie's nose, her lip split open.

Bruce turned back to the suitcase and clicked it closed, all the while listening to Julie's rasping breath and the blood gurgling in her throat.

CHAPTER 38

BRUCE SLAMMED THE front door. Julie lay semiconscious, blood drying on her face. Ten minutes later she was awake. She turned her head to the left, and blood streamed out of her mouth. She felt as if she were a drowning victim who had just been saved. The blood was the salt water she had swallowed. But where was the ocean? Where was the lifeguard? She spat more blood, and instead of thinking about Bruce and the horror of what had just happened, she began thinking of her father.

She saw him in her mind's eye. Her dad, Jim—he would have sorted Bruce out. God, how she had loved her father. Loved him as much as she'd loathed her mother, Sheila.

Jim had been a cop in Sandsville. Julie's favorite memory of him was the day he took her to work and showed her around the Sandsville police station. She was ten and very proud of her dad.

They'd gone to the forensics labs in the basement. A man in a white lab coat had shown her the machines and racks of test tubes, told her about fingerprinting and a new thing—DNA profiling. She hadn't really understood any of it. But the next day she took a book from the local library. It was called *Forensic Investigation,* and she read every word of it.

Julie had begun to hate her mother when she realized Sheila didn't love her dad. There was another man. Julie wasn't sure if Jim knew about him, but she sometimes overheard her mother talking to her boyfriend on the phone when her dad was out. And once she followed her and saw her kissing a heavyset man with a brown beard. How could any sane woman prefer this guy to her dad?

The day she'd seen her mother kissing her boyfriend had been the worst day in Julie's life. That is, the worst day until the really worst day arrived. The day two cops came to the door of their house and told them her dad had been killed on duty—knifed trying to stop a burglar. Jim was thirty-four.

CHAPTER 39

LATER THAT NIGHT Julie began to plot Bruce's murder. It all seemed perfectly logical, perfectly justified. She planned everything as meticulously as a not-very-meticulous person could. And as she took one step after the other on the road to killing her ex, she started to enjoy herself.

Bruce was a sex pig. She believed that all men thought with their dicks, but Bruce's sex drive was more powerful than most. So he was a bigger pig than most. She knew she could use that knowledge to her advantage.

Bruce always had a liking for what he called "class ass." So Julie went to an Internet café and, using the "class ass" name Sabrina, sent an anonymous e-mail to Bruce's phone. She was sure he wouldn't reply right away. But she'd give him some time. "Sabrina" would send another e-mail.

At first, he was cautious, but after half a dozen messages all sent from different computers, Sabrina ensnared him, and the exchanges became more explicit. For Julie it became a delightful task. It was like writing pornography. She described what she would do *to* him and *with* him and *for* him. The asshole stepped into the trap. Soon he was begging to meet her in person.

She coaxed and teased like a pro, made it clear she liked rough sex in scary places. The more depraved, the more it turned her on. She had Bruce salivating.

She called in to him at an Internet café in Balmain and typed a message: "I want you...TONIGHT!"

"When? Where?" he responded almost immediately.

Finally "Sabrina" gave him the place and time: nine p.m., at a condemned house she had already staked out. The burned-out house was fenced off with wire mesh. On the perimeter of the property stood a large notice board that detailed the new development planned for the site. Another sign told the public to keep out.

The windows and the front door were boarded up, but Julie was prepared. She made short work of a couple of planks, securing one of the side windows in the living room. The room was strewn with crack pipes and newspapers and pigeon droppings.

She'd found everything she needed in the local hardware store, and she arranged it neatly in the corner of the dilapidated bathroom—a powerful battery-powered lamp, a hammer, and a new knife. She surveyed her purchases.

Then she waited patiently. Maybe it was a half hour.

Maybe he wasn't coming. Finally she heard someone approach the door. She recognized Bruce's sounds—the heavy tread of his feet, the irritating whistling—almost as if she were hearing him come into their own apartment.

"Sabrina?"

She didn't reply.

"Sabrina?" There was a nervous edge to his voice.

"In here," she called from the bathroom down the hall, and flicked on the battery-powered lamp. She stood behind the half-opened door.

Julie let him take two steps into the room, crept up behind him, swung her new hammer low, and said one word: "Bruce." He made a half turn, and Julie smashed him behind the right knee with the hammer.

He yelled and stumbled, grabbing the edge of the tub. She leapt on him and brought the hammer down hard on his head. Then once more. Her reward for her efforts was a bubbling little fountain of blood coming from the back of his skull.

The ridiculous haircut of his was soaked with his blood. He looked up into her eyes as she stood over him. He slowly twisted his head and saw her face.

"Julie!" he gasped. Then nothing.

She knelt beside him and pushed him over, onto his back. His eyes rolled back and up into his head. They were the eyes of a dead man.

Julie didn't know whether to laugh or cry. So she did both.

CHAPTER 40

GREASE-STAINED CARGO pants, heavy brown boots, a black, sleeveless top, and a bandanna. That was Mary Clarke's wardrobe choice when she walked into the Golden Wheel restaurant and bar in Campbelltown.

As soon as she took a seat at the bar, the place turned completely silent, the way it happened in saloons in old Western movies when the really bad "bad guy" or the really good "good guy" walked in.

"Coke, please. No ice if it's cold."

"Maybe you in wrong place, miss?" the Chinese bartender said.

Mary smiled sweetly. "Pretty sure I'm not. Now... Coke?"

The bartender walked to the fridge. Mary scanned the room. Thorogood had given her a pretty thick file to study on the new Triads. So she recognized a few of the Golden Wheel patrons from those classified photo-graphs and documents.

Mary knew that there were two main gangs, one more important than the other. Latest intel was that they tolerated each other because each was run by two blood brothers who'd fought. At the moment the two broth-ers were on good terms. So apparently, the gangs were working together—for the moment.

The bartender broke Mary's concentration. "Six dol-lar."

She put the coins on the counter, lifted her glass, and continued surveying the room openly, even brazen-ly. One of the brothers was here, she noted. Lin Sung. A homely bastard with a pie-shaped face and eyebrows that should be trimmed with a lawn mower. She had studied his mug shot, sent over from Hong Kong that morning. When she'd seen his picture and Craig told her the guy was one of the two brothers leading the Sydney Triads, she'd joked that the poor bugger had ob-viously inherited the ugly genes. Then she saw the image of Sung's brother, Jing, and laughed out loud. Lesson learned: you don't have to be pretty in order to be a gang leader.

She felt a familiar ripple of power as she looked around. They knew she was either a cop or a PI. Most of the guys in this bar were not dumb. And even the dumb ones had street smarts. Whatever their intellectual makeup, they all had the brains not to lay a finger on her, at least not yet.

A man got up from a table. It was Lin Sung. He was

all smiles, wire thin, snappily dressed, if you happen to go for shiny fabrics and narrow ties, circa 1979.

"Do I know you?" he asked. "What're you drinking?" He flicked a glance at the bartender.

"I don't think you do, Mr. Lin," she said. "And I'm enjoying this Coke—don't need another, thanks all the same."

Lin gave a slight bow. He looked at her again. "Well, then," he said, "is there anything else I can do for you?"

"Nope!" Mary said, smacking her lips. "Just here to have a Coke. Seemed like a nice place...from the outside."

Lin straightened up. The fake smile disappeared. He turned and walked away.

She drained her glass of the much-discussed Coke, pulled herself off the stool, and walked toward the restroom. What she actually wanted was a look at the outside rear of the building.

She opened the bathroom door and locked it behind her. Filthy basin, filthy toilet. But there was a square frosted-glass window covered in wire mesh. The window was stuck closed. She moved her right palm over the frame, found just the right spot, hit it with the flat of her hand. The entire window frame collapsed. She climbed through.

Outside, behind the bar, it was pretty much as anticipated—stinking, overloaded bins, empty steel beer barrels, a fish skeleton ground into the dirt.

There was a small, falling-apart shack across the alley. She crossed the alley and tried the door handle. Locked.

A solid kick knocked it in; the bolt snapped, clunked to the ground.

A storeroom piled high with large cartons. Chinese writing on the sides. She hoisted one down, plucked a Swiss army knife from her pants, and slit it open. It was filled with bags. She moved one aside, sliced along the seam. Rice spilled out, over her heavy boots. She closed the knife and slipped it back into her pocket.

A sound from outside. She ducked down beside a tower of boxes.

Two men, both Chinese, walked through the space that had been created by the missing door. As soon as the men stepped closer in, Mary charged at the doorway. Once outside, she heard someone shouting in Chinese. One of them tackled Mary. She fell. She used her elbow with all her strength and hit the temple of the guy who had tackled her. The aim of her elbow was absolutely perfect. The guy was out—guaranteed concussion. Also guaranteed was that the other guy would be right on top of her.

She was correct about that. And the guy on top of her was Lin Sung, his hideous face broad with a big grin and a mouth full of bad teeth.

Suddenly she felt a sting of pain in her left hand. Mary ignored the pain and managed to use that same hand to retrieve the knife from her pocket.

She had her knife out in three seconds. As she snapped it open, she managed to slash Lin Sung in his left forearm. It was barely worse than a scratch, but it grabbed his focus for a moment. That gave Mary the few seconds she needed to shove him off, turn him over. Now she was kneeling on his shoulders, pinning him against the gravel. His smile had not disappeared. He looked at the point of Mary's blade. It was a fraction of an inch from his Adam's apple.

Lin lifted his head a little.

"Who killed the Ho boy?" Mary asked quietly.

"Who is Ho?"

Mary touched his skin with her knife.

"The Ho boy?" Lin said, slowly and sarcastically. "I'm afraid that name is new to me."

"I would slash your face open," Mary hissed, "but it would do your looks a favor."

Lin chuckled. "What do you people say? Sticks and stones—"

"Who killed the kid?" And now she cut his throat just enough to let some blood drip out. It was as gentle as a nick from shaving.

Beads of sweat broke out on his forehead.

"You'll kill me before I speak," Lin Sung said.

Mary stared him out for ten, twenty seconds, becoming more and more aware of her own pain, her hand throbbing. She flicked a glance downward and saw a puddle of blood. She stood up. She looked down at Lin Sung and sneered at him.

The moment she turned to walk away, Lin Sung, still on the ground, began to laugh.

CHAPTER 41

YASMIN TRENT'S THICK, black hair was held in place on top of her head by two ruby-studded antique combs. Casual chic—that was her intention, and it worked. Other jewelry? A small, gold Rolex on her left wrist, a bunch of skinny Elsa Peretti silver bangles on her right. Roberto Cavalli jeans. Her beige shirt was made from a fabric that was just one small step away from being see-through.

She walked briskly from the SupaMart through the parking lot. Her small tote held a container of no-fat cottage cheese, a spit-roasted chicken, a small box of green tea, and a bottle of Tanqueray gin. She had no reason to notice Julie O'Connor, standing a few yards from the rear door of Yasmin's Toyota Land Cruiser.

Julie was in a remarkably good mood. In a local stationery shop an hour earlier, she'd overheard women talking about the "serial killer." It was exhilarating, but, of course, it made her realize that people were on the alert now. So she had to take extra care in her next murder.

Yasmin Trent touched the remote. The car beeped and flashed. Yasmin pulled herself into the driver's seat, placed her tote on the passenger seat, and shut the door. Just at that moment, Julie jerked herself into the back.

Yasmin started to turn. Then she screamed.

"Don't move, bitch!" Julie hissed, and Yasmin felt something hard and cold at the nape of her neck. She screamed again.

"Once more and I'll slice your cute little head right off."

Yasmin shut up.

She could see the figure in the back reflected in the mirror. It was a woman in a hoodie: bleached, crispy blond hair protruding from under the fabric, no eyebrows.

"Drive," Julie said quietly.

Yasmin froze.

"Okay," Julie said a little louder. "I get that you're terrified. But you *will* turn the key. You *will* pull out of the parking lot. And you *will* drive along the road, or I'll not only slice you up, I'll come back for your kids."

Julie saw Yasmin turn the key, and the engine fired up. The car pulled out of the parking space. Julie kept the eight-inch blade she was holding tight up against Yasmin's slender, tanned nape.

"Good," Julie hissed. "You're being a very good little girl."

CHAPTER 42

YASMIN DROVE. SHE was amazed at how driving was such a reflexive endeavor. In her sweating, shaking, stomach-turning fear, tears continuously filled her eyes. But she noticed that her driving was impeccable. She stopped at the stop signs. She slowed down at the yellow lights.

A few minutes into the drive, she found enough saliva in her mouth to actually speak: "What is this all about?"

There was still a noticeable tremor in Yasmin's voice. That pleased Julie, and by not replying she only heightened Yasmin's anxiety.

They were driving down the main thoroughfare from the eastern suburbs toward the business district. Following Julie's instructions, Yasmin pulled the Land Cruiser off at the next junction, through a toll booth, and onto the freeway, heading west.

"Please—what is this about?" Yasmin asked.

"It's about you and me."

"What's that mean?"

Julie chuckled. "Power, Yasmin. Everything in life always ends up being about power."

"I don't..."

"You don't understand? Maybe you're as stupid as you look."

Yasmin had no response. She just kept driving.

"So, the Rolex, Yasmin?" Julie said slowly.

Yasmin touched her wrist involuntarily.

"How many blow jobs did that take, eh?"

Julie could see Yasmin's horrified face in the mirror. "Everything costs something, Yasmin. Come on. Everything costs—"

"Is that it? You want my watch? Here, have it..." She reached for the clasp.

"No, you stupid bitch! I don't want your shitty watch."

The car swerved. So much for reflexive driving.

"Careful, honey," Julie mocked.

The car swerved again. This time it was deliberate, and Julie knew it. Julie pushed the tip of the blade a fraction of a millimeter into Yasmin's neck, making her squeal.

"Stop doing that shit...NOW!"

The car swayed once more. Horns blared. The Land Cruiser crossed lanes. Yasmin cut in front of another car. More horns, screeching tires.

Julie pulled her mouth up close to the woman's ear.

"Here's some info: If you don't stop this shit, I will take your twins from preschool. I will take them somewhere very private..."

Yasmin slowed the car immediately. It felt to Julie that Yasmin was about to pull over onto the shoulder of the road.

"Don't..."

Julie watched Yasmin's face in the rearview mirror, white as dead flesh. She was staring fixedly at the road ahead.

Then Yasmin spoke very softly.

"You're the killer!" Yasmin said, shocked at her own discovery.

Julie felt a stirring of pride in the pit of her stomach. "Just drive," she said. "Not much farther now. It'll all be over very soon."

CHAPTER 43

A VARIETY OF disgusting objects lay across the steel-top counter—a pile of filthy and bloodstained sheets, takeout cartons that reeked of rotted food, cigarette stubs, crumpled Kleenex, used condoms, empty booze bottles, plastic pieces of what was once a TV remote—all collected from the deserted Triad apartment in Parramatta.

Mary pulled up a chair as Darlene turned away from the monitor to face her.

"I could tell by your tone on the phone that you're disappointed," Mary said.

Darlene shrugged. "Look, perhaps we were hoping for too much."

Then she noticed Mary's bandaged hand. "What happened there?"

Mary glanced down. "Oh, a stupid accident. Don't ever use the pointed end of a knife to remove an avocado pit."

"I'll keep that piece of advice on file," Darlene said. Then she handed Mary a pair of rubber gloves. Mary stood up next to Darlene.

"The blood on the sheets matches Ho Chang's, of course. His prints are all over the bedding, on the food cartons, chairs in the kitchen."

"What about other fingerprints? The guys who abducted him?"

Darlene paced back to her workstation, Mary in tow. She tapped at a keyboard. The image on the monitor changed to show several sets of prints.

"I've found four distinct sets in the apartment, excluding Ho's. I've also separated out three samples of DNA."

"That's great...yeah?"

"Not really. One set of prints and one DNA sample belong to a plumber who'd worked in the apartment a few weeks back. He had a record—petty theft in 1990; meant he was in the database. Another set of prints belongs to the manager's wife, Betty Griffin."

"Could she or her husband be involved?"

"She died last month. Ovarian cancer."

Mary snorted. "And the other two?"

"According to my analyzer, the DNA comes from two different Asian males."

"And?"

"That's it—no matches in any databases. Same for the prints."

"So we've narrowed it down to—what?" Mary declared. "About a billion men?"

"Actually, I think it's closer to two billion."

CHAPTER 44

"TO OUR WONDERFUL Greta!" Brett Thorogood said as he lifted his crystal flute of Veuve Clicquot. He clinked it with Greta's and those of their two closest friends, Deborah and Barry. The doorbell rang.

"I'll get it," Greta's son, Serge, called as he ran from the playroom, his younger sister, Nikki, close behind.

"That should be Christine, the babysitter," Greta said.

"You're so lucky, having a regular sitter," Deborah said.

"Christine's great. She works in the bakery at the local SupaMart. The kids love her. I think Brett likes her a little too much too."

Brett laughed and said, "Wait till Barry sees her. He'll love her too. She looks like the sweetest cupcake in the bakery."

"You sound just like an idiot schoolboy," Greta said.

Footsteps echoed from the hallway. Serge came in with a woman who was clearly not a "cupcake" or, frankly, any kind of fantasy confection. Greta stared at the chubby woman with spiked blond hair and mottled skin. She was clearly confused.

The woman stepped forward and held out her hand. "Hi, I'm Julie—Julie O'Connor."

Greta noted the SupaMart uniform and badge.

"Christine went home sick from work. She called you, right?"

"No, she didn't," Greta said.

"Oh. Well, I've got a lot of experience. I sometimes babysit with Christine. We're old friends—"

"It's not that," Greta said, as pleasantly as possible. "It's just, I don't know you..."

Julie let out a gentle sigh. "Okay...I understand." She turned to leave.

Brett stood up, touched Greta's arm, and whispered in her ear. "We're stuck, darling. It's your party—we have to go now, but we can't leave the kids on their own."

"Just a sec, Julie," Greta said. "Just let me try Christine." She plucked her cell from the table and hit the speed-dial number. It rang five times, then went to voice mail. Irritated, she snapped the phone shut.

"We'll be good," Serge said.

"It's not that, sweetie."

"Too late to get anyone else," Brett muttered.

"Okay! Okay!" Greta put her hands up resignedly. "Julie . . . ?"

Julie's face was expressionless.

"I apologize. Would you ...?"

Julie smiled sweetly. Then she spoke.

"I understand your concern. But, listen. Don't worry."

"I'll try not to," Greta said. "Our cell numbers are on the pad near the kitchen phone, and the children should be in bed by nine and—"

"Calm down, Mrs. Thorogood. Have a good time," Julie said.

Brett smiled and said, "We will. Sorry for the confusion."

CHAPTER 45

SHE CLOSED THE door. Nikki and Serge were standing together, eyeing their babysitter.

"Where'd your eyebrows go?" Nikki asked.

Julie tilted her head to one side, touched her face, and feigned surprise. "Aaaggghhh! They've vanished!"

Nikki didn't even smile.

Then Julie said, "Truth is . . . I woke up this morning, and they were gone!"

Nikki was highly skeptical. "No, you didn't!"

"Honest, I did! I think my cat ate 'em while I was sleeping." Julie clapped her hands together. "So, what's your favorite game, kids?"

The siblings argued about whether they should play Pocket God on the iPad, Xbox, or the interactive game that came with the latest Harry Potter DVD. In the end, the wizard won out.

Julie indulged them for an hour. Then it was bedtime and Julie's turn for some fun.

She wanted to see the inside of a house like this, see how the bitches around here lived. Earlier that day, she'd told Christine, the Thorogoods' regular sitter, that Greta had dropped into the store and asked her to pass the message on that she had to cancel tonight. Then she'd slipped Christine's cell from her pink work smock.

The plan had worked, and now that she was here, she was stunned. She'd never been in a house like this and couldn't get her head around the fact that only four people lived in it. It did nothing for her state of mind.

She walked through the main living room. She picked up crystal vases and marble ashtrays, elaborately framed photographs and silver bowls. She settled the things back down carefully. The stairs beckoned. She spun round and walked up the wide metal-and-glass steps to the first floor. The kids were asleep.

She took the second flight of stairs to the top floor, a single, expansive area devoted to the parents. A vast bedroom decorated in navy blue and white, a wall of windows looking out onto the ocean. A marble bathroom bigger than most people's living rooms. *Holy shit.* There was a shower that could fit about twenty people in it. *Two* tubs, *two* basins, and a whole separate room for the toilet.

The wife's closet had endless shelves, along with a sliding ladder attachment; that way the bitch could get to the Jimmy Choos on the very top shelves. Julie slipped between the rows of clothes. She ran her hand along the parade of dresses and skirts and suddenly realized that they were hanging and separated according to color.

Beyond the walk-in was a small room. Well, what the hell was this? Greta's personal dressing room. A counter, a chair, necklaces hanging from stands, makeup set out in precise rows. It looked like the cosmetics counters in the fancy boutiques on Castlereagh Street North.

Julie squatted down and chose a lipstick—Guerlain Rouge d'Enfer—applied it carefully, and studied the result in the mirror over the counter. She gave herself an approving little nod, found the Dior mascara, and stroked it on. Then she walked back to the clothes.

She took her time, sifting through the garments carefully. She read the labels—Lanvin, Chanel—chose a bright-red dress, slipped into it, and managed to zip it up halfway. It was ridiculously tight on her, but she didn't care.

She picked a pair of leopard-print Blahnik shoes, crammed her toes into them, and strode into the bedroom, where a mirror occupied half a wall.

"I was born for this," Julie said to herself, and did an ungainly twirl, almost falling off the shoes. That was when she saw Nikki Thorogood staring at her. Nikki's mouth was wide open.

Julie reacted with incredible speed, whirled on the girl and grabbed her before she could take a single step back. She brought a rough hand to the girl's mouth and pulled her backward against her body. Nikki's petrified squeals were muffled by Julie's fat fingers.

"Shut up," Julie hissed in Nikki's ear. She twisted the little girl to face the mirror. She slipped the stiletto off her right foot and lifted the bladelike heel to the kid's throat. "Tell anyone about this, Nikki...and I will come for you in the night and I will kill you very, very slowly. Do you understand me?"

The kid was too terrified to move. Julie tightened her grip. "DO YOU UNDERSTAND ME, NIKKI?"

The girl nodded, and slowly Julie loosened her grip.

CHAPTER 46

THE PLACE WAS a great choice. Icebergs is, I gotta say, the best restaurant in Bondi Beach. Plus, it sits on the side of a cliff, has an amazing, panoramic view back across a spectacular stretch of ocean. The Thorogoods had booked the entire restaurant for Greta's birthday party. One hundred people.

Justine was a knockout in a tight-fitting red cocktail dress. She'd put her hair up, Audrey Hepburn–style circa *Breakfast at Tiffany's*.

I felt her tug on my sleeve and lead me toward a balcony across the room. I plucked two champagne flutes from a surf dude who had put on a waiter's uniform for the night.

"Greta seems to be having a fun time," I said. She was dancing with Brett, and they both looked happy. Greta was laughing at something her husband was saying close to her ear.

"It's good to see. Hasn't been having a good time recently, since the murder."

We stared out at the darkness, broken up by the lights of Bondi. In the sky was a sliver of moon, something my late wife used to call a "toenail moon."

"Ice," Justine said suddenly.

"What?"

"We seem to have a thing for ice, you and me. You took me to the ice bar, and now I get you here at Icebergs." She produced a gorgeous smile.

"Where next?" I said. "Would you like dinner somewhere with 'ice' in the name?"

"Ah," Justine said, "I'm flattered, but..."

"Sorry."

"No, don't be. But..."

"You're taken...Jack's a very lucky man."

There was an awkward silence. Then she said, "So, Craig...How did you end up here, doing what we do? This crazy job?"

"Nice diversion, Justine!" I laughed. "Long story."

"Got time." She took a sip. I turned, leaned on the balcony. "I was born in England. Mum died when I was twelve. I never knew my father. I was sent to Australia to live with my uncle and his family."

"And why PI work?"

"Ah—well, that was thanks to the love of a good woman."

She raised an eyebrow.

"I studied law, but when I actually got round to practicing it, I found it bone-dry. Let me rephrase that: it sucked. Then I met my future wife, and I fell in love. Becky was the one who pushed me into trying something I really wanted to do. So I set up my own little company: Solutions, Inc."

It was clear from Justine's nodding that she knew something of what had happened to my family.

My cell trilled. I recognized the Private Sydney number. "Darlene—you're working late."

"Sorry to call you at the party. Just had a call from police HQ. I thought you'd want to know. There's been another murder."

CHAPTER 47

"REPETITION IS SO bloody boring," Darlene said.

We were standing over the dead woman. Same story—face disfigured with multiple cigarette burns, skirt up and over her legs, a roll of fifty-dollar bills in place—only this time the victim was an almost-black-haired brunette.

"This bastard's getting me down," Darlene said as she knelt beside the body.

The victim's blood had pooled on the concrete beneath her, drenching her clothes red. I'd already learned that her name was Yasmin Trent: forty-one, mother of three young boys, lived on Gervaine Road in Bellevue Hill, about five hundred yards from Stacy Fleetwood and Elspeth Lombard. Yasmin had been a homemaker, and her husband, Simon Trent, was a dentist. So that pretty much wiped out the finance-motive theory. Most dentists made a nice living, but they didn't have the dough that the finance guys had.

There were two Police Forensics officers working on Yasmin Trent's body. They'd mellowed toward us recently. I guessed they realized we weren't going away. Plus, they'd benefited from Private's lab resources.

As I looked around myself, I caught a glimpse of Mark at the wheel of his car, the door open. He was talking to a sergeant.

I left Darlene and nosed around. It was a patch of waste ground behind a gas station in Sandsville, in the western suburbs. The late-evening traffic was light on the freeway beyond the forecourt. The place was scrappy and grimy. A rusting car stood to one side. A few weeds poked through the concrete nearby. A dead palm stood close to the rear wall of the gas-station building.

The MO had altered here slightly. It was another new, disconcerting aspect to this case. Killers rarely change their MO, even subtly. Like the other victims, this dead woman was from the eastern suburbs. She'd probably never even been to Sandsville before today, maybe just seen it on TV when channel 9 news carried an item about a knifing or a house blaze to the west. It was only, what? Thirty miles from here to Bellevue Hill? But the two places might as well have been in different solar systems.

So the question was: what was Yasmin Trent doing here? Was she killed here or in Bellevue Hill? This was different. On the other hand, some of the MO was the same—facial disfigurement, multiple stab wounds to her back, vaginal ATM-in-reverse. We were looking for one sick motherfucker.

I felt a tap on the shoulder, turned to see Darlene. She had her box of forensics equipment in her left hand.

"That was pretty quick."

"I've learned what to look for. That part of it's predictable. The hard work comes later. But you know what, Craig? There's something not quite right about this."

"You mean the body being here in Sandsville?"

"No, it's that, but it's more than that. I can't put my finger on it. But I will. I've got very sensitive fingers."

CHAPTER 48

HO DAI WAS thinking about sleep. He was almost dreaming about sleep. He'd just gotten back to his apartment after leaving his father's house, walked into his tiny kitchen, gotten a glass of water, and heard a sound. He drank the water.

The noise came again. Footsteps? Voices? Whatever the noise was, it was also soft. But it was real. He saw two shadows pass by a glass wall close to the front door. Then Ho Dai watched as the handle turned and was released.

He padded across the floor and into the bedroom, reached the built-in wardrobe, pulled himself inside, and eased the door shut. It was dark, but he knew where he kept the gun his father insisted he have. He felt the grip just as the intruders made it through the front door and into the tiny hall.

Dai pulled the weapon down from a shelf and pointed it directly ahead. He heard someone enter the room.

"Mr. Ho," a voice said, "we know you're in here."

"I have a gun!" Dai shouted. "Open the door and I'll shoot."

A bullet thudded through the door and smacked into the wall a foot to Dai's left. He felt his bowels loosen, just managed to control himself. A second bullet sent shards of wood flying in the dark and crunched into the wall at the back of the wardrobe. It was so close that splinters flew into Dai's arm, making him cry out.

"Open the door a crack and drop the gun outside, or we'll shoot again," said the same male voice.

Dai stood rigid, trying to think, trying to rationalize.

"I'm counting to three. One…"

Dai was wreathed in sweat and breathing hard. He couldn't win. Whatever he did, he was dead meat.

"Two…"

He could barely make himself move. Had to force his arm forward. The door opened an inch, two inches. He tossed the gun onto the carpet and slammed the doors outward, propelling himself into the bedroom. He tripped, crashed to the floor, and felt the cold barrel of a gun on the back of his neck.

CHAPTER 49

ANTHONY HILARY WAS feeling horny as hell. Everything had been arranged with Karen. He would surf at six a.m. with his buddies, Chad and Frankie, and then he would meet her at the empty old house he'd found the day before. When he'd first suggested it, Karen was reluctant, but he'd eventually persuaded her.

"I can promise you the most comfortable and cleanest sleeping bag in Sydney," he'd told her with a grin.

"Oh! I'm touched!" she'd responded. "I must remember to mention that to my parents when they ask me why I'm leaving for school an hour early." But then she had shaken her head and smiled. "Okay, Ant. Seven a.m."

The surf was excellent this morning, but Anthony's mind wasn't on it. He wiped out way more than usual. Even Frankie and Chad noticed.

"Dude, what's with you? You totally wasted that wave."

"Yeah, sorry, man," Ant responded. "Look, I'm gonna bail."

"What?"

"Can't focus. I'll put the board in your car, all right, Frankie?"

His friend waved and slipped back into the surf.

Half an hour later, Anthony was standing outside the house on Ernest Street, in Bondi, watching the shifting morning light on the roofs across the road. He didn't normally do this sort of thing. He and Karen were good kids from the same coed school. He loved her, and he believed she loved him. They were seventeen. Yeah, he rationalized, some kids their age were parents already, but he and Karen could never be alone together, were watched over 24-7. It pissed him off to no end.

Karen was fifteen minutes late, and Ant was growing increasingly frustrated. When she arrived, he just managed to stay cool.

"Okay, lover boy," she said, sidling up to him and reaching on tiptoes to kiss him full on the mouth. He looked down at her tanned face and dark curls. He was hard almost instantly.

"Come on," he said, and took her hand.

The front door was broken, and, although it looked like it was closed securely, it actually hung halfway off its hinges. Ant escorted her down a narrow passage to the second room on the left. She could hear music drifting along the hall and glanced at her boyfriend as she recognized the tune, Angus and Julia Stone's "Big Jet Plane."

Karen stood at the entrance to the room, holding Ant's hand. He knew he had her. She was entranced. He had cleaned it up, swept the floor, made a bed of sleeping bags. The curtains were drawn; two dozen candles glowed. An iPod played softly through a portable speaker system. The song ended and was followed by Karen's favorite, Alicia Keys's "No One."

"Oh, Ant. This is the best." She turned and kissed him again, sliding her tongue between his teeth and producing a low moan in the back of her throat. Ant felt he would burst there and then. He swept her up, lowered her gently onto the soft layers of the sleeping bags.

It all went a little faster than Karen would have liked. But it was still good for her. Ant was pretty sure of that. When it was over, they lay together, looking joyfully and contentedly up at the shabby, pitted ceiling, as if they had just finished making love in the Sistine Chapel.

"Back in a sec," Karen said softly. She pecked Anthony on the cheek and pulled herself up. "Bathroom."

"Hey, take this." Ant reached into his bag for a large bottle of water. "No main supply."

Karen looked pained and then crouched down to kiss Anthony again. "That's very thoughtful," she said.

He watched the girl's naked form in the candlelight and threw his head back onto the makeshift pillow. He really thought that this was the high point of his life. That things could never be better than this.

Then he heard Karen scream.

CHAPTER 50

INSPECTOR MARK TALBOT felt like shit, and days like today, the ones that started out really bad, were almost impossible to bear.

He'd woken up at six a.m. with a sore head from a big night out with two of his tequila-loving buddies and had dragged himself into the station by seven thirty. Forty minutes later the call had come in—another grisly find. This was getting to be fucking ridiculous. Back in the car.

The traffic was terrible all the way to Bondi, and around eight o'clock it turned stormy—black clouds rolling in over the ocean. He switched on the radio, pushed the button for classic-rock FM, and felt better as Steely Dan's "Reelin' In the Years" filled the car.

"All right, what's the story?" Talbot said as he got out of his car and followed a sergeant into the empty house, the rain crashing down around them.

"Best see for yourself, sir."

Talbot dashed into the hall, his jacket soaked. The forensics people were everywhere. Huge spotlights blazed, powered by a portable generator. None of it did his head much good. At the end of a corridor, there was a bathroom, with two officers in plastic suits crouching down. The tub, toilet, floor, and white walls were splashed with dried blood. A lab guy was photographing the scene. Talbot saw a line of dry red-black dots leading from the room, out toward the kitchen and the rear of the property.

The stench hit him as he entered the yard. The smell of death. He knew it well.

The blood trail stopped on the west side of the back garden. There was a large stain on the patio, close to the fence. His team had already lifted the paving stones and dug away some soil. Talbot, hand over his mouth, could see part of a corpse—a woman, faceup in the dirt.

He waved over one of his sergeants who had been standing on the other side of the shallow grave. "The basics," the inspector said, his voice phlegmy.

"Young guy called us about seven thirty. By the time we got here, the place was deserted."

"What was he doing here?"

"Looks like the kid was a vagrant—evidence someone had slept in the front room last night."

"Obviously wasn't here long. Probably nothing to do with the crime. Needs checking out, though."

The body was no more than a couple of feet beneath the surface. Three men in blue forensics suits lifted the dead woman out of the opening and laid her on plastic sheeting.

Talbot and his sergeant took two paces toward the body.

One of the forensics officers leaned in and brushed away some soil.

Most of the woman's clothes were decomposing. Her flesh barely clung to her bones.

"Dead for weeks," the forensics guy muttered, his voice muffled by his mask.

"Clear the soil from her pubic region," Talbot said.

The officer moved the brush down the dead body, swept away the sand and grains of soil. Some skin and flesh came away with it. A roll of fifty-dollar bills had been wedged into her vagina.

"You want me to call Private?" the sergeant asked.

"No, I don't think so," Talbot said. "Not this time."

CHAPTER 51

COOKIE POKED HER head around the door and into Private's lab. She was afraid of disturbing Darlene. So Cookie quietly said "Knock, knock" in that cute voice that some young women can use without sounding like idiots. Cookie always got away with it.

"What's up?" Darlene asked. She saw a tall, skinny guy with hair like a giant bird standing just outside the room, trying to peek inside.

"Er...this is—what did you say your name was again?" Cookie asked, turning and deliberately obstructing the doorway.

"I-I-I'm S-S-Sam," the man said.

Darlene looked at him blankly for a second, and then the name registered. "Software Sam? Mickey's friend?"

"The very s-s-same."

Cookie glanced at Darlene, then at the tall guy, and stepped aside.

"Mickey reckons you're a whiz with computers," Darlene said, leading Sam into the room. Cookie disappeared with an equally cute "Bye-bye."

He was gazing around, taking it all in approvingly. "Yeah...I-I-I am. So, w-w-what's your problem?"

"Look, I don't mean to be rude, but this equipment—well, it's all pretty new. Most of it's one-off stuff, custom made. I wouldn't expect you to be able to help with it."

"I could g-g-give it a go."

Darlene studied him. *You look ridiculous,* she thought. *But, then, so did Einstein!*

"Okay. I'm having a problem, primarily with my image-enhancing software."

She led him across the room.

"I'm working on some blurred images from a security camera." She pointed to a large Mac screen, sat, and tapped at the keyboard. Sam stood beside her chair.

A pair of indistinct faces came up.

"Th-th-they're the o-o-originals, r-r-right?"

Darlene looked up. "No, Sam, but they're the best I can get."

He whistled. "What s-s-software package you using?"

"It's a custom-made one from a friend of mine in L.A. He calls it FOCUS."

"Yeah, well, it's c-c-crap, isn't it?"

Darlene produced a pained laugh.

"C-c-can you open up the p-p-program for me?"

Darlene shrugged. "Okay." She brought up the appropriate screen. Then she offered her chair to Sam.

The screen filled with symbols and lines of computer code.

"I'll c-c-clone this first," Sam said. "As a b-b-backup." He tapped at the keyboard with extraordinary speed. Darlene watched as the algorithms and rows of letters and numbers shifted. Sam paused for a second, peered at the screen. Then his staccato key stabbing started up again.

Two minutes of concentrated effort, and the visitor pushed back Darlene's chair. "Th-th-that sh-sh-should do it," he declared.

"What did you do?"

"B-b-boosted the r-r-response parameters, r-r-realigned the enhancement s-s-software to concentrate on th-th-the contrast and the w-w-warmth c-c-components."

Darlene returned to her chair and clicked the mouse a couple of times to bring back the main screen. She opened the FOCUS software package, clicked on the image from the security camera, and pressed Import. A new screen opened, showing a crisp, sharp image of two Asian men, the picture so clear you could almost count their eyelashes.

"That's incredible!"

"I-i-it is pretty c-c-cool, i-i-isn't it?"

Darlene stood up. "I'm so sorry I ever doubted you."

"No prob." Software Sam looked a little embarrassed. "Oh! Almost forgot. M-M-Mickey gave me these." He held out a bunch of invitations. "H-h-half a dozen p-p-passes to his b-b-birthday bash, tomorrow night at the V-V-Venue."

"Fantastic!" she said.

"I'll be there too," Sam said.

"Fantastic!" Darlene repeated. And she meant it.

CHAPTER 52

I WAS STARING at the monitor on Darlene's desk.

"That's just amazing!" I exclaimed as I studied the piercingly clear image of the two men who'd killed Ho Chang.

"I'd like to take credit for getting it up," Darlene said, "but it was Mickey Spencer's buddy, some guy they call Software Sam."

"Yeah, Cookie told me he'd been here—kind of a weirdo."

"A weirdo genius. Actually, he's kind of a cutie," she said. Then she quickly added, "In a weirdo-genius sort of way. You know, when the class nerd takes off his glasses, and suddenly you think, *He's not so bad.*"

"I know the situation. As the class nerd...but not with the same results you describe," I said.

"Oh, yeah. I'm sure," Darlene said. Then she got back

to business: "So, what do we do now? We going to share this with the cops?"

I contemplated the image. "Oh, I don't think so... Not yet, anyway."

Darlene gave me a quizzical look—quizzical but satisfied.

"If we do that," I went on, "someone will blab, and these bastards"—I waved a hand at the monitor—"will disappear. No, this is ours, Darlene. At least for the moment. You been able to do anything with it?"

"I've tried. Spent all afternoon attempting to match up facial characteristics with databases all over the world. Not getting very far. Same old problem. The Triads bribe the authorities in Hong Kong. So nothing's on record. If there's nothing on the two men, then the CIA, MI Six, the Australian intelligence agency can't get a handle on them. These guys have no DNA records, no fingerprints or photo presence at all. As far as the investigative agencies are concerned, they don't exist."

CHAPTER 53

I WAS IN the New South Wales police pathology lab with Darlene. She was looking over the rotting remains of the dead woman discovered in the old house in Bondi. And I was looking at Darlene. No matter how long I was in this business, I could never get used to the human forensics.

As I watched her work methodically, I felt myself growing more and more pissed off. Private hadn't learned about the corpse for at least five hours after it was found. Even then, it was only because Darlene heard about it thirdhand from a friendly cop at police HQ.

The victim was Jennifer Granger, thirty-eight, from Newmore Avenue, a street that happened to be perpendicular to Wentworth Avenue in Bellevue Hill, where Elspeth Lombard had been found. It was within spitting distance of the other victims' homes. Although, of course, in Bellevue Hill, nobody spat on the street.

"I spoke to one of the sergeants at the station in the CBD," I said. "Jennifer Granger was reported missing three weeks ago, on December fifteenth." Darlene didn't look up, but she couldn't have missed the anger in my voice. "Who reported it?"

"Her husband. She was supposed to be on a girls' weekend in Melbourne but didn't show. Her girlfriends didn't tell her husband, a gynecologist called Dr. Cameron Granger, until Sunday morning."

Darlene lifted her head at that bit of info.

"Two of them knew Jennifer was having an affair. So they figured she had used the weekend as a cover, without telling them. The same two women tried to text her. When they got no reply, they phoned her cell. No response. Straight to voice mail. We've followed up on the calls; their story holds up."

"Probably dead at least twenty-four hours by then," Darlene said.

I stared at the mess of rancid flesh that smelled of newly applied chemicals. I tried and failed to imagine her as a beautiful, wealthy woman engaged in an affair.

"What's the husband been doing all this time?" Darlene asked.

"The sergeant at the station told me that Dr. Granger called them at least twice a day," I said. "Went to the station half a dozen times, offered a reward of ten grand for any info. That was all in the first week after she vanished. One of Jennifer Granger's friends finally enlightened her husband about the affair. But he still kept up the pressure on the cops. In fact, he doubled the reward."

Darlene raised an eyebrow. "Here's an informed guess: this poor woman is the first victim."

"Is that based on anything empirical? Apart from the fact that she died three weeks ago?"

"No, just a hunch. The murder is a bit different from the others...done with less confidence."

I tilted my head and frowned.

"The murderer got the woman to come to him...in a derelict house, away from Bellevue Hill. Now, though, he literally goes straight to the victims' doorstep."

"What about Yasmin Trent?"

"I'm convinced she was snatched. Probably close to where she lived. The cops found her car fifty yards from her body."

It was my turn to look surprised. "I didn't know that."

"They checked the odometer. The last journey in the car was thirty-one miles. Precisely the distance from Bellevue Hill to where Yasmin Trent's corpse was discovered in Sandsville. I reckon our killer is beginning to feel the heat in Bellevue Hill and mixing it up to keep us off his scent."

I was about to reply when the door opened and Mark Talbot walked in.

"Just passing." My cousin smirked.

"We need to talk," I said.

CHAPTER 54

"WHY THE HELL didn't you tell us about this woman?" I said.

Mark and I had walked to a deserted storage area at the back of the building.

"One of my officers caught a pickpocket in Darling Harbour this morning, Craig," Talbot said. "Should I have told you about that?"

He moved toward me, stepping right into my personal space. But he apparently had a whole routine starting.

"Oh, and that pesky graffiti artist who keeps spray painting a wall just off George Street in the CBD? Got him too. Sorry...forgot to mention—"

"Maybe you think you're being clever, Mark," I said calmly. "But we have a deal with the police, don't we?"

"*You* have a 'deal' with the deputy commissioner."

"And you have to abide by it."

Talbot came even closer. He was about my height. We were eye-to-eye.

"This morning I used my professional discretion."

"No, you didn't. You did this deliberately, to screw me over. And you just showed up here to continue the fun."

He shrugged. "Well, yeah, maybe I did."

"Thanks to you, we lost five hours of precious investigation time."

He laughed. I could feel his breath. "Just listen to you…you fucking smart-ass. 'Precious investigation time'! Who the hell do you think you are? You're a PI. You can fool the deputy commissioner, but not me."

"I'm very disappointed."

"You what?"

"I'm disappointed."

He leaned in, his eyes narrow. "Disappointed! You cocksucker! Who do you think you're talking to?"

I went to gently push him back. And that was when he took a swing at me.

I blocked his fist, and he stumbled back a step, went for me again, his right arm swinging round.

I had learned something about fighting since I was eight years old. Better yet, Mark wasn't in the best of shape. I dodged his fist so easily, it was embarrassing— which enraged him more. His left fist came up, slower, but at an oblique angle. It grazed my shoulder. I grabbed his wrist and bent his hand back.

"Don't, Mark!" I said in his ear.

His breath was on me again, his mouth close to my

left cheek. I bent his hand a little more and sensed him shift position, his right knee moving up toward my groin. I turned my body away, and his knee hit me in the hip. It hurt. Still gripping him with my left hand, I swung round, sending a right hook to his face.

He fell back and landed heavily on the floor, blood streaming from a cut just below his left eye. He began to get up.

"Stop!" I hollered, but he wouldn't listen.

"Asshole! You always have been…!" He growled, got to his feet with surprising speed, and rushed me. I whirled round, elbow out, and he ran straight into it, nose first. I heard the cartilage crunch. He spun, hit the floor again, lay still for a few moments. In the police business we call that "victim supine."

I heard him groan, crouched beside him, keeping my guard up. He glared at me, blood streaming from his nostrils. His left eye was already puffed up.

I offered him a hand, but he spat at it. His saliva landed on the floor between us.

"Suit yourself," I said. Then walked away.

CHAPTER 55

WHEN I RETURNED to the morgue, I tried to look cool, calm, and composed. I was none of these.

"You all right?" Darlene asked.

"Yeah, fine."

"You look like you've been in a fight."

"You're perceptive. You should go into detective work."

She smiled and then pointed to Jennifer Granger's corpse.

"It's very similar to all the others," Darlene said. "Face burned and cut, stabbed in the back repeatedly. The same money dump—*fake money* dump. No sign of sexual assault. No DNA."

"You're leading up to the word 'but.' Aren't you?"

"But . . . ," she said. Then paused.

"You've found something, haven't you?"

This time she grinned. "You should go into detective work. I've found a partial print on one of the photocopies."

"Oh."

"Which convinces me even more that Jennifer Granger was the first victim. The killer was less practiced. He made a mistake."

CHAPTER 56

I KNEW THAT the dark-silver fabric suit Dr. Cameron Granger was wearing was expensive. I knew because I'd seen it up close in the Armani store the week before. I knew because I also found the price tag hidden in the suit and examined it. Then I stepped quickly away, as if the mannequin wearing the suit were about to mug me.

Let me put it this way: Cameron Granger was *annoyingly* handsome. The square jaw, the big head of blond hair, the blue eyes, the broad shoulders. He had the whole annoying deal going for him. Plus, I knew that he had a big house in the eastern suburbs, a tennis court in the backyard, and, I guessed, a million-dollar yacht moored somewhere where other people were paid to take care of it.

I had to quickly remind myself that Dr. Granger had

just learned that his wife was cheating on him...and dead.

He indicated a plush, gray suede sofa, sat on one end, with me at the other. He looked suitably morose.

"I've been to the morgue. Been briefed. Given my report to the cops."

"If you don't mind my saying so, you seem very contained, Doctor."

"What can you do? I've had some time to absorb it all. After Jennifer failed to show up with her friends, I assumed she'd either run off with her lover or she was dead."

I appraised the man again. Was he using fake courage to overcome his grief?

"You had no idea your wife was involved with another man?"

"Oh, right...What more traditional motive for murder is there than being cuckolded?"

I held his eyes, and he looked away.

"Again, I apologize, but it strikes me as a little odd," I said. "Why would a wife risk losing such a lavish lifestyle by messing around?"

Granger surprised me by simply shrugging. "You tell me, Mr. Gisto. Maybe she thought she'd never be caught."

"When did you see your wife last?"

"I went through this with the police." He sighed. "I kissed her good-bye in the hallway of our home. Waved as she got into her car. She was leaving for the airport— or so I thought—to see her girlfriends in Melbourne."

"Then, later, you got a call from one of them."

"Yes, Maureen Miner, over thirty-six hours later, actually. She'd tried and failed to reach Jen by phone... Got worried... Stupid bitch."

"You sound pretty angry. Wasn't this Maureen Miner doing you a favor?"

"Oh, yeah! The sisterhood, keeping my wife's infidelity a secret. Great favor. Remind me to send her a thank-you note."

"Right," I said evenly, thinking about all the times men had closed ranks and kept their buddies' secrets to themselves. "Well, you obviously would like the killer brought to justice—you've doubled the reward."

"I doubled it once again earlier this afternoon."

"Is there anything you can think of that might help us... and the police?"

"Look, Mr. Gisto, I've told the police everything I know. I saw Jennifer leave the house. I assumed she was doing what she said she was going to do and met her mates in Melbourne. I didn't hear a thing until Maureen called. That was three weeks ago. Maybe you should speak to the guy Jennifer was fucking."

"As a matter of fact, Dr. Granger, we've found the guy. My colleague is with him right now."

The doctor didn't even ask the name of his wife's lover. All he said was:

"Really? Do me a favor. Give him my very best wishes."

CHAPTER 57

THIS GUY WAS Jennifer Granger's lover? This was Nick Grant?

You've got to be kidding.

This was the guy who stole Jennifer Granger from her husband?

Justine studied the man sitting in front of her and wondered how any woman could find him attractive. He was about fifty years old, tall, almost sickly thin. He wore a brown vest and cargo shorts. On his left arm was a full-sleeve tattoo of grapevines interspersed with hearts and stars.

Nick Grant had agreed to meet on "neutral ground"—a pub on Napoleon Street in Bondi.

"Look," he said, fixing Justine with a confident gaze. "Me and Jen—it was a casual thing, right? She was getting quotes for an extension on her house in Bellevue Hill.

Took a shine to me right off." He gulped his beer, gave Justine a faintly flirtatious smile. Then his expression turned serious. "I was sorry to hear what happened..."

"She was with you the weekend she was murdered?"

"No! That's just it. I hadn't seen her for weeks. As I said, it was casual. I think we only did it four times, five max. She'd arrange everything and call me up with half an hour's notice. Tell me to put on something clean...that she was in room one thirty-one at the Four Seasons, or room four twenty-eight at the Hyatt, wearing nothing but high heels." He grinned stupidly. "Well, what do you do?"

"And the weekend of December fourteenth? You were in Sydney?"

"No." Nick Grant shrugged. "I weren't."

"So where were you?"

"In Melbourne."

"Melbourne?"

"Yeah—you look surprised."

"No, no, go on."

"Rugby piss-up. Me and the lads. We went to see the Waratahs at AAMI Park. Fantastic game—and afterward! Sunday...whoa...a complete blur. Took Monday off. Went back to work Tuesday. We're on a big job in Mona Vale." He nodded toward the Northern Beaches.

"So when did you hear that Jennifer Granger had gone missing?"

"One of her friends called me out the blue. I didn't know what the woman was talking about at first. She was another stuck-up bitch—sorry. I mean she was—oh, fuck! You know what I mean!"

Justine stared at the man.

"This woman," he went on, "Maureen? She said Jennifer hadn't shown up for a girls' weekend. 'Why you telling me?' I said. Apparently, Jen had mentioned my name and the company I work for, and this Maureen tracked me down. Cheeky bitch. I got a bit pissed off with her. Told her she'd better not tell anyone where to find me, especially Jen's bloody husband."

"And nothing else happened?"

"No. Not another word till this morning."

"So when was the last time you saw Jennifer Granger?"

Nick Grant took another gulp of beer and pondered the tabletop.

"Well, let me think . . . Must have been two weeks before the Melbourne weekend. Yeah—early December, at the Sheraton."

Justine shivered. She couldn't help but recall the gruesome and sad, shallow grave where Jennifer Granger was found.

She suddenly found herself saying aloud what she was only thinking. "What a terrible mess some people create for themselves," she said.

Nick Grant didn't seem taken aback.

"I'll agree with you there, ma'am. I'll agree with you there."

CHAPTER 58

THE PARTIAL PRINT from Jennifer Granger's body appeared two feet wide on the flat-screen. Darlene studied the lines, what analysts call whorls and loops. She remembered a stat from college—there's a one-in-64-billion chance that any two people share fingerprints.

The partial on the screen looked completely unremarkable. It was, perhaps, two-thirds of a full print, limited in value but better than nothing.

Darlene double-clicked the mouse and highlighted the image. Then she moved the picture to an icon on the screen. The file disappeared, and a box came up with the words GLOBAL DATABASE ANALYSIS IN PROGRESS. Beneath this, a line, a tiny red dot to the left, and the words ESTIMATED TIME REMAINING: 42 MINUTES—the time it would take for the Private computer system to compare the partial print with prints in every database throughout the world, some two billion records.

Darlene pushed her chair back, ran her fingers through her hair. She was extremely frustrated. Here she had some of the best forensics equipment in the world, yet she'd spent three days drawing a blank on four connected murders. At the back of her mind, something was nagging at her. It'd been needling her for at least twenty-four hours, but she couldn't pinpoint it.

She got up and walked across the lab to a bench. She'd filed every piece of data she had on the four murders. Most of the info was on the computer, and there were a few coded written reports kept in a filing cabinet. Here on the bench stood ninety-six test tubes in twenty-four racks. Each one was meticulously labeled. Each one contained something from the murder scenes.

She scanned the racks. There were slivers of cloth, particles of soil, fragments of body tissue, blood-soaked fabrics, hairs. Hairs! She moved the racks forward, one after the other, taking care to keep everything in the correct order. Then she saw what she was looking for—a test tube containing a single, whitish-blond human hair.

Darlene then walked to a powerful drive that stored all the crime-scene photos. She tapped the mouse and brought up the photo collections from the past three days. Clicked a folder entitled "Yasmin Trent." Scrolling down, she stopped over image number 233. A smile spread across Darlene's face.

CHAPTER 59

DARLENE DROVE STRAIGHT from her lab to the house in Bondi where Jennifer Granger had been found. She knew the Police Forensics team would still be there, and she wanted one more search around the place herself.

Darlene recognized the cop who met her at the front door. He gave her a warm smile. "Darlene," he said. "Back again?"

"Can't keep me away from a good murder scene, Sergeant Heller," she said, reading his ID badge. He was young and good-looking. She'd spotted him at the earlier murder sites, and she was certain that he'd noticed her too.

"It's Brian," he said, and he followed her through the hall. They stopped at the door to the bathroom, the bathroom that was obscenely splattered with blood.

"The murder was committed here," the sergeant said.

"You don't say!" She laughed. "So, I heard you got tipped off by a vagrant who slept in the front room last night."

"That's what we thought at first. A young guy called us early this morning. We followed up, traced the cell call. Turns out he's a seventeen-year-old high school guy. He and his girlfriend snuck in here for an early-morning quickie. They're both respectable kids from good families. But they picked the wrong spot. Their parents were real pleased to hear about it all."

Darlene gave a small laugh, and then she and Sergeant Heller walked outside, into the intense afternoon sun. Darlene saw four men in boilersuits digging up the lawn and the overgrown flower beds at the rear of the house. Two others were sifting through the soil, searching for further clues.

Then Darlene heard a cry from one of the diggers. She ran across the yard.

Two of the men were bending over an opening in the ground. Darlene skirted the edge and crouched down. Decayed human bones. Patches of white caught the light of the sun—a forearm, protruding from the dirt.

The forensics guys ran over, saw the bones, and squatted down beside Darlene.

"Keep digging, real gently," one of them said to the men with the shovels. They had to clear the soil near the arm with different spades, spades no bigger than a soup spoon.

The grave was shallow, not even three feet deep, and soon the outline of a large man could be seen. A few patches of gray-brown flesh remained on his dead bones. Strands of red hair clung to his skull.

CHAPTER 60

IT WAS PAST six p.m. and Johnny was leaving the office when the phone rang. A young female voice told him she was calling from Bonza Records and inviting him to a "VIP concert" starring Mickey Spencer, starting at eight thirty that night.

He just had time to get home, get changed, and get a cab to the concert site—a rather macabre place called the Old Quarantine Station, near Manly.

The cab pulled into the drop-off lot. Johnny paid the driver and walked toward the noise. He knew this place from when he was a kid. For more than a century—since it was built, in the 1820s—it was the place where visitors to Australia were quarantined before being allowed into the country. Thousands had suffered terribly in this place. Decades ago it'd been turned into a theme park, "the most haunted place in Australia."

Close to the old shower block and the mortuary, the original boiler house had been converted into a swish restaurant and conference center. Johnny emerged onto a cobbled courtyard lit up by massive lights on rigs. Directly ahead stood a stage strewn with musical equipment, men in black jeans and T-shirts testing mics. There were perhaps a hundred people milling around in front of the stage. Most were wearing suits, drinking champagne, chatting animatedly.

Johnny walked over to a waiter carrying a tray, took a glass of orange juice. A leggy blonde approached with a clipboard. Johnny gave her his name.

"Ah, yeah!" she said. "I was the one who called you earlier. I'm Melanie." She extended a hand.

"So, what's this all about?"

"Promo for the suits. Even stars as big as Mickey need to lay on a show for the execs and the sales guys."

Johnny nodded. "Strange choice of venue."

"Oh, we like to be a bit different!"

There was a sudden hush as the strains of a famous classical piece Johnny couldn't put a name to flowed from the speakers on either side of the stage. A man wearing a cream linen suit and a Mickey Spencer T-shirt walked out stage right, radio mic in hand. It was Ricky Holt.

"Ladies and gentlemen…welcome." His voice was deeper and softer than Johnny had imagined. He smiled at the crowd, pointed at someone at the front, laughed good-naturedly. "Thanks for coming along. It's a sort of celebration of Mickey's birthday tomorrow. Now, Mickey's well and truly wired, and he is RARING TO GO! So, please, give it up for my boy—Mickey Spencer."

The lights died, the entire stage turned black. A drum rhythm started, and a bass guitar came in. Then the lights burst on, thousands of watts of color. And there was Mickey Spencer, dressed entirely in white, crouched, microphone in hand. He screamed and the music came crashing in.

The crowd, lubed on expensive champagne and free cocaine, went wild. The song rocketed along, growing more and more powerful as it went.

Johnny had seen videos of Mickey Spencer, of course. His latest song already had a million hits on YouTube, but seeing him live and only fifty yards away was something else. He looked around and saw Mel nodding appreciatively. Then he turned back to the stage. Johnny was hardly able to believe that the demure, shy character he'd met at Private could transform himself into this massive personality, this rock god, parading in front of them.

CHAPTER 61

I WALKED INTO Darlene's lab and caught her doing crazy little dance steps. She looked as excited as a little kid waiting for Santa Claus.

So of course I couldn't resist saying, "What's happened? The newest edition of *Forensics Now Journal* arrive early?"

She gave me a smile and tilted her head to one side. "Just got back from the house in Bondi. And guess what? There's a second body in the garden."

"Really? Are you shitting me?"

"Nope. It's a man. From the level of decomposition, I'd say he's been dead two, maybe three months. Severe facial disfigurement, multiple stab wounds. Sound familiar, Mr. G.?"

Since being a detective meant always playing devil's

advocate, I said: "But it's a totally different MO—a male victim. It doesn't make sense."

"I've taken samples. Police Forensics is all over it. There must be some link. Has to be the same killer."

Then Darlene said: "There's some other news."

"Lay it on me."

"I think I *have something* on this killer."

Darlene walked to her desk and picked up a file.

"Something was always bugging me about these crimes."

"Yeah, you said something in Sandsville—Yasmin Trent's murder."

"It came to me a couple of hours ago." She pulled a test tube from the pocket of her lab coat and held it out.

I took it and lifted it to the light.

"A strand of hair?"

"Specifically, bleached-blond hair. Found on Elspeth Lombard's blouse."

"She was blond. Not one of hers?"

"I don't think so. I've just had it under the scope. A particular bleach was used. Every brand is slightly different. This is a cheapie—slightly higher peroxide level than the more upmarket dyes. Doesn't sound like the sort of stuff a woman like Elspeth would use. Also, see how a good third of the hair is dark? The woman this hair came from doesn't keep up with her color. She let it grow out. Again, doesn't fit Elspeth's profile."

"I don't see what—"

"Okay...The thing bothering me was that when I first arrived at the scene of Yasmin Trent's murder, I ran off a couple hundred shots on my camera and must have subconsciously noted a strand of blond hair lying across the dead woman's arm. I was distracted by something and had to talk to one of the cops for a minute. By the time I got back, the Police Forensics guys were packing up, and I set to work."

"You'd forgotten about the hair?"

"I don't think I really registered it consciously."

"But the camera did."

Darlene pulled a photo from the folder. It showed a magnified white-blond hair lying on a piece of dark fabric.

"And Yasmin was a brunette," I said.

"She was." Darlene took back the photo. "I called Forensics straightaway. I got one of the good guys there, Gabe Ruggie. He's okay, seems to like me. He checked their files. Sure enough, they have a blond hair from the Yasmin Trent murder scene."

"Holy shit!" I said.

"Yep. They profiled a DNA sample from the hair. Couldn't match it with any database. They sent the profile over."

She pulled a piece of paper from the folder and held it out. It was a chart showing the analysis of the sample. "And this," she said proudly, "is the profile I have from the hair on Elspeth Lombard's body." She handed me a second sheet. The two charts were identical.

"Hair from the same person."

"Absolutely no doubt—and the DNA does not match either blond victim. Oh, and one more thing."

"Okay. Lay it on me."

"Absolutely no Y chromosome in the profile."

"You mean..."

"You got it, Sherlock. The DNA is definitely from a female. Our killer is a woman."

CHAPTER 62

JOHNNY TOLD ME what had happened to Mary at the Triad place. So when I ran into her on my way to my office, I just nodded to her, and she followed me inside. She had to know—Mary was as bright as investigators come—that I wasn't happy.

Just to make sure, I started by saying, "I'm really pissed with you. What the hell were you thinking?"

She sat down and tried hard to keep her bandaged hand just out of sight.

"Information gathering, Craig. I went into places worse than that friggin' Triad dump all the time in the force."

"You could have gotten yourself killed. You might as well have put up a billboard on George Street: 'Triads— we're after you!'"

"They knew already. Word travels fast in this city. Besides, that's exactly the desired effect. I wanted to give them the shits!"

I let out a deep sigh. "Okay." I put my palms down flat on the table. "It's done. So how's the hand?"

"Just a scratch."

"Yeah, right! A sixteen-stitch scratch!"

"God!" Mary exclaimed. "Can't a girl keep anything secret around here?"

The phone rang.

"Mr. Gisto?"

It was Ho Meng, and he sounded a little out of breath.

"I need you to come here to my home immediately. There has been . . . a development."

CHAPTER 63

JOHNNY WAS WALKING toward the exit gate at the Old Quarantine Station where the cabs were lining up when he heard someone call his name.

He turned just as a huge, black Mercedes SUV pulled up. Mickey Spencer had his head out the window, a big grin on his face.

"Jump in, mate."

Johnny peered inside. Even more impressive than the car was the girl in the backseat next to Mickey. She had legs as long as the Mercedes and her exquisite face wore a perfect model's pout. The ubiquitous Hemi was in the front passenger seat, next to the driver.

"I'm good, Mickey."

"Dude! You're coming to the after-party, right?"

"Party?"

"My place. Come on, hop in." He spread his arms. "Plenty of room."

"Okay."

The car pulled away as the door closed, and Johnny landed on a seat facing Mickey and the girl. There was an ice bucket in the middle of the floor, two uncorked bottles of champagne inside. On the fold-down tray was a mirror with half a dozen lines of coke. Johnny noticed white powder on Mickey's upper lip.

"Johnny, meet Katia, my girlfriend. Katia, this is Johnny, a good friend of mine."

The girl looked at him seriously, didn't move a muscle. She had jet-black hair cut in a severe bob with a high, straight fringe; huge, dark eyes; and of course those comes-with-the-total-package cheekbones. She was dressed entirely in black except for what looked like a miniature sword about an inch long on a pink ribbon at her incredibly pale throat.

"I know you don't drink, Johnny, but do you . . . ?" He nodded toward the cocaine.

"No, thanks, Mickey."

"How dull," Katia said, but she did smile after she said it. She had one of those nonspecific "Continental" accents.

"Each to his own," Mickey said. "Katia is a brilliant guitarist, Johnny. She's Russian and was in a band in Moscow. They were called Khuy."

"Which translates as 'penis,'" the girl said. Again the smile.

"Isn't that fuckin' great, man? I fell in love with her

when I learned that. Six months ago...longest relationship I've ever had!" He turned to the girl. "And I love her."

Katia leaned in to kiss Mickey. They stayed glued together for a few minutes while Johnny looked out the window at the buildings flashing past.

Finally Mickey pulled away, wiped his mouth, and refilled his and Katia's glasses.

"So, man, you like the show?"

"I was knocked out," Johnny replied earnestly.

"Excellent. Excellent." Mickey downed the champagne in one gulp. "Well, I think you'll enjoy the party even more." And he gave one of his huge smiles.

CHAPTER 64

MICKEY'S SYDNEY CRIB was a penthouse in Wool-loomooloo. Gray, minimalist, clean lines, massive windows looking out toward the harbor, all at a $10-mil price tag.

By the time the SUV got there, the place was packed. About two hundred people in various states of weird wardrobe—women and men in midthigh shorts with neon-bright T-shirts, assorted piercings and tats, fur boas and garden-party hats. Insanely loud music (apparently John Mayer and Justin Timberlake were back).

Mickey and Katia vanished, and Johnny wandered around the huge room. This was his night to consume a few pints of orange juice.

He was still somewhat amazed that Mickey Spencer was actually his buddy, his client, his source for coke, should he ever want it.

Johnny knew he was a poor kid from a middle-class suburb. But Johnny was determined—through school, through his job at Private—to leave the crummy background behind him. And meeting Mickey—well, that had been a totally unexpected piece of great luck.

He felt a tap on the shoulder and turned to see Katia.

"Can I speak with you?" she said.

"Sure."

She led the way across the main room. During that little walk Johnny caught a couple of famous faces from TV and YouTube, as well as a lot of not-so-famous but very beautiful young women. Johnny also noticed Ricky Holt talking to Mickey on the far side of the room. Katia motioned toward one of the balconies just as Johnny saw Holt hand Mickey a small package wrapped in brown paper.

"I'm sorry I was so rude earlier," she said. "You know, when I was on 'automatic bitch' and said 'How dull.' "

Johnny shrugged. All he could really think of was how lovely and refined her voice was.

"I didn't mind . . . Plus, I *am* pretty dull."

Katia smiled at his self-effacing charm.

"I didn't realize you were the guy from Private. Mickey's been singing your praises." Johnny's face could not conceal his pleasure at that comment.

"I'm very concerned for him," Katia went on.

"Because of this Club Twenty-Seven business?"

"Of course."

"He's convinced that Ricky Holt—" Johnny said.

"I'm very aware of that," Katia said. "But . . . Oh, I just

don't know...Let me be straight about this. I'm worried that Mickey's losing it."

"Drugs?"

"Everything, Johnny. Everything. It's almost as though he has some weird death wish."

"So you think Ricky Holt has nothing to do with it?"

"You're the private investigator."

He fell silent, looked back to the room, filled with people. There was a sudden commotion. A woman ran over from a doorway in the far wall. She was shouting something, but Johnny couldn't hear anything over the thumping music.

Katia's instincts kicked in immediately. She barged her way through the packed room. Johnny followed her. Some drinks went flying.

The music stopped abruptly, and a hundred threads of conversation stopped with it.

CHAPTER 65

THE SILENCE IN the room was being replaced by the low, nervous rumble of voices as people pointed and whispered. As soon as they arrived in the room, Johnny followed Katia through a door into a cavernous marble bathroom. Three men stood around Mickey, who was lying faceup on the floor. A fourth man was kneeling beside him. He opened a metal briefcase.

"Fuck—*yob*—*govno!*" Katia screamed, madly mixing her languages. She also knelt on the floor.

Mickey was semiconscious. He was drenched in sweat. Foam surrounded his lips. His arms and legs were twitching.

Katia spoke to the man who was opening the metal case: "Dr. James, you've got to..."

The doctor ignored her.

Katia went to grab Mickey.

"Please!" the doctor snapped.

Dr. James pulled a syringe from the case and squeezed the plunger a fraction of a millimeter. A tiny squirt of liquid now dribbled from the tip of the syringe. Then the doctor leaned forward.

With one shockingly violent movement, the doctor plunged the syringe into the middle of Mickey's chest, right through to his heart.

Mickey jolted upright. Then, as the doctor withdrew the needle, the rock star slumped back, his eyes snapping open. He rolled to one side and vomited.

It was then that Johnny noticed the package he'd seen Holt hand to Mickey minutes earlier. It was open on the floor, a used syringe and an empty vial lying on a piece of brown paper.

CHAPTER 66

HO BLENDED IN almost perfectly with the cream-colored sofa he was sitting on. He was dressed in a beige polo shirt and wore silky cream-colored chinos that could have been made from the same material that covered the sofa. He stood up, shook my hand, but it was apparent that he was upset.

"What's happened?" I asked.

"Dai has disappeared. I called his cell and home numbers half a dozen times. I went to his apartment and rang the bell. No response. I let myself in. There were signs of a struggle. A gun had been fired into the wardrobe."

"Any blood?"

Meng shook his head. He looked down and stared at the plush, white living-room carpet.

"And you haven't contacted ...?"

Ho looked up. "No, Mr. Gisto, I haven't called the police."

I sighed. "There's more, isn't there?"

"A ransom note. Same as before. Either I do as they say, or my son dies."

The unforgiving light from the ceiling halogens made the man appear almost transparent.

"Is there an ultimatum?"

"Midnight tonight. I say yes, or Dai..."

I nodded.

"And there was this."

He leaned over to an ornately carved side table and picked up a small cardboard shoe box. He removed the lid and handed the box to me. I looked inside and— *Holy shit!* I saw an ear nestled on a bed of bloodied cotton.

"We can't fuck around, Ho. Forget about us trying to catch the two goons who kidnapped and killed Chang. We have to get the police involved and go much higher up in the gang hierarchy."

Ho closed his eyes for a second.

"This has gone too far for Private to deal with alone," I said. "And, actually, by not going to the police, you're in danger of breaking the law yourself."

He sniffed at that, but a moment later he nodded and said, "I know."

CHAPTER 67

TENSE. ANGRY. CONFRONTATIONAL.

If you could ignore those three poisonous moods darkening the atmosphere in the briefing room at Sydney Police HQ, we were just a bunch of guys hanging out together.

Ho Meng and I were sitting around a steel table with the very pissed-off Brett Thorogood, the very pissed-off Mark Talbot, and a senior detective in charge of the police assault force, Evan Freitas.

Deputy Commissioner Thorogood was commanding proceedings from the head of the table. It was no-nonsense all the way.

"Mr. Ho," Thorogood said, looking directly at the man. "You know these gang people better than any of us. Do you have any idea of the identity of the men?"

Ho sat completely still. He now possessed some sort

of Zen-like calm that I thought covered a seething anger and horrible pain.

"As you are aware, the lead operatives in Sydney are the Lin brothers, Sung and Jing," Ho said stiffly. "They are Four Twenty-Sixes."

"Which means?"

"The Triads have clear distinctions between ranks and positions in the gang. They are each given numbers based upon the I Ching numerological system. The leader of the Triads is Four Eighty-Nine. His name would be 'the Mountain' or 'the Dragon.' I believe the gang in Sydney is a fragment of the Noonan, perhaps the most powerful of the Triads. The Dragon, the Four Eighty-Nine, is a man named Fong Sum. I met him once in Hong Kong. He's there now."

"So he'd be like a don in the Mafia?" Talbot asked.

Ho nodded slowly. "There are many differences, but, very broadly speaking, yes, he would. He controls a global network. The Sydney gangs are just a small part of it."

"And the Lin brothers—how many people work for them?" Freitas asked.

"That I do not know for certain."

"Ballpark?"

"I would estimate perhaps forty to fifty foot soldiers in the city," he responded.

"Foot soldiers are the rank and file, right?" Thorogood asked.

Ho nodded again. "They are known as Forty-Nines. I would suggest the men who abducted Chang and Dai would have been their best Forty-Nines, men who are working their way up in the pecking order. This would have been a big job for them."

"As this whole heroin project is for the Lin brothers too," I remarked.

"Indeed," said Ho.

"Okay," the deputy commissioner said. "So, do we have a consensus as to what to do next?"

Ho apparently felt he was a participant in answering Thorogood's question. He spoke: "I have come to the conclusion that the only chance we have of saving my son is to convince the gang that I will do what they want."

"And that could provide us with a platform for a sting operation," I added.

Mark looked at me with suspicion. "Us?"

"We're here to do anything we can to help," I said directly to Thorogood. "But we can't do it unless we're armed—like the rest of you. My assistant Mary Clarke and I are licensed to carry firearms."

"I appreciate your contribution," the deputy commissioner responded. Then, to make sure his opinion registered, he looked directly at Mark Talbot and said, "I think we can work together on this."

CHAPTER 68

WITHIN A FEW hours, the cops were at Ho's house, setting up tracking equipment for landline and cell calls. There was quite a crew from our side too. Talbot, Freitas, and Thorogood were there to babysit, and I had Mary and Darlene with me this time.

At eleven p.m., Ho Meng made first contact from his landline.

He tried to keep the call going, but the foot soldier at the other end wasn't dumb. The call ended before the police expert could locate the caller within less than a square mile. Ho gave the anonymous Triad member a mobile number. The guy clicked off before saying when he would respond. We just had to wait.

"We brought along some technology that might help," I said. Mark gave me a contemptuous look (surprise!), but Freitas and Thorogood were full of hope and full of enthusiasm.

Darlene walked across the room with two small boxes. She stacked them on a low table and opened the lid of the top box. Then she plucked out a cell phone and removed the back cover. "Put your SIM in here," she said to Ho Meng. "When they call you, we can get a better trace on them than with the conventional gear." And she flicked a glance at the police operator, with his suitcase-sized tracking unit, which he'd set up on the sofa, close to the home phone.

Darlene picked up the second box and pried open the lid.

We could all see inside. A white pad with a black dot the size of an aspirin on top. "A microtransmitter," she said.

"We can place this anywhere on Mr. Ho's body, and it'll pick up conversations and relay them to a receiver. You'll be close by in a van, right?" Darlene asked the cops.

"I'll be with the assault unit," Freitas replied. "Inspector Talbot will be in the van."

I glanced at him. Mark looked away.

"Okay." Ho nodded. "So, what happens now?"

Thorogood looked up. "We're ready when they are. Just need them to give a call."

CHAPTER 69

JULIE HAD FALLEN asleep in front of *Australian Idol* and, as usual, was dreaming about her father. In her dream, all the bad things had never happened. Dad was still alive. Julie had finished school, gone to college, become a police forensics officer.

"Geeeeee-na Esposito!" the announcer shrieked, and as the *Australian Idol* winner was announced, the audience began to cheer, and Julie woke to the strains of Sheila Watson singing "I Dreamed a Dream."

Gina Esposito wept for joy as the horror of Julie's own life came rushing toward her. She closed her eyes again, and there was her mother, screaming at her. When Sheila felt that Julie had misbehaved—that was when the torture began. She had kept her locked in her bedroom for days, a plastic bowl for a toilet. Sheila gave her only beets to eat.

Later, the torment increased. Sheila would tie Julie to a chair in the kitchen, gag her, and burn her arms with cigarettes.

On her eleventh birthday, her first since her father's death, she received nothing. Then, just before bedtime, Sheila tied her to the chair again and told her if she made a sound, she would put her feet in the fire in the living-room fireplace. Then she pulled out one of Julie's incisors with a pair of pliers.

This treatment continued for four years. She could never say a word for fear of torture. She hid the scars and the marks, made excuses for every lost tooth, every bruise. Then, one day—she knew it would happen one day—Julie snapped.

On the evening of her fifteenth birthday, Julie knew she would be in for her traditional "gift." As Sheila busied herself, getting ready to go out, Julie slipped a medium-size kitchen knife into the back pocket of her jeans.

Her mother appeared in the doorway to the kitchen. She was wearing a clownish amount of cheap makeup. There were two lengths of cord in her left hand.

"In the chair."

When she didn't move, her mother began to smile. Took a step toward her.

Julie pulled the knife from her pocket and swung it around. She stopped just before her mother's face.

The woman screeched, the smile vanishing instantly.

"You...! In the chair!" Julie hissed. And when her mother didn't react, she moved the knife a tiny bit closer.

She tied Sheila with the cords, gagged her with a tea

towel, then brought the knife to the center of her forehead.

Sheila was shaking, her eyes filled with terror and hatred.

Julie moved the knife another fractional distance closer, scoring her mother's flesh. The woman screamed under the cloth, but it came out as nothing more than a muffled hum. Julie heard a rush of liquid and saw her mother's urine flow over the front of the chair and onto the floor.

"You never made me do that, even once, you useless bitch!" the girl announced proudly. She pulled the knife away and pocketed it again, turned, and walked out.

CHAPTER 70

LIN SUNG CALLED at midnight.

Ho managed the call deftly, and I could understand how he'd been such a successful cop in Hong Kong and snowballed his skill into a lot of money with his businesses in Australia. He was quick and smart and calm.

Darlene's app was able to pinpoint the caller in under ten seconds. It was impressive but actually not much help. Lin was calling from a pay phone outside Luna Park, in North Sydney.

"We would like to meet you," Lin said, his voice coming into our individual earbuds. Of course, his words also went straight to a digital recorder.

"You will have my son?"

"Not this first time."

"Then there will be no meeting."

Silence from the other end. I held my breath.

"You are hardly in a position to negotiate, Mr. Ho."

Ho paused for a moment. "I entirely disagree."

Lin gave a small laugh. "Don't begin a game of bluff with me, Mr. Ho."

"I'm not bluffing." Ho's voice was stony.

Another, longer pause.

"Very well. We'll bring the boy. But we will only consider an exchange if all our conditions are met. Do you understand?"

Ho said nothing.

"I'll assume that is a yes, Mr. Ho. And if you invite a third party to our meeting, your son will be killed before your eyes."

When Ho still did not speak, Lin said. "Blackball Reserve, forty-five minutes."

Then Lin hung up.

CHAPTER 71

WE WERE ON the freeway, ten minutes short of Black-ball Reserve near Manly, when the agreed-upon rendezvous was changed. I was in my car, Mary in the police surveillance vehicle with Mark, and, next to him, a plainclothes officer, driving.

Two hundred yards ahead of them was Ho. He looked like a lonely old man, driving alone in his Bentley.

My cell clicked on to speaker. It was Mary.

"New destination," she said. "A green-and-chrome warehouse near the airport."

We all turned off at the next junction and headed south. I couldn't see the Bentley, but I had to assume that the cop directly ahead of me could. My car was fitted with a police tracker set to a broad range of frequencies. I could hear their comments, and I knew that Central

Control had quickly redirected the chopper assault team to the new location.

We reached the place in thirty minutes, pulling up a hundred yards away from the warehouse. I parked behind the surveillance vehicle and ran over to join them as Ho's car vanished into the shadows. Mary opened the sliding door, and I climbed in. Mark and an operative were at the controls. We could hear every sound Ho made through the tiny transmitter.

"Assault Officer One," the operative in the van said. "This is Control, come in." AO1, I knew, was Evan Freitas.

"Control. We're in position. AOs Four, Five, Six, and Seven are in a small room across from the main warehouse building. I'm with AOs Two and Three, on the opposite side. I have visual contact with Mr. Ho's vehicle."

A screen on the wall of the control room of the van lit up with a night-vision video feed from AO1's helmet. It showed a fuzzy image of Ho's Bentley entering the derelict warehouse, lights ablaze. It stopped, Ho dimmed the lights, and the image improved dramatically.

Now a black Mercedes with tinted windows, registration LS1, entered through the north end of the dilapidated building. It crunched over the pitted floor, strewn with pieces of metal and crushed concrete. It stopped about fifty yards short of the Bentley.

Ho stepped out of his car. He took a couple of steps toward the Mercedes. The car's engine was still running; both rear doors were opened. Two men slipped out. They were slender, black-haired figures. The slightly taller one of the pair was Lin Sung. He was dressed in his usual vintage, narrow-lapelled shiny black jacket and skinny tie. His brother, Jing, was wearing a blue track-suit and white trainers. They walked slowly toward Ho as the driver clambered from the front of the Mercedes to stand by the hood.

"It's a pleasure," Lin Sung began, and put out a hand, which Ho ignored.

"Where is my son?"

Lin Sung chuckled and flicked a glance at his broth-er. "There is great value in patience, my friend."

"I'm not your friend." Ho looked from one brother to the other. "I'm here to make a deal with you, as we agreed."

"Yes, and—"

"I want my son released. Then I will cooperate."

Sung sighed, cackled.

"You find it funny?" Ho asked coldly.

"You don't?" the younger brother butted in. His voice was oddly effeminate, completely at odds with his ma-cho stance.

"Ho's hanging tough," I whispered to Mary, who was standing beside me in the police van.

"Hope he doesn't overdo it."

I turned back to the screen and saw Lin Sung take a step closer to Ho. "We have the boy," he said slowly. "But we need assurances. Surely you understand that? If we return him to you, what is to say you will cooperate?"

"You have my word."

It was the younger brother Lin Jing's turn to produce

a half-assed laugh. "Ah! Your word!" he said, nodding. In an instant his mirth had vanished, and he pulled a gun, a Chinese Type 64, from his waistband. Lin Sung saw it and glared at him, but he didn't flinch.

Ho looked from one man to the other.

"In case you couldn't tell, this isn't going well," Mary hissed in my ear.

Freitas's voice came through. "Hold positions. No one move till I say."

Sung deliberately moved closer to his brother and slightly in front of him.

"We are all reasonable men," Sung said, and he tilted his head slightly as he stared at Ho Meng. "I understand you want your boy back, but you have to put yourself into our position, Mr. Ho." Then he turned and snapped his fingers at the man standing by the hood of the Mercedes. He walked to the back door and opened it.

"You may see your son."

The driver leaned in and helped Ho Dai climb out. The young man's hands were tied behind his back, and he was shaking, weeping, petrified. He had a large, bloody wound where his left ear had once been. He saw his father and began to speak. "Say nothing!" Lin Jing barked, then whirled around to Ho again, his gun raised.

"There. Your baby's safe. Now we talk."

"What is it you want from me?"

"At last—" the younger gangster exclaimed, but his brother cut in over him.

"Your business provides a perfect cover for one of our...trade plans."

"Drugs...You want me to get heroin in," Ho said.

Sung smiled, nodded.

"And in return?" Ho flicked a look at his son, who was still standing by the car, the driver gripping his right arm.

"When you have proven your worth, he will be released."

Ho gave Sung a venomous look. "No deal," he said, and started to turn.

"You motherfucker!" the younger brother screamed. He was clearly about to squeeze the trigger of his Type 64.

"Go!" yelled Freitas.

CHAPTER 72

SENSORY OVERLOAD PLUS. Shouts from the assault team, yells and thuds from the warehouse floor. On the screen, a smudge of movement through the night-vision lens.

Ho fell to the floor. I couldn't tell if he'd been shot or had hit the ground to avoid a bullet. Sung reached toward his brother. Ho rolled to one side as the younger brother fired a second bullet. Sung was yanking Lin Jing's arm down when the assault team, in full body armor, burst into the warehouse from two different directions. They screamed as they ran. Their Enfield SA-80s were leveled and ready.

The younger Lin reacted instinctively. Pumped up, he jumped for cover, into a pile of metal drums. Then he fired at the approaching cops. Before he could reach the barrels, he was ripped open by at least three different shots. He crumpled in a heap.

Sung whirled round, ran, and reached the Mercedes. Dai and the driver were crouching behind the car. The driver had pulled a gun. The kid looked like a puppet—big cartoon eyes, limp limbs. Sung reached cover and pulled out a semiautomatic, Bulgarian-made Arcus 94.

Lin grabbed Dai, and we all heard the gangster yell something that I couldn't understand.

"Hold your fire," Freitas's voice boomed through the speakers.

On the screen, I could see the fragmented image of Lin Sung rising slowly from a crouching position. He had the semiautomatic at Dai's temple. The driver shuffled out of the scene. He slipped behind a huge pile of rusting plant machinery. Then Ho Meng stood up slowly, apparently unharmed. He started to walk toward his son.

"Let my boy go!" he yelled.

Lin Sung ignored him and took a step forward. Then he opened the driver's door with one hand and shoved Dai inside the Mercedes. Lin Sung moved in beside him. They disappeared from view behind the tinted windows.

Ho reached the car, but it made no difference. The car roared away. The cops had their machine guns raised, jumping aside as Lin accelerated toward them. The car skidded on the uneven floor, drifted for a second, tires screaming. Lin got it under control and apparently pushed his foot to the floor.

I didn't wait another second. I slid open the door of the surveillance vehicle and ran across the gravel to my Mas. Then I hit the remote.

CHAPTER 73

I SPUN THE car backward on the gravel, turned into a pitted lane beside the warehouse, and shot away.

I couldn't see the Mercedes, but I knew I was racing in the right direction. It was the only route to the perimeter fence. Careering round a bend topping sixty, I hit a yard-wide hole in the tarmac, bounced out, the suspension stretched to the breaking point. I almost lost my grip on the road as the rear end came out. I just pulled it back.

The entrance to the freeway was about fifty yards ahead. I caught a glimpse of Lin's car as it shot through the gates and accelerated up the on-ramp. I dodged a stupid fucking pothole, swung left, then a hard right. I opened up the engine and tore onto the M5, headed west.

The Mercedes was quick, but the Maserati was quicker,

and, driven by someone in my crazed state of mind, it was *fantastically* fast. Lin may not have been aware of my advantage, but he learned of it immediately when I began to gain on his car, halving the distance between us in less than thirty seconds. The M5 freeway was almost deserted, and I had the Mercedes in my sights, only twenty-five yards ahead. The speedometer read 120.

Lin took the next exit. His car went screaming onto Princes Highway, toward Rockdale. It was a smart move: a slower road, a greater chance of urban traffic, plenty of turnoffs. It leveled the playing field—a little.

At 1:15 a.m., the street was pretty much empty of traffic. Lin pulled the Mercedes onto a side street, took it wide, and just missed an oncoming car. I screeched after him, barely missing the same car.

It was a narrow suburban street—rows of modest houses, parked cars to the left. Lin jumped the lights. I slowed and checked, followed him over the junction. He took a right, a left. More residential roads, a church, a McDonald's. I caught a sign for a sports field and saw a line of trees.

Lin waited until the last possible second, roared into a narrow lane just before the park. I braked and flew around the corner.

The Mercedes had disappeared from view. Then I realized I'd shot straight past it. Lin had taken a hard right off the road and pulled up onto a rutted track at the edge of the field.

I reversed and caught some movement in my rearview mirror. Lin was out of his car, gun in hand.

He rushed around to the passenger door. He yanked it open, dragging Dai to the ground.

I stopped, slipped out, kept low. The Merc was ten yards away. Lin was pulling Dai up, the barrel of his gun at the kid's temple.

I was in the shadows, but Lin certainly knew precisely where I was crouched. He could have taken a pop at me, but then he risked losing Dai. "Stop!" he shouted into the night. "Or I'll kill him."

I pulled back and crept behind a line of bushes. He couldn't be sure where I was now. I moved fast. Lin and the boy dropped out of view for a few seconds. Then I found an opening in the bushes and saw that they hadn't moved.

I picked up a stone, tossed it to my left. Lin whirled around. He had his free arm around Dai's throat.

"Stop the stupid games," Lin said, an edge to his voice now. I was getting to him.

I moved to his very far right and could see the back of his neck, wet with perspiration. I leveled my gun to his head.

"Let him go."

Lin spun around.

"Let. Him. Go."

"No!"

Some instinct told me I'd pushed him too far. I fired, and his gun went off simultaneously. Lin flew backward. The hood of his car broke his fall; a cloud of red exploded from his head. Dai jolted, screamed, and collapsed to the ground.

I rushed over, expecting the worst. Blood was running down Dai's cheek, dripping from his jaw. He must have thought, like me, that Lin had been about to shoot. Dai had moved just in time. Lin's bullet had just grazed the boy's temple.

I pulled Dai to his feet. He was shaking fiercely. I untied the cord around his wrists. He started to cry, tears streaming down his cheeks. He put a hand to his face and came up with bloodied fingers. I thought I might start crying myself.

We could hear sirens. "It's okay," I said, and I knew I was saying it as much for myself as I was for Dai. "Just a scratch. You're going to be fine, Dai. It's all over, buddy."

CHAPTER 74

I SPENT ABOUT three hours at police HQ. I didn't get the "full hostile" interrogation treatment, but no one was especially easy on me. As expected, Mark Talbot could barely contain his pleasure at witnessing the intense, relentless questioning.

Finally everyone agreed: I'd handled the situation with Lin as wisely as possible.

Brett Thorogood summed it up: "An impossible situation with a reasonable outcome. In fact, I'd say the good guys won." Mark looked disappointed.

From HQ I drove directly to Private. I was exhausted, and I was filthy. I showered and shaved in the workout locker room and stepped back into the grungy clothes that had traveled with me to hell and back. Then I called all parties into the conference room. Frankly, they didn't look much fresher or better rested than I did.

I started the meeting by holding up the front page of the *Sydney Morning Herald:* SYDNEY SLASHER CLAIMS NEWEST VICTIM.

"We're getting nowhere fast with this one, gang," I said.

Then I looked at Darlene. "Anything, Darlene, anything? Please tell me you've got something."

"Only what I said yesterday afternoon. I'm sure the killer is a woman."

No one said anything. They'd all been updated on Darlene's DNA findings.

"Not conclusive, though," Mary said. "We know the victims were all acquainted. The blond hairs could have come from a mutual friend."

Darlene looked at the table, nodded.

"But what if they *were* the killer's? Let's run with that for a sec," I said.

"There's no match in the database," Johnny commented.

"Means nothing. Maybe the murderer had never committed a crime until..."

"All right," Justine said suddenly. "What if she happens to be a 'respectable' bleached-blond friend of the dead women and part of the same social circle? Maybe the motive was some relationship mess or simple jealousy."

"The wife of a banker or a corporate suit gone crazy?" Darlene looked interested. "Maybe it *is* a sex thing. An eastern-suburbs mum taking revenge on women her husband's slept with?"

I raised my hands. "Hang on, let's calm down!"

"Actually, I don't believe that," Darlene backtracked.

"Why?"

"For a start, the hair was not recently bleached. There was significant regrowth. That in itself suggests the woman doesn't pamper herself. How many wealthy women walk around with weeks of roots growing out?"

"Search me!" Johnny said.

"And my sister insists Elspeth and Stacy weren't messing around," Justine said.

"Besides," I added, "the banknotes don't fit the theory, do they? The very fact that the notes are fake suggests the killer isn't a rich woman living in the same area as the victims . . . unless that's a trick."

"Oh, for God's sake!" Mary exclaimed. "We're going round in bloody circles!"

"No, no . . . rewind," I said. I was suddenly excited. I stood up and started pacing close to my chair. "Let's say it's *not* a trick and the killer *is* poor—a woman from outside the area. She can't afford real fifty-dollar bills. She photocopies them. Yes!"

I surveyed the room, the faces of the team. For a moment they all looked confused.

Then I remembered something. "Darlene, you told me the other day that the fakes are high-quality photocopies. What if our killer photocopies the notes at a shop instead of at home? And what if . . . what if the murderer, this woman whose bleached hair strands have been discovered . . . what if she doesn't live in the eastern suburbs but works there?"

"I'll get on it—visit all the copy shops in the area," Johnny said, as excited as me. "I think you're on to something, Craig."

Then Mary spoke: "Hey, Johnny, before you start making the rounds, let me give you some advice."

"What's that?" Johnny asked.

"It'll be a lot easier to drive if you remove your lips from the boss's ass."

For the first time in a long time, everyone in the room laughed.

CHAPTER 75

JOHNNY MAY HAVE been an ass-kisser, but he was a hardworking ass-kisser. He was back in my office with a report by midafternoon.

"There are five copy shops within a three-kilometer radius of Bellevue Hill. First three shops I visited drew a complete blank. Guys there had no idea what I was talking about when I asked them if any odd-looking, memorable, cheesy blond women had been in. Made me feel bloody stupid, actually!"

"What about the other place?"

"Fourth shop was on New South Head Road, about a mile from Bellevue Hill. The manager was a nice guy. Said he'd seen one particular woman come in a few times during the past three weeks. She didn't look 'odd,' exactly, just miserable, run-down. But get this. He described her. Above-average height, well built, bleached blond."

I rubbed my hand over my chin and stared at Johnny silently. "And the fifth shop?"

"Jackpot! A very sweet girl running the place."

"Yeah, yeah..."

"She'd seen the same woman at least twice during the past month."

"Don't fuck with me, Johnny. You've got more. I can tell by your tone."

"The last shop keeps surveillance-camera records for a month at a time. I gave the girl a hundred bucks, and she ran off a copy of the disk for me."

He handed me the disk as if he were presenting an award. I slipped it into my PC.

It was a crappy-quality recording but good enough. It showed a woman coming into the copy shop, moving from the counter to a self-service machine. She placed something indistinct on the machine's tray and watched as half a dozen copies emerged. She then paid for them and left.

"Quite a powerful-looking woman," I said.

"And piss ugly," Johnny said.

I exhaled.

"Sorry!"

"Can't see much of her. But she definitely has bleached her hair."

"First thing I noticed," Johnny replied.

"Take it through to Darlene. See if she can do anything with her magical imaging equipment."

CHAPTER 76

DARLENE WATCHED THE short clip taken at the copy shop. Johnny was leaning on the back of her chair, peering at the screen over her shoulder.

"It's pretty bad quality," she mumbled.

Johnny said nothing.

"But, thanks to my new buddy, Software Sam, I might get something out of this. It works just as well for video as it does for still images."

She ran her hands over the control panel of the image enhancer. Then she turned back to the computer keyboard and moved her fingers over the keys.

The screen went blank for a second. Then the film spooled back to the start. Darlene tapped another couple of keys. The clip was now 500 percent clearer.

The woman lumbered into the shop. She was wearing a shapeless navy-blue sweat top, handbag on her right shoulder. The camera caught her straight on. She had a wide face, a flat nose, small eyes. Her shoulder-length hair looked greasy. It was blond. Not dyed well—a bottle from a pharmacy, badly applied a long while ago. She wasn't wearing makeup. Then Johnny said something that Darlene had already noticed: "She doesn't have any bloody eyebrows."

"Not the prettiest specimen," Johnny said, a little more diplomatically this time. "What would you say? Five seven, five eight? Hundred and seventy pounds?"

"Five nine, one seventy-five."

"I bow to your superior skills," Johnny retorted.

"I used to work in a carnival," Darlene said.

Johnny laughed at the joke. Then they continued to watch the video of the woman walking towad the photocopier.

"Can you close in on her just a little bit more?" Johnny asked.

Darlene played her fingers over the keyboard, slowed the film, zoomed in and adjusted the enhancer to sharpen the picture. She was pushing the software to its limits.

Tugging the mouse gently, she moved the center of the image to see what the woman was placing on the copier. They both noticed she was wearing latex gloves. She plucked a sheet of paper from her bag. It was impossible to see what was on it.

Darlene slowed the film, then let it creep forward a few frames. The first insert began to emerge. She shifted perspective, closing in on the paper spewing from the copier. It appeared slowly. She moved in closer still. She toggled the controls on the enhancer, prayed the software would hold up.

And there, in the plastic collection tray of the photocopy machine, lay a sheet of paper containing the image of four fifty-dollar bills.

"Excellent job," Johnny said.

"We still don't know who she is," Darlene commented. "I'll get this over to the police. They may know something about Blondie."

CHAPTER 77

IT WAS A good thing that the door to my office was wide open when Darlene came rushing in. If it had been closed, she'd have crashed right through it like Bugs Bunny.

She was waving a paper file.

"Better sit down for this one, Craig," she yelled at my empty desk.

"I am, Darlene," I called from the sofa.

"Just off the phone. Sergeant Tindle called. They've ID'd the remains of the man at the Bondi house."

She sat at the other end of the sofa from me, opened the file. "Name's Bruce Frimmel."

She handed me a photograph of the man from police records.

"He'd served time. Assault charge five years ago. His DNA was on file. He vanished two months ago."

"And you reckoned the guy in the garden had been dead for two to three months."

"Police Forensics also identified two distinct sets of blood splatter in the bathroom at the house. One is Frimmel's, the other is Granger's blood. They were both killed in the same room."

"Interesting."

"Just wait. It gets much more interesting. Bruce's girlfriend, Lucy"—Darlene glanced at the file again—"Lucy Inglewood—was questioned when Frimmel vanished. She told the police he had crossed a few people. There was a biker gang in Blacktown he'd upset, and a few months earlier, he'd broken up acrimoniously with his last girlfriend, who he'd lived with for a few years."

"The police looked into these, I take it?"

"They interviewed everyone who'd known Bruce Frimmel. Sergeant Tindle worked with Inspector Talbot on it. They talked to twenty-odd of Frimmel's associates and those close to him, including his ex, Julie O'Connor. The sergeant called me, Craig, because he had just seen the security-camera stills of the woman in the copy shop I sent over this morning."

She plucked two sheets of photographic paper from the file and handed one to me. "This," she said, "is the best image from the security camera."

I stared at the photo of the woman walking toward the copier.

"And this is the woman Sergeant Tindle interviewed two months ago? This is Julie O'Connor?"

I glanced at the second photo, then held the two images side by side. "We have our killer," I said.

"And you know the best bit? According to police records, as of two months ago, she was working at Supa-Mart in Bellevue Hill."

CHAPTER 78

"GOOD NEWS," MARY said as we pulled up outside the SupaMart in Bellevue Hill.

"Yeah? What?"

"Iceberg lettuce is on sale for a dollar nineteen a head."

I wasn't in the mood to laugh.

I checked my watch. It was just past noon as Mary moved from the car to the sidewalk. She pulled on her shades and waited a moment for me to step out of the car and lock it. I led the way to the store, keeping the keys in my hand.

The manager's office was at the back. A girl standing on some steps was stacking spaghetti-sauce jars on shelves and pointed the way.

"Take a seat, take a seat," the manager, Jimmy Kocot, said.

Obviously bored, I concluded. *Slow day in Bellevue Hill.*

"We're looking for Julie O'Connor. Understand she works here."

"Julie? Yeah, she does. Should be here now, but she isn't."

"What do you mean?"

"Didn't turn up for her shift this morning." He frowned. "What's this all about? You cops?"

"No," Mary said. "We're from an investigative agency. We've had a call from one of Julie's relatives," she lied. "Miss O'Connor's aunt way over in Perth has died. The family want to reach Julie."

"So maybe the old girl's come into some money," he said.

"Maybe."

"Well, of course...I understand...Mustn't assume anything."

"No," I responded. "Would you have Julie's address? Maybe a phone number?"

Kocot looked doubtful for a few moments. "That might not be possible. There's a certain confidentiality—"

"Sure," Mary said in her sweetest voice. "It's just, the family is *desperate* to get in touch with Julie. She apparently left her relatives in Perth under a cloud, years back."

"I didn't know that," Kocot responded. "Might explain a thing or two."

"What makes you say that?" I asked.

"Well, I like Julie, but she's never been the most... communicative of my staff. Never made friends with the others. She's a bloody good worker, though—that's why I kept her on." He paused.

"Okay—I can't give you her phone number, 'cause she doesn't even have a phone. But the address..." He turned toward a mini filing cabinet on top of his desk. Flicked through the cards. "Yeah, here it is: Six Neptune Court, Impala Road, Sandsville. Let me know what the outcome is, will you? It'd sure help me to know if Julie will ever be coming back."

CHAPTER 79

JULIE WAS SITTING on her beer-stained, grease-stained, bloodstained sofa, watching TV with the sound off. It was the only way to watch, because the voices of everyone on *Australia's Next Top Model* could make you crazy with anger.

Beside her lay her scrapbook and a notebook. She picked up the notebook first. She kept this in her overalls pocket at work. In many ways, she had the perfect job for her purposes. Working at the checkout of Supa-Mart in Bellevue Hill each day, she was on the lookout for potential victims. Each day held a constant parade of spoiled wives of successful eastern-suburbs bankers, brokers, and doctors. These women floated into Supa-Mart, Gucci-clad and dripping Tiffany, to buy zero-fat milk and goat cheese with their private-school uniformed brats. To them, Julie was either invisible or an object of contempt. Julie loathed them.

But Julie also had access to their personal details. She had their credit-card data, she caught their names when they bumped into their snooty friends and had a little "chat" at the checkout. She noted everything she heard. The same women came in several times a week. A month of listening and note taking, and she knew a great deal about Samantha, Sarah, Donna, and dozens of others including Yasmin Trent, Stacy Fleetwood, Elspeth Lombard, and, of course, Jennifer Granger, the wife of the bastard who'd started it all.

She returned the little notebook to the top pocket of the lumberjack shirt she was wearing, and she picked up her scrapbook. She'd devoted a double page to each of the murders, numbered them.

1. JENNIFER GRANGER
2. STACY FLEETWOOD
3. ELSPETH LOMBARD
4. YASMIN TRENT

Beneath these names: descriptions of each murder, re-counted in her scratchy misspellings. Interspersed with the words, Julie had pasted in pictures of adorable, chubby babies, pictures she had cut out of magazines.

In the middle of the scrapbook, she sorted and listed the info she had scattered in her notebook. Here she neatly arranged rows of credit-card numbers, addresses, friends' names, husbands' jobs, husbands' offices, kids' schools. All of it had been routinely transferred from the notebook.

Now she turned through the pages of the scrapbook slowly, as if it were a religious manuscript. She studied all the information she'd transferred over the months.

"Tabatha," Julie said aloud. "Married to Simon, a 'very handsome' broker at Stanton Winslow. Address: Eight Frink Parade. Four kids—shit! Busy girl!"

Turning the page . . . "Mary—ah, nice Catholic girl, Mary. Irish ancestry, no less. Works for a local charity— Homes for Rejected Pets. How lovely! Two kids, Fran and Marcus. Husband, a spinal surgeon at Royal North Shore Hospital . . . Tempting, very tempting."

She flicked to the last page. A newspaper article about the murder of Jennifer Granger. She had read it hundreds of times. She had memorized it.

Then Julie's eyes drifted downward as she slowly read all the factual material she had collected on this woman.

"Well, hey . . . will you just look at this," she said in a whisper. "Just look at this. I'd almost forgotten this one . . . Oh, this one would be perfect!"

She leaned forward, the scrapbook on her lap, turned back to her pages listing the murdered women, flicked to a fresh page, and wrote: "NUMBER 5." Then a name.

CHAPTER 80

"SOMETIMES I CAN'T believe how easy all this has been," Julie announced to the empty living room.

Then she looked up at the silent television screen and at once felt a shiver pass through her body. She immediately ramped up the sound.

"...the body has been identified as that of Bruce Frimmel," the newsreader said. The TV camera held the image of the dead man—an old police mug shot, Julie imagined.

The newsreader continued: "Frimmel is thought to have disappeared in November. A police spokesman said he was most likely killed around that time."

Julie jumped up at the sound of tires screeching outside. She ran to the small window of her first-floor apartment and saw a white car pull up near her entrance in the small scruffy courtyard.

She snatched up the scrapbook, ran into the bed-room, and tossed it on the bed. Then she scrambled to the bottom of her wardrobe, where she had her back-pack already prepared with the things she knew she might need when it was time to leave fast.

Back in the living room, she moved to the filthy kitchen area. She picked up a book of matches, darted back to the bedroom, struck a match, and held the flame over the end of the scrapbook.

At first the paper resisted. It felt to Julie that seconds were passing as minutes. She had to quell her rising panic. The match expired without the flame catching. She'd just singed the edge of the flimsy cardboard cov-er. She struck another match and steadied her fingers by gripping her wrist with the other hand, blowing gently on the flame.

It caught. Julie couldn't wait a second longer. She dashed out of the room and into the tiny hallway, leaving the door ajar. She could hear footsteps on the stairs, a woman's voice. She puffed her way up to the second lev-el, then around the bend and onto the next flight. Now she was on the top floor. Only the flat roof was above her.

She leaned over the railings and saw two people, a man and a woman, approach the door to her apartment. The pair moved along the wall and then disappeared. Julie turned, rushed as best she could up the final flight of stairs, and pushed the exit door onto the roof.

The roof was supremely quiet—just the hum of traf-fic from the main road, the occasional squawk of a lorikeet. Julie crouched beside a utility pipe running along the edge of the roof, felt around for the brick she knew was there, found it, shifted it, plucked up the key.

She ran back to the shed, slotted the key into the lock, pulled open the door. The inside of the shed was so dark that it seemed almost black, but her eyes adjusted quickly. She scanned the shelves of jam jars filled with nails and screws, tins of paint, rolls of wire, bits of plastic tubing, and a bench scattered with tools. On the floor stood a five-gallon plastic drum with FLAMMABLE written in large, black letters around the middle. She locked the door from the inside and crouched down, keeping her breathing shallow and listening for approaching feet.

CHAPTER 81

MARY AND I had the brains to drive to Sandsville in her smartly sensible Toyota instead of my stupidly extravagant Maserati. In case you don't know what most of Australia knows—Sandsville is, hands down, the most dangerous section of Sydney. It's all gangs, all the time.

The seedy apartment blocks of Neptune Court looked as though they could collapse at any moment. There were three buildings clustered around a scrap of land, the grass worn to nothing. The music of the place was people fighting, babies screaming, occasional gunshots, rap tracks blasting.

Of the three buildings, we knew we were headed to the one that housed apartments one through twenty.

The door into Julie O'Connor's block was closed, but the steel-reinforced glass had been smashed in. I climbed through the hole, Mary half a second behind me.

Number six was on the first floor, but I smelled the smoke before I was halfway up the flight of stairs. Mary moved ahead, leaned on the wall next to the door, then swung inside. I was right behind her. She turned into the living space, swept the room, then moved to the only other part of the apartment, a tiny bedroom.

Yellow flames swirled up from blackened sheets. The fire was small—a pile of papers, but smoke had filled the room. We grabbed a pillow each and smacked at the fire. Then I found a quilt on the floor, threw it over the small blaze.

"This was just started," Mary said.

"Must've missed her by seconds. You keep looking around. I'll be back in a minute."

I ran onto the landing. No one. I noticed half the doors were boarded up. There were two more floors above this one. I ran up the first flight, saw no one, reached the top floor. There was a ROOF EXIT sticker on a door. The door had been pushed outward.

I eased out onto the roof. It was deserted. I spotted a workman's shed in one corner, paced over to it slowly, carefully. I tried the handle. It was locked.

I did a three-sixty, saw the black metal railings of a ladder descending from one corner. Walking across the roof, I peered over the edge. The ladder dropped three floors to the ground. No one. Nada. Nothing.

CHAPTER 82

WHEN I RETURNED from the roof, I found Mary sitting at a kitchen table that had been shoved up against the wall between the stove and an ancient fridge. She'd pulled on latex gloves and was leafing through a clutch of charred papers.

She fished out a second pair of gloves from her cargo pants. Tossed them over. The place still smelled of fire and ash.

"Tried to open a window," Mary said. "They're sealed tight."

"So we can just die of smoke inhalation? I don't think so," I said, and I picked up a kitchen chair and threw it against the small kitchen window. A shattering of glass and a bit of fresh air.

"Checked every cupboard. No one in any hidey-holes. Looks like Julie O'Connor left in a hurry. No sign of a handbag or purse. Found this on the floor over there," Mary added, picking up a five-dollar bill.

"Probably dropped it after snatching notes from this," I replied, indicating a jar lying on its side on top of the fridge. A few coins had been left inside.

"So, what do you think she was burning on that bed?"

"It's hard to tell." Mary nodded at the crispy papers. "Some of it's just burned to nothing."

She pointed to a pile of black, fire-ravaged paper. Then she carefully sifted through a few pages of what looked like some sort of photo album or scrapbook.

"Don't want to damage it more; Darlene'll kill me," she said. She opened the pages meticulously to the only section of the book left untouched by the fire. It was about the halfway point in the book.

I walked around and looked over her shoulder. There was a scorch mark running across the paper. "Personal info, descriptions," I said. "That set of numbers halfway down the left side." I hovered a finger over the damaged papers. "List of credit-card numbers—always sixteen digits, batches of four."

Mary nodded, turned a page carefully. "She's headed each double page with a woman's name."

I felt a tingle pass up my spine as I saw the name at the top of the first pair of pages. "Elspeth Lombard."

"All right," I said, "let's bag this stuff. Get it to Darlene." I glanced around to search for a plastic container. That was when we both heard, from the hallway, the sound of smashing glass.

Then an enormous explosion.

CHAPTER 83

"IT'S A GODDAMN Molotov cocktail!" I yelled.

Mary was up in a flash, her chair flying across the kitchen floor as she ran for the bedroom. I scanned the room desperately and spotted a plastic trash bag resting against a garbage can. I picked up the bag. Moving as fast as I could, I poured the contents of the bag onto the floor, then tucked the bag inside my jacket.

Before I'd finished, Mary was back in the living room, clutching a pair of blankets. The flames from the hall had spread, fiery tendrils reaching toward the ceiling. A ratty sofa close to the hall end had caught fire; the cheap foam melted quickly and added to the choking stench.

Mary ran to the sink, pulled on both taps, twisting them to the max.

"Got to wet the blankets!" she hollered, and then threw the blankets under the running water. Then she threw one of the sodden blankets to me. Following Mary's lead, I ducked my head under the stream of tap water. Then I wrapped the wet blanket around my shoulders, across my front, letting the bottom edge flap against my shins.

"Go!" I bellowed, and without wasting another second, I ran straight for the flames and the hallway.

The fire had engulfed about half the living room. I could sense Mary a foot behind me as we stumbled into the hallway.

The heat from the fire hit me like flames from hell. I knew I had to keep running. The floor was scorching the soles of my shoes.

Gripping the blanket, I reached for the latch and twisted. It was locked.

Panic rose up in my chest. It was getting harder and harder to breathe. I turned to Mary. I'd never seen her scared before. Then we both reached the same decision at the same moment and charged forward, slamming into the door together.

I heard the wood splinter and managed to stagger back. My chest was screaming at me. It was like walking barefoot on hot coals, but I knew that if I didn't keep going, we would both die.

We ran for the door again. A pain shot across my shoulders and up my neck. The door gave, but only opened a fraction. We charged a third time. The door fell outward, and I collided with Mary as we crashed onto the concrete landing.

We pulled ourselves up, but I tripped on the blanket,

falling heavily against a door the other side of the landing. I did my best to ignore the pain. I threw the blanket aside and felt something hit me hard across the face and chest. I looked up and saw Mary leaning over me, beating out a line of fire across the front of my shirt.

CHAPTER 84

MARY AND I staggered out onto the dirty ground between the buildings. I was leaning forward, hands on
my knees, gasping for air. A couple of teenagers ran to
us. Mary was coughing from deep in her gut. Then she
turned away and vomited.

Now the first teenage guy approached, and I suddenly felt a terrible pain in my jaw. I stumbled back
and caught a glimpse of the other kid as he jumped on
Mary's back.

Before I could take in that the bastard had hit me, he
swung his fist again. I dodged it, lashed out, and caught
him on the side of his face.

I heard a crash from behind and saw the kitchen window of Julie O'Connor's apartment shatter outward, a
great sheet of flame spewing out. The teenagers were
distracted, and Mary had apparently recovered. She

whirled round, a string of vomit running down her vest top. She threw the teenager from her back. The little bastard crashed to the ground face-first. I landed a second punch to the side of the other kid's face. As this kid fell, Mary connected her right boot with his balls. He doubled up, moaning.

I noticed that the bandage around Mary's hand was bloodied. "You okay?" I gasped almost inaudibly.

"I've had better days, Craig. You?"

I started coughing and couldn't stop for at least ten seconds. Fire alarms in the apartments began to wail.

Mary had taken her cell from her pocket. She nodded toward the car as she called 000. We ran toward our vehicle, leaving the two thugs groaning in the dirt.

I watched a group of people running out of the building.

Mary was giving instructions into the receiver as we crossed the patch of ground. I was limping like an injured footballer leaving the field, and I was totally in awe of how incredibly fit and powerful Mary was.

It was only as we got ten yards from the Toyota that we realized all four tires had been slashed.

CHAPTER 85

JULIE O'CONNOR CAUGHT the train from Sandsville and headed for downtown. She had close to two hundred bucks, a fortune to her. She also had a stolen basic green American Express credit card. But the most important thing she had was a plan.

She was still feeling the buzz, the thrill she had experienced—making the gas bomb from the materials in the shed, tossing it into the apartment, descending from the roof of her block using the metal ladder, and slipping away in the commotion.

Ten minutes into the train journey, she left her seat, walked calmly past a disgusting young family—cute wife, cute husband, cute twin girls—in the next aisle and into a corridor. She pulled open the door to the washroom.

Yanking her backpack from her right shoulder, she let it drop to the floor. Leaning down, steadying herself as the train swayed, she found the plastic bag she'd put in the backpack earlier. She placed it on the small sink.

Pulling out a dark wig, a fake mustache, and a baseball cap, she arranged them on the side. Tugging on the wig, she tucked a few loose strands of bleached-blond hair beneath the edge, found the tube of glue she'd purchased, ran a line of it along the back of the mustache, and put the mustache in place. Then she tugged on the cap. Looking at her reflection in the mirror, she had to smile. Now, that wasn't hard at all.

She was wearing jeans, boots, and her lumberjack shirt. She felt around the inside of her handbag and pulled out the roll of banknotes—real ones: three fifties, plus a twenty, a ten, and a few coins. There was a second roll wrapped in an elastic band—ten fifties. This second batch, however, was photocopied money. She planned to use that later.

She then removed the AmEx card, a packet of mints, and her favorite baby picture, one she had salvaged from her scrapbook. It showed a real cute kid, about nine months old—a cuddly baby girl wearing diapers and pink shorts. She had an adorable fat tummy and was crawling toward the camera, a big smile on her face.

Julie stuffed all these items into the pockets of her jeans, opened the window of the washroom, and tossed out her handbag. Then she checked herself in the mirror again and brushed a stray bit of wig under the cap. Taking a deep breath, she leaned into the mirror, real close, her face filling her view. She bared her teeth. "You can do this, Julie O'Connor," she hissed. "You can do this...*baby!*"

CHAPTER 86

"JUST GOT THIS in from one of our cars out in the western suburbs, sir," said Sergeant Raj Petigara. He then handed a sheet of paper to Inspector Mark Talbot. "Thought you might find it interesting."

Talbot scanned the report and grinned, touched the Steri-Strip across his nose. Craig Gisto had almost been barbecued, then beaten up by a couple of teenagers in Sandsville.

"He's not, by any chance, in the Serious Burns Unit of the Royal North Shore Hospital?"

"Not this time, sir," the sergeant replied.

"Shame," Talbot remarked under his breath. He glanced at his watch. "Hell. I'm late." Then he turned and walked quickly down the hallway.

He crept into the conference room just as Brett

Thorogood was about to start talking. Talbot found a seat and manned out Thorogood's glare.

There was a buzz of excitement in the room. Even Talbot could sense it. He could feel his own adrenaline pumping. This was why he'd joined the force: a manhunt—well, a womanhunt in this case.

"This is the suspect," Thorogood announced, pointing to a large photo of Julie on the whiteboard. "A snap taken when she started work at SupaMart."

Hideous bitch, Talbot thought.

"Don't have much on her," the deputy commissioner went on. "Name: Julie Ann O'Connor. Age: twenty-seven. Current address: Six Neptune Court, Impala Road, Sandsville. No record. So far, so ordinary. Her father was a cop, Jim O'Connor—killed in the line of duty in 1996. She disappeared in 2000, off the radar until 2004. Cropped up in state records as a cleaner for a small engineering firm, Maxim Products, in Campbelltown. Our friends at Private have come up with some useful stuff."

Talbot felt a knot in his gut. He hated even hearing the word "Private."

The DC clicked a remote, and footage from the copy shop came on screen.

"Appears the woman is underprivileged, lives in a slum, works in one of Sydney's most affluent areas. Could be some sort of motive for her killings. She copies the banknotes using a couple of different copy shops near Bellevue Hill."

" 'Underprivileged'?" Talbot said, and looked around at the five other officers in the room.

"Yes," Thorogood replied. "Your point?"

He had none, just hated the term. This bitch was dumb as dirt. Didn't she know you could photocopy at home on a printer? But she probably didn't have a computer—a big satellite-TV dish, for sure, but no computer. She'd probably never touched one, had no clue. Douche bag.

Thorogood was talking again. "Private has confirmed a positive DNA match to place this woman at two of the murder scenes for sure. She was also in a long-term relationship with the male victim, Bruce Frimmel, whose DNA was found at the same murder scene as Jennifer Granger's. Both victims' bodies were found in the yard of the house on Ernest Street in Bondi."

Talbot wanted to retch. That word again. *"Private."* Thank God it had been one of his boys who'd put the pieces of the puzzle together, matching the photos of the O'Connor bitch.

"Any idea where this Julie O'Connor is now, sir?" It was Chief Inspector Mulligan, Talbot's immediate superior. He was leaning back in his chair, arms folded across his chest.

"Good question. We don't know. But we will. I've just heard that about an hour ago, Craig Gisto and Mary Clarke from Private almost got O'Connor at her apartment in Sandsville. Ended up, though, that they were lucky to escape with their lives. The bloody woman firebombed the place with them inside."

Mark exhaled loudly. Thorogood gave him an odd look.

"I'm pulling out all the stops," the deputy commissioner went on. "Closing the airports, putting up roadblocks ringing the city, every spare man out on the streets. We'll get her, and when we do, she'll live out her days in a ten-foot-square cell."

Not if I get her first! Talbot thought.

CHAPTER 87

JULIE GLANCED AT her plastic Little Kitty digital watch: 5:03 p.m. It sure as hell had been a busy day.

She had left the apartment hours earlier, thrown in the Molotov, slashed the car tires. Now she was walking around town dressed as a man, feeling increasingly confident. No one seemed to notice. She just blended right in...blended right into the pool of humanity around her. She, of course, knew she was not *like them,* not *like them* at all. She was a different breed from the people she brushed shoulders with, different from all these assholes she stared at, all these people who merely glanced at her and moved on with their normal, happy lives.

They all had homes to go to. In those homes were people who loved them, people they loved. They had lives, careers. Julie had nothing, and it made her feel...it made her feel...For the first time in her life, she actually felt liberated. Free. Totally free. She was her own powerhouse. Why, look at that, there was some dumpy, middle-aged rich broad who smiled at her, a flirtatious sort of child. Yes, she was free. She could do anything. *She* could even be a *he*.

CHAPTER 88

"OKAY. I KNOW I'm interrupting."

Johnny looked up from his desk and saw Katia, Mickey Spencer's girlfriend, standing at the entrance to his cubicle. She looked even more stunning than she had the night before. She was dressed entirely in white—a long, flowing skirt that reached almost to her ankles, a snug-fitting white T-shirt, and the miniature sword on the pink silk ribbon, still around her neck.

"A visit from you could never be called 'interrupting,'" he said. *Mr. Suave is in the building.*

She gave him a faint smile.

"How's Mickey?"

"Oh, he's absolutely fine."

"He's fine?"

"Up by two this afternoon, and off to a rehearsal at three."

"But...?"

Katia gave him a broader smile. "You're pretty naive, aren't you, Johnny Ishmah? That's so sweet."

God, he hoped he wasn't blushing.

"I don't know much about the rock world, but I'm not totally naive."

"Mickey has an incredible constitution, *and* he keeps Dr. James close by. Ricky insists upon it. Mickey can't stand the doctor. Thinks he's grossly overpaid."

Johnny perched himself on the edge of the desk and decided to go for what he wanted.

"Last night, you were starting to tell me what you thought about this Club Twenty-Seven thing."

She paused, bit her lip. Then she spoke.

"You know, Johnny, I really don't know what to think anymore. I've been with Mickey for six months. He was a user when I met him. He drinks heavily. But...you know...he's a rock star...That's what rock stars do, isn't it? The difference now is—well, he's become a lot worse in the last two months."

"And you think that's because he's approaching his twenty-seventh birthday? Or do you think Holt is pushing him into killing himself?"

Katia folded her arms and looked as though she were about to burst into tears.

"Look, Katia," he said, "last night I saw something."

She fixed her huge, dark eyes on him.

"The smack. I saw Holt give it to Mickey just before he went into the bathroom."

Katia exhaled through her nose. "Of course he did,"

she said, her expression cynical. "Mickey was a prize racehorse. He used to be Ricky's most valuable asset. Now, though, even with his career on the slide, Ricky's still Mickey's supplier for everything... especially first-class drugs."

CHAPTER 89

JOHNNY HAD BEEN tailing Ricky Holt for over two hours. After all that time, he ended up at Kings Cross—the cheesy stretch of strip clubs, ugly discos, and dumb-luck gambling haunts called the Strip.

Holt had ducked into a joint called the Roxy. Johnny stopped outside, nodded to the bouncer at the door, and pulled out his wallet as he walked in. He approached a woman in a significantly short black dress. The dress also had a significantly plunging neckline. She was sitting at the business end of the bar. Her legs were crossed, and a large sign above her nearby cash register stated simply: ENTRANCE FEE, $50. Johnny paid up.

Some nameless dance track, all bass drum and bubbling synthesizer, thumped away. Spotlights on a small, circular stage moved in a random pattern and sent splashes of color across a couple of girls wearing G-strings and nothing else. Several punters stood near the edge of the stage, looking up at the girls and the glare. A smaller bar near the stage was surrounded by UV lights.

Johnny scanned the room, but he had trouble making anything out. He moved slowly around the edge of the space, trying not to make himself obvious to the half dozen men sitting at tables. He did not see Holt. Then he caught some clear movement in the corner of his vision, a man slipping under an arch. A notice to the side said PRIVATE ROOMS.

Johnny made his way over, slowed as he reached the arch, and took a couple of paces into a narrow corridor lined with closed doors. At the end of that corridor stood an emergency exit. The door was open and led into an alley. The music was quieter here, just the thud of the bass drum. Johnny paced along the corridor and heard voices coming from beyond the exit. He recognized Holt's voice. Then he pulled in close to the wall and held his breath, straining to hear what was being said.

Then came a thumping sound, a groan—and suddenly Ricky Holt was flying toward the emergency exit. Ricky grabbed on to the door frame, trying to break his fall. Johnny couldn't help himself. Stupidly, reflexively, he jumped aside and into full view of the men in the alley.

CHAPTER 90

JOHNNY RAN THROUGH the doorway and cut right. He was suddenly in the alley, and he hoped he'd gain a few seconds' lead before the men realized what was happening.

The dark passageway was cratered with potholes and strewn with garbage. Johnny tripped on—what the hell was that? A battered television set. He almost went down but steadied himself and kept going. He glanced over his shoulder and saw two thugs running toward him through the shadows. Beyond them, the rear lights of a car.

Another dark alley was on his left. He turned and ran through the black back street. He could hear that the two men had reached the same left turn and were coming after him, gaining on him.

His eyes burned with perspiration. *Am I too young*

to have a fucking heart attack? he thought. Somehow he found some backup energy. Where the hell had that come from? He ripped along the narrow lane and came out onto a brightly lit road. People were walking—couples, children, friends out with other friends. He saw restaurants and bars and shops. He could merge, maybe. He could disappear into all these faces. But these guys would get him somehow. It was their turf.

Directly across the street, a dark entrance to another alley. He darted across the road. Horns blasted. Johnny swerved, gained speed, and flew into the passageway. But the men pursuing him were just as fast. They crashed into the lane a few yards behind him. Johnny put on a final burst of speed, reached the end, a T-junction. He swung left and tripped. He hit the ground with a skin-scraping thud, and he heard a very unpleasant snapping sound. His back. He knew something had snapped in his back.

CHAPTER 91

THEY YANKED HIM up and rammed him against a wall. One of them pushed his hand tightly at Johnny's throat.

"A little nosy, aren't we, kid?"

Johnny stared into the man's face. His head was shaved, and his eyes were like two dirty pools of water. His eyebrows could have benefited from a trim with a power lawn mower.

"I was just leaving the place."

"Uh-huh."

"Look, I'm not interested in what you were saying."

The other guy laughed and took a step forward. The first man loosened his grip on Johnny's neck, grabbed his left arm, pulled it up hard behind his back. Johnny cried out in pain.

"A little word with the boss is in order, I think," the

guy with the big eyebrows said. He pushed Johnny forward, and in a few moments, they were back on the busy main thoroughfare.

Two minutes later the two men had marched Johnny to the rear entrance to the Roxy. A big, black BMW stood in the lane.

Johnny struggled to get away, even though he knew he had little chance of that. The two men each had an arm on him. They came around to the side of the vehicle, and the one on Johnny's right opened the door with his spare hand, pushed down on his head, and shoved him into the car. Then he slipped in beside him. The other guy ran around and jumped into the driver's seat.

"You a little out of breath?" the boss asked, turning to the henchman in the back. "Gave them a run for their money, eh, Johnny? *Johnny Ishmah?*"

Johnny stared at the boss. He had a flabby face, small, black eyes, and a big, nauseating grin.

"Jerry Loretto!" Johnny said, amazed. "It's been a long time..."

CHAPTER 92

"ALL RIGHT, YOU two—piss off," Jerry Loretto said, and so they quietly stepped, pissed off, into the alley and slammed the doors shut.

"Well, well!" the youthful-looking boss exclaimed. "Never thought I'd see you again, Johnny. What the hell you doin' here?"

Johnny had regained some composure, took a deep breath. "Could ask the same of you, Jerry. You watching one of your dad's places?"

Jerry snorted. "My own, you cheeky little bastard. I'm a big boy now!"

Johnny knew Jerry Loretto was only twenty-four, although his expensive outfit—striped suit and navy-blue polo shirt buttoned to the neck—looked like it would be perfect for a fifty-year-old undertaker. Yes, that was what Johnny thought, but he kept his observation to himself.

Johnny had known Jerry in high school. Not that Loretto had shown up at school very often. Even then he'd been a petty criminal—newsstand holdups and purse snatchings.

Johnny had studiously avoided the guy. Jerry Loretto was one of the school thugs, a thoroughly nasty piece of work, even at the age of eleven. But one day Loretto crossed the path of another tough kid from a neighboring school who had intruded into Jerry's "patch," selling weed and Ecstasy. Loretto had been jumped, knifed, and dumped by the roadside. Johnny had found him, and Jerry had begged him not to call an ambulance because he didn't want anyone to know what he'd been up to.

Johnny had helped Jerry get home, and after that, Loretto was his guardian angel.

"I'm here on an investigation," Johnny said, a little embarrassed. "I'm a PI."

"Holy shit," Loretto said. Then he burst out laughing. "Well, I guess that figures. Johnny, you always were a little pussy." Then Jerry added, "You're not investigating *me*, are you?" Johnny thought the question was half-joke, half-serious.

It was Johnny's turn to laugh, a nervous edge to it. "Nah, I'm keeping an eye on your buddy, Ricky Holt."

"That shyster?"

"He manages one of our clients."

"Mickey friggin' Spencer?"

Johnny nodded.

"So, what do you want to know about Holt, then, Johnny boy?"

"Well, he's obviously up to his neck in it."

"Up to his eyeballs, more like—up to here." And then Jerry indicated a level six inches above his head.

"Gambling?"

Loretto nodded. "Stupid bastard must be the worst punter in history, but he don't give up."

"How much does he owe you?"

Jerry frowned, then tapped his nose. "Client confidentiality," he said, and laughed loudly. "Let's just say *a lot*."

"And you've given him an ultimatum?"

"One he probably can't meet."

Johnny nodded. "He really is up to here…" He imitated Loretto's earlier gesture.

"Oh, yes, Johnny boy. I sure as shit wouldn't want to be Ricky Holt in three days' time."

CHAPTER 93

AT TEN P.M., Darlene was alone in Private HQ. She kept unsociable hours, always had. And she never saw anything odd about rising at noon and staying awake until seven a.m.

Darlene approached the large metal table that dominated the center of the lab. The powerful light above the table bleached the gray steel bench to a near-white color. Under that light, on the steel counter, lay remnants of Julie O'Connor's papers, the papers that had been salvaged from the apartment in Sandsville.

Darlene had already spent several hours sorting and sifting through the material. She'd compiled three separate groupings. Group one: useless ashes. Group two: almost-useless scraps of paper worth examining. And, finally, group three: a small heap of material that might prove helpful.

This last pile included about a dozen pages of a scrapbook. Wearing latex gloves, Darlene carefully turned these pages. It was a peculiar mess. Many of the surviving pages contained pictures of Julie holding babies. Then there were pictures of babies cut from magazines, ads for baby strollers, baby clothes, disposable diapers.

A few pages in, she saw a crude drawing of a nursery. Then, on the following pages, names. A long list, two columns to a page. At the top of the left column, Julie had written "GIRLS." Topping the right column was the word "BOYS." Under these headings were dozens of names, alphabetized, some crossed out and written over, many misspelled.

A set of double pages from the scrapbook had separated from the spine. She saw familiar names. One said, "WHORE NUMBER 3: ELSPETH LOMBARD"; the other, "WHORE NUMBER 4: YASMIN TRENT." Beneath this were details of the murders from Julie O'Connor's perspective. Crude in their descriptions, shocking in their candor.

Darlene carefully continued to leaf through the notebook. Then she suddenly stopped.

On the brightly lit counter lay another double page that had slipped away from the others. She could see three words: "WHORE NUMBER 5." Next to that heading was a deep brown scorch mark.

CHAPTER 94

A SHORT, STOCKY man with a mustache walked from the train station, south along Seymour Avenue, then right onto Sebastian Road. He'd walked this route many mornings before. It was 10:15 p.m. as he entered the parking lot of SupaMart. No one had seen anything odd or distinctive about the guy. It was, of course, Julie. And the only one who knew that . . . was Julie.

Julie strode straight past the entrance, the rectangle of glass fronting the store, then down a broad alleyway toward the other parking lot, the rear parking lot. Hanging a left, she found the darkened doorway at the back of SupaMart. The door was bolted and padlocked.

Julie slotted a key into the padlock, turned it, found a second key for the lower Yale, twisted that, pushed— and the door swung inward.

She now stood in a corridor, flipped a light switch. A

fluorescent strip buzzed and sputtered into life. Concrete floor, concrete walls, concrete ceiling. She pulled open another door, took three paces along the passage, stopped at yet another door. It was marked STOREROOM 1.

It was unlocked, the light on. It was filled with boxes of canned goods—soups and gravies and vegetables for the shelves in the store. At six a.m. tomorrow, a three-person team would arrive to take the goods out onto the shop floor. Later tomorrow, a threesome from a truck would arrive to unload their cargo of more boxes to be put into this storeroom, to be put on the store shelves. It was a long and boring cycle.

Julie knew that there was a concealed cupboard at the back of the third shelf up from the floor. She had spotted it weeks ago when she was sent to the storeroom to bring out a carton of Heinz beans. She yanked on the handle. Inside were a few items she'd put there two days ago—clothes, a sleeping bag, a thermos, and some basic toiletries.

Julie gathered the things up, unfurled the sleeping bag on the floor, and lay on it. She was used to sleeping rough. After walking out on her evil mother, she'd lived on the streets for four years. She'd been raped twice, had her skull fractured as she slept in a park, and almost died on the operating table. No, unlike the stupid, soft bitches she delighted in killing, she knew Julia Ann O'Connor was as tough as they came.

She leaned back against the wall and pulled out her crisp, new, virginal notebook. At the top of a double page, close to the back, a name. Beneath this an address, followed by a list of people—the woman's family and friends. Then a collection of phone numbers. Last, some notes, a set of things she thought might one day be useful information about the woman she'd targeted: "Favorite restaurants," "Gym address," "Phone number," "Habits."

Under "Habits," she'd written: "This whore likes to run. She runs and she runs . . . silly bitch. She runs around Parsley Bay, a couple of miles from her house. Always same time—early riser, this babe . . . six a.m. Easy!"

CHAPTER 95

THE YOUNG MAN knocked on the lab door.

"Come on in, Johnny," Darlene said.

"How'd you know it was me?" Johnny asked.

She looked up from her microscope.

"I just knew. I just know everybody's knock, everybody's footstep," she said. "I guess I was born to have this kind of job."

"Seems kinda creepy," Johnny said with a smile.

"Whatever," Darlene said without a smile.

She pulled back from the scope and said, "Take a look."

He peered into the eyepiece. "Means nothing to me."

"And not much more to me," Darlene said. "It's part of Julie O'Connor's scrapbook, but it's so badly charred, I can't make out the words. I'm getting really pissed with it, to be honest."

"Not surprised." Johnny paced over to Darlene's desk. He saw the small pile of invites Software Sam had left yesterday.

"I heard about these," he said, picking up the tickets. "Mickey Spencer's birthday party...right? Craig mentioned them."

Darlene nodded. "Yeah, that guy...Friend of Mickey's dropped them in. With all the stuff going on here, I'd forgotten."

Johnny stared down at the invitations. "It's tonight." He stared into Darlene's eyes.

"It is?" she said.

Then Johnny was surprised to hear himself say: "Darlene? What is wrong with you? How could you forget? We should be there to watch out for him. What if Ricky Holt—"

He stopped shouting. He was panic struck.

"Shit," Darlene said.

"Come on. Let's get moving," Johnny said.

"Johnny Ishmah," Darlene said, "you're not asking me out on a date, are you?"

He flushed red. Maybe it was embarrassment. Maybe it was fright. Probably it was both.

"Oh my God! You're blushing!" Darlene said, hand to mouth. "How..."

"Don't say 'cute.' "

"All right...How *not* cute!"

CHAPTER 96

NO DOUBT ABOUT it. Darlene was a bundle of contradictions, and all those contradictions intrigued Johnny. To put it mildly. Darlene's job was messing with blood and body parts, but underneath her lab coat, she always wore Prada or Chanel. A trust fund from her rich dad bought her a three-bedroom apartment with a harbor view, but she drove a seventies VW Beetle that she'd lovingly restored herself. Johnny was definitely intrigued, but he also knew that Darlene was way out of his league. This "date" for the Spencer party was a totally unexpected bonus for the lad.

Darlene, with Johnny in the passenger seat, chugged the old VW through the exit gate of the garage. The security guard smiled and gave her a shy wave.

"Sweet bloke," she said to Johnny. "After his concussion he came to work in just a few days. He insisted."

It was 11:32 p.m., and the sidewalks of the CBD were crowded and busy. They passed a club on George Street called Ivy, a line out the door stretching two blocks.

Johnny leaned in toward the radio—an original sixties collectible. He pointed to the machine. She nodded, and Johnny nudged down the On switch. Classical chamber music came out from the speaker.

"You ever been to anything like this before?" he asked, picking up the invitations.

Darlene shrugged. "Once or twice, but it was a while ago."

Craig had told Johnny that Darlene had been a model for almost a year after graduating from college. Darlene had never brought up the subject. So Johnny assumed it hadn't been a good experience.

"How do you change channels on this thing?"

"You don't like Brahms? The dial."

Johnny slowly turned the knob. He passed through a jazz station, the ABC late program. Then some pop music came on. He went past it, backtracked, tuned it.

"Unreal!" He turned to Darlene.

"What?"

"Only Mickey Spencer's new single. Heard it on Spotify this morning."

"The song is happening all over," she said as she turned off George Street. The two of them fell silent for a few moments. They just listened to Mickey's new song.

She hung a right onto Castlereagh Street and then

looked at Johnny. "Pretty catchy tune. Why so quiet? What's up?"

He was pale, staring at the radio. Held up a hand. "Sssh! Listen!"

The music swelled; Mickey repeated the chorus: *"I just wanna die at midnight in your arms. Like Jimi and Janis and Kurt... Club Twenty-Seven charms."*

"They'll be playing it at his funeral service if we don't hurry up," Darlene said.

CHAPTER 97

THERE WAS A long line to enter Mickey's celebration, but Darlene and Johnny simply showed their invites to the bouncer at the head of the line. He glanced at the papers, stared briefly at Johnny and significantly longer at Darlene. Then the big guy nodded to the double doors.

"How'd you get us in so fast?" Johnny asked.

She handed him the invitations.

"Look closely," she said.

Sure enough, he saw a tiny engraving at the top right: "Very VIP."

The club was huge. Music throbbed from powerful speakers. Lights swept and flashed. One vast wall was covered with an early Pink Floyd–esque display of psychedelic colors.

"We've got to find Mickey fast," Darlene said.

"Good luck with that."

It was packed. Darlene and Johnny pushed their way across the main floor.

They reached the bar. Johnny leaned in and tried to get the attention of the bartender.

Darlene wasn't paying much attention; she was busy looking for Mickey. She very quickly caught the eye of the bartender. She was good at doing that.

"Hello, darlin'," he oozed. "What can I interest you in?"

She switched on the charm. "Listen, I need to find Mickey. I'm a friend."

"Of course you are, sweetheart!"

She flashed her invite, and the guy changed his tone and his tune.

"Okay. Cool. So, how can I help?" the bartender asked.

"Where's Mickey right now?"

The man shrugged. "How should I know?"

"I *really* would like to know," she said. "And I *really* think Mickey would like me to know too. Okay?"

He straightened. "Upstairs in his suite. Two twelve. Second floor, far end . . . I'd use the stairs; the heads are taking the elevator straight to the washrooms on the second floor."

He smiled and tapped his nose.

CHAPTER 98

MICKEY'S PARTY WAS part heaven, part hell. Part porn flick, part Disney cartoon. Part fun house, part madhouse. You get it. The party was precisely what you'd expect of an international rock star on his twenty-seventh birthday.

Barely clad, kohl-eyed women tottered around holding flutes of champagne. A dealer sat at a corner table, dispensing his drugs as if they were Big Macs. A voluptuous female dwarf wearing nothing but a yellow bikini bottom carried a tray on her head. The tray was heaped with cocaine.

Meanwhile, Mickey and Katia held court in the bedroom. He strummed an acoustic guitar and sang one of his lesser-known songs. A spliff dangled constantly from the corner of his mouth.

Hemi overflowed an armchair located close to

where the bedroom spilled out into a vast lounge. He'd positioned himself there deliberately so he could follow the action. He was drinking his usual sparkling mineral water. Hemi spoke to nobody, and nobody spoke to Hemi.

Mickey was on the last repeat chorus of his song when he saw Hemi roll forward and collapse onto the carpet in a wobbly, groaning heap. He stopped strumming immediately and turned blankly to Katia. She hadn't seen the big man crumple, but she, like everyone else, had heard the sound of him reaching the floor. She was the first up and across the room. Mickey came around the end of the bed, still holding his guitar.

Katia crouched beside Hemi, and together Mickey and Katia managed to roll the big guy over. He was out cold and began to snore. She raised her head to Mickey, and she burst out laughing. The rock star looked concerned for a moment, but then he started laughing too.

"Too much sparkling water, Hemi," he mumbled.

Katia stood up and came around to hug Mickey. "Let's get outta here."

He looked down at her, eyes swimming. "But it's my party."

"I want to take you somewhere quiet and lick you all over."

Mickey giggled stupidly. "Well, that's an offer I ain't gonna refuse...am I?"

"Ricky's room is empty. He's banned everyone—"

"Ricky's?" Mickey said, and he suddenly looked frightened.

"Don't worry—he's downstairs schmoozing. I got the key earlier from Reception. I wanted us to see in your birthday together...just you and me. I want to protect you. No one can touch you till after midnight."

CHAPTER 99

THEY STUMBLED DOWN the corridor. They fell. They giggled. They stood up again and stumbled some more. Once they reached the door, Katia slipped the key card into the lock slot, opened the door slowly, and then pulled Mickey inside. Ricky Holt was getting up from the end of the bed, a bottle of Wild Turkey 15 in his hand. He had a split lip and a line of Steri-Strips across his cheek.

"Ah!" Katia said.

"Don't mind me," Holt mumbled.

Mickey began to jabber. His words made no sense. He pointed at Holt.

"What's he saying?"

Katia shushed Mickey and guided him to the bed.

Holt looked at the bottle and frowned, turned it upside down. "Damn!"

"I'll get you something." Katia left Mickey sitting up on the bed, his head back on a mountain of pillows. He was gazing at Holt warily. A few moments later, Katia was walking back from the drinks cabinet with a bottle—this time Jack Daniel's—in one hand and a tumbler almost full to the brim with amber liquid. She handed the tumbler to Holt. He made a grab for the bottle. "No, no," she tutted, and crossed over to Mickey.

Holt pulled himself into an armchair and took a gulp of Jack.

"I've got a story," Katia announced. Holt looked at her blearily.

"Oh, I like stories," Mickey said, swigging from the bottle.

"There was a pope. I can't remember which one. It was a long time ago, maybe in the tenth century, sometime like that. Anyway, he wasn't a very popular pope, and so he decided to go on a tour of all the papal dominions, to try to buy the favor of his flock with indulgences. He reached Verona on Midsummer Day and was dispensing his promises and his money to the people of the city, when a woman who was known to be a witch stood up and yelled to the crowd that the pope would die on October second of that year. That would be just over three months later."

Mickey was looking at her, rapt as a child listening to *Goodnight Moon.* Holt had his eyes closed. His chin was on his chest.

"They arrested the woman, of course, burned her at the stake in front of the pope. But even though the witch was dead, the pope was terrified by her curse. He returned to Rome immediately and tried to put the memory of what had happened in Verona out of his mind. But it was no good. As October second approached, the pope became more and more agitated. On October first, he gave strict instructions to his staff and to the cardinals and locked himself in his private chambers. He would see no one, and he would not eat or drink anything until just after midnight on the morning of the third.

"The pope's servants followed his every wish, and as the clock struck midnight and October second passed into October third, the room was unlocked. The elated pope sprang from his bed, walked toward the servant, tripped, smashed his head against the leg of a table, and died instantly."

Mickey looked horrified and was just about to say something when Holt tumbled to the floor.

"Shit!" the rock star exclaimed. "We've lost another one!" He turned to see that Katia had taken off her pink silk-ribbon necklace and had the sharp tip of a very sharp, very small sword at his jugular.

CHAPTER 100

THE STAIRS STOOD at the far side of the dance floor, and that dance floor was packed with heaving, sweating bodies. Music seemed to make the walls and ceiling actually shake.

"Must be a back way," Johnny yelled into Darlene's ear.

She glanced at her watch. It was 11:55 p.m. "No time to look for it." She made for the edge of the crowd, forcing her way between the revelers and the wall of mahogany paneling. It was almost impossible to move.

Johnny took out his Private ID and squeezed past her. Under the pulsating light show, he looked like a plainclothes cop holding up his badge. The sea of humanity more or less parted before him.

He reached the stairs, and Darlene almost fell over him. "Neat trick," she said.

The first floor was dimly lit, the noise from below still incredibly loud. A red carpet led them down a corridor of guest rooms. They ran for the second flight of stairs.

It was quieter—no one around. Then they heard a sound—laughter, a girl squealing. Darlene glanced at her watch: 11:58.

On the far wall, a sign: SUITES 208–215, an arrow pointing left. Darlene turned on her heel, headed off, Johnny close behind.

The door to 212A stood ajar. They slowed, turned in, and almost fell over a couple of girls rolling around on the floor and kissing passionately. Three people were passed out on the bed. No Johnny. No Katia.

Darlene ran through the bedroom, into the lounge, and then on into the second bedroom. The bed there was a tangle of limbs, groans and moans audible above the music coming from a beat box in the corner.

After checking that Mickey wasn't one of the bodies on the bed, she did a one-eighty and charged back into the main bedroom.

"Anything?" she asked Johnny.

They tore along the plush carpet, careered around a corner, pulling up just short of an elderly Asian maid pushing a cart filled with toiletries. She was wearing earplugs.

"Whoa!" she shrieked. The woman pulled out the earplugs, grimacing at the noise.

"Sorry," Darlene said. "Can you help? We're looking for Mickey Spencer."

"Who?"

"The pop star?"

"Never 'eard of him," the maid said irritably. "Just can't stand this awful noise." She paused. "Oh, I know who you mean! It's his party . . . right?"

Darlene nodded.

"He's got suite two twelve B. Terrible mess he always makes."

"He's not there."

"I saw him a few minutes ago. He went off with a girl."

Johnny stepped forward. "Tall, skinny, black hair?"

The maid nodded. "They went that way. The older man—his boss."

"Mickey's manager?"

"Whatever you call him . . . His room is down there . . . two fifteen. That's where they were headed."

CHAPTER 101

DARLENE AND JOHNNY ran down the corridor. The door to 215 was locked. Johnny whipped a penknife from his pocket. Darlene stood aside as he flipped a blade out and slid it into the lock. He twisted it right, left, back, then left again. They heard a click, and the door opened.

Katia was on the bed, crouching over Mickey. She appeared to be almost supernaturally huge. Mickey was frozen in fright, rigid. He was eyeing the tiny but deadly sword at his throat.

It took Darlene and Johnny a second to absorb it all. They saw Mickey's manager, Ricky Holt, unconscious on the floor.

"Okay, everyone, whatever's happening needs to stop happening," Johnny said.

"Yeah...what *is* happening?" Mickey said drunkenly.

His brain obviously knew that it should sober up, but his voice hadn't gotten the message yet.

Katia blew the singer a kiss. "Dear Mickey," she said softly. "You see...just like all pop stars, you could never keep your cock in your pants, could you?"

"What?"

"You probably don't even remember her, do you?"

"Remember who, Katia?"

"In 2010 Fun Park played a gig in Moscow. You must remember that!"

"Yeah."

"After the show you met a young girl."

"I've met a lot of—"

"Don't!" Katia screamed, and she moved the blade in her hand forward a fraction of an inch.

Mickey's fists clenched. "Agh!"

"Don't be a fucking baby all the time." She was angry. She kept shouting.

Mickey took a couple of deep breaths. He was wet with sweat.

"You bitch!"

She blew him another kiss and smiled sweetly. "I mention the girl because—"

"What fucking girl?" Mickey turned his eyes to Johnny and Darlene and gave them an imploring look.

"That girl was my sister, Anaïs. She got pregnant. You made her pregnant."

"What! I didn't—"

"You didn't what, Mickey? Didn't screw her? I know you did."

"I had no idea—"

"She e-mailed you. She tried to get to you and 'your people.' Never a single reply. You discarded her, simply brushed her off."

Katia was staring down at the singer, her face contorted, eyes ablaze. Johnny and Darlene knew that the best they could do was to do nothing.

"Katia," Mickey pleaded. "Please . . . I didn't know. No one told me. Maybe I can help now . . ."

"She's dead, Mickey. Died having a backstreet abortion."

There was a stillness in the room. No one spoke.

"I'm so sorry—" Mickey began.

"Sorry?"

"I didn't know . . ."

"Anais suffered so much." As tears filled her eyes, she relaxed her grip.

Mickey moved in the bed and placed his hands gently on Katia's cheeks, wiped away the tears. He looked into her eyes.

"I really am . . . ," he said.

For a moment, Katia began to respond, closed her eyes, went to kiss the pop star. But then her eyes snapped open. She seemed to explode. She shoved him back and brought the tiny dagger to his throat again.

"I could have killed you anytime, Mickey, but I wanted you to *suffer*. I filled your tiny brain with the idea of you joining Club Twenty-Seven a few months ago. You've been too drugged up to remember that. And I could also blame it all on Holt. I made you think that too."

Johnny and Darlene were scared. Katia had suddenly became frighteningly calm. A soft smile turned her mouth upward. Her teary eyes were suddenly gentle. She leaned back slightly. The calm was more frightening to Johnny and Darlene than the shouting and cursing. They could see her tighten her grip on the miniature sword.

There was a movement from behind the woman. Darlene and Johnny managed to stay still, to show no reaction.

Katia shot them a glance. "I have to kill him, you see," she said, now way too calm. "An eye for an eye... and I loved Anais."

She went to push her hand forward, and Ricky Holt's fist swung around. Whether Katia reacted fast or Ricky's aim was sloppy, Katia managed to avoid contact with the fist. She shot her hand out, away from Mickey's throat, running the tiny blade across Holt's face. He yelled, fell back, hands to his face, blood gushing between his fingers.

Katia was off the bed, ramming straight into Darlene, knocking her into Johnny with surprising force. Johnny grabbed for Katia as he tumbled, but she sidestepped him and was out the door.

CHAPTER 102

"DARLENE, STAY HERE. Call 000," Johnny snapped, turned and headed after Katia.

She'd vanished, but there weren't that many places she could run to. Johnny turned a corner and saw Katia yank open the door to Mickey's suite. He heard screams from the room. Johnny ran to the door.

She was like a storm trooper plowing through the party, pushing people aside. Drinks were flying, men and women falling. She turned, saw Johnny no more than ten feet behind her, and pushed even harder against the crowd. A woman fell to the carpet, smashing her head on a chair leg. Katia almost tripped over Hemi, who had been left to sleep on the floor.

For a second she didn't seem to know what to do. Then she reached for a champagne bottle, smashed it on a table, gripping it in her right hand. She spun round. Half the people were so stoned, they moved like zombies. A few looked petrified. Katia grabbed the closest girl to hand, a near-naked waif with cocaine powdered all over her tiny breasts. The kid screamed as she was pulled back and Katia held the jagged spikes of the shattered champagne bottle to her face.

"Get back!" Katia bellowed as Johnny approached.

Someone killed the music, and the place fell silent.

"What are you doing, Katia?" Johnny took a step toward her.

The woman was glowing sweat, her eyes wild, hair stuck to her exquisite face.

"This isn't you, Katia."

"Get back, I said. NOW!"

"Katia." Johnny stopped and crouched down a few feet in front of her. The young girl in Katia's grip began to sob violently.

"This is a young kid," he said, flicking his eyes toward the terrified girl. "Just like your sister...just like Anais."

"You don't know anything about Anais," she spat.

"I know she suffered. You said so yourself."

Katia screamed suddenly. "Shut up! I don't want to hear it." She went to move her hand to cut the girl's face to shreds. Johnny dived forward, grabbed Katia's hand with his left hand, and smashed his right fist into her gut.

She lost her grip on the bottle. The weeping girl slumped to one side, and Katia groaned but kept on her feet, stumbling backward. Johnny rushed forward, smacked her across the face, hard. She fell backward and slammed into a cabinet of glass shelves. The shelves tumbled down on top of her, shards cascading all around her unconscious body.

CHAPTER 103

THE COPS ARRIVED within minutes, and Mickey Spencer's twenty-seventh birthday party came to a close.

Katia was taken into custody. Mickey and two cops rode with Ricky Holt in the ambulance to St. Vincent's Hospital. Darlene and Johnny, because of their Private connection, managed to talk their way out of going to police headquarters for a grilling. Even so, the interviews at the club took hours.

So it wasn't until 3:30 a.m. that Darlene pulled her VW Beetle away from the club to take Johnny to the station in the CBD. He had five minutes to catch the first morning train home.

"Funny how this goofy little bug of a car can make the world seem like a happy cartoon," Johnny said.

"I'm glad you feel that way. Maybe I'm just used to

riding in this goofy little bug. So the evening seemed pretty horrible to me."

"I understand," Johnny, suddenly the wise old man, said. "I understand."

The station was in sight when Darlene spoke next.

"I've just got to say something, Johnny. And I mean it. You did some fantastic work tonight."

"Thanks," he said softly.

They arrived at the station, and Darlene went with him to the ticket machine.

"One more thing I need to tell you," Darlene said as the train was coming into view.

"I'm ready for it," Johnny said.

"We make a great team." And she leaned in and pecked him on the cheek.

He blushed.

"You're doing it again, dude!" Darlene laughed.

He turned and went for the stairs down to the platform, raising his hand as a wave good-bye. His back was to her, and he had a big smile on his face.

Darlene walked to the goofy little bug of a car. She sat behind the wheel, staring silently for a moment at the leafy, deserted avenue running toward the bridge. She hadn't felt this good and fresh and alive in a long time. She wasn't certain what the future was going to bring. In fact, she was only sure of one thing. Sleeping tonight was absolutely out of the question.

CHAPTER 104

EVERYTHING IN THE lab was as Darlene had left it over four hours earlier. On the central counter lay the collection of singed papers and piles of crispy, black remnants from Julie O'Connor's scrapbook. A few feet above it hung the microscope.

Darlene slipped on her lab coat, took her glasses from the right pocket, and stared into the eyepiece, pulling over the last page she'd viewed earlier, the words "WHORE NUMBER 5." The name wiped by fire, the entire page brown.

"Superficial burn, though," Darlene noted to herself. "Which makes it all the more frustrating. If only..."

Her mind was racing. She could try solvents. "No—too dangerous. Might destroy the thing entirely.

"Ultraviolet?" she whispered. "What about ultraviolet?"

She pulled up a chair and sat down. Sighed heavily. The sigh was so dramatic and loud that she smiled at herself.

"No...wouldn't work...wrong sort of disruption of the paper fibers."

All these processes involved "peeling away" the upper layer of flame damage. But if she could do that, she could see what was underneath. But, no, there was no way...

She froze.

"Yes!"

She pushed back her chair and got to her feet. Suddenly she was feeling a little bit giddy.

The giddiness turned to mild elation. She just had to say something out loud.

"Easy, girl...But you *are* a genius, Darlene Cooper."

She smiled as she walked—almost ran—across the room to the storage cupboard.

"You are a bloody genius."

CHAPTER 105

IT WAS CALLED a Saser, and two months earlier, when Darlene was giving Craig a wish list of equipment for the lab, she'd almost deleted it as something they should requisition. It was, she thought, terribly expensive, and she wouldn't be using it very much, and if she really needed it she could...

Now she was thanking all that was holy that she had kept the Saser on the list. Even with a price tag of twenty grand, tonight it might prove to be a very solid investment.

For all that money, the machine didn't look like very much. It wasn't even very large, just a couple of shiny buttons on the front of a six-by-six-inch steel box. It looked something like a small photocopier.

But talk about appearances being deceptive. The Saser was an amazing invention, and there were maybe only half a dozen in the world.

She found it on the second shelf on the right of the storeroom. It was quite light, easy to lift down. She placed it on the counter below the overhead microscope, plugged it in, and watched a small screen light up.

She pulled over her chair and started programming the device. She remembered the spec. A Saser, she recalled, was, according to the technical review she'd read in *Forensics* magazine, a little like an X-ray machine. But—and this was its USP—it didn't see *right* through things to show the bones of the body or the contents of a suitcase, like an airport scanner. A Saser could be finely adjusted to penetrate beneath the surface to any predetermined depth. In skilled hands, it could reveal layer upon layer of any object. It was exactly what she needed now.

She lifted the lid and picked up the final pages of Julie O'Connor's scrapbook.

The contents appeared on the screen. The pages were covered with scorches; almost all the writing was totally wrecked. Darlene adjusted a few parameters and pushed the Scan button.

The Saser made a hissing sound. It was almost human. Darlene studied the screen. The initial image appeared to be almost identical to the original. But after a few seconds, small patches of scorched paper cleared. She could trace the lines of a few letters that had been invisible.

She altered the penetration depth and upped the resolution. She pushed Scan again. A new image appeared.

"That's better," she said, stunned by the quality. The

picture had sharpened dramatically. She could see numbers, letters, a few entire words. She scrolled up. The top of the page was looking better, but still not enough to show what she was after—the damn name.

Darlene adjusted the parameters a third time. Now she was anxious and nervous and had numbers and quotients running through her brain. She had to get the depth right or she would overshoot, go straight through.

She pulled back on the resolution and doubled the depth of penetration to one five-hundredth of a millimeter, pushed the Scan button again.

The waiting actually made her stomach hurt. Her eyes held almost madly to the screen. She could hear her own heart thumping.

As she read two words at the top of the page, Darlene felt a shudder move up her spine and through the nape of her neck.

GRETA…THOROGOOD.

CHAPTER 106

JULIE HAD SET her phone to wake her at 4:30 a.m. It went off on time, but she was already awake. She hadn't slept—too lost in wonderful thoughts, thoughts of blood, rolled-up banknotes, revenge...sweet, sweet revenge. She got up, changed into fresh clothes, threw the wig, mustache, and men's things into a plastic bag.

It was still dark as she tugged open the door onto the parking lot at the rear of SupaMart. Totally deserted, of course. Just two cars left over from the previous night. She tossed the plastic bag into a nearby dumpster.

It was three miles from here to where the silly bitch went jogging every morning. Six a.m. Parsley Beach.

"How typical," Julie said aloud. "Just when she goes out *running,* I'm on the frigging train from Sandsville to wait on stupid bitches like her."

She turned onto Sebastian Road and just kept walking, anger building with each step. She could feel the long knife through the lining of her jacket, and her smile broadened as she contemplated what she would do to Greta Thorogood.

CHAPTER 107

THE PHONE RANG, and I did what any normal person who'd been woken from a deep sleep would do.

I looked at the bedside clock. It said 5:14 a.m.

I said a grumpy "Oh, shit."

Then I said a grumpy "Hello?"

"Craig?" the voice asked.

"Don't you ever go to bed, Darlene?"

"Sorry, Craig. But I think you'll wanna hear this."

I was out the door in ten minutes, cell phone to my ear as I pressed the remote for the car.

Greta's cell just rang and rang and finally went to voice mail. I left a message.

"Greta. It's Craig. If you get this message at home, stay where you are. Got that? Stay put and call me back. I'm heading over to your place right now."

I searched for the Thorogoods' home number as

I pulled onto Military Road and headed toward the bridge, found it, punched the preset. No one picked up. I disconnected, tried again. Waited, waited...still nothing.

Even at that early hour, the traffic was beginning to build. I put my foot down. *Bugger the cameras,* I thought — and if I got stopped? Well, then, I got stopped.

I sped left onto Warringah Freeway, with the black colossus of Sydney Harbour Bridge in the distance, the towers of North Sydney to my right, a much-larger collection of skyscrapers directly ahead, over the bridge.

Three minutes later, I was on the Cahill Expressway. I shot down the off-ramp, weaving between slower cars, ignoring the blaring horns, ignoring the speedometer. I tore down onto New South Head Road and just went for it. I saw two traffic surveillance cameras go off. Slowing, I pulled onto Stockton Boulevard, the Thorogoods' house a little way down on the right.

Lights were on. I tried the home number again as I stepped out of the car and ran along the sidewalk. No response. I reached the doorbell, leaned on it. Nothing. Tried again. Banged on the big mahogany door.

The door opened, and I almost fell into the hall. Brett was standing barefoot in a bathrobe, hair wet, bewildered.

"What the—?"

"Where's Greta?"

"What do you—?"

"Where is Greta?" I yelled.

"She's out on her run...why?"

"Your wife's the next victim."

His expression changed to one of horror. I didn't wait for a response.

"Where does she run?" I yelled.

"Parsley Bay, about three miles away," he said, his voice cracking with shock.

"I know it."

"Always the same route—along the beach, up through the reserve, along to the parking lot. Jesus Christ! Look, go...Craig! I'll get a team there immediately."

CHAPTER 108

GRETA CLOSED THE door of her BMW and turned to the path down to the beach. It was already seventy degrees plus, and she loved the summer.

She ran down the path, and two minutes later, she was on the sand, the sun casting a fresh morning glow all around. The ocean was so perfect—little whitecaps on the waves, a fat orange ball of sun over the horizon—it looked like it had been Photoshopped.

She found her rhythm and ran close to the water, where the sand was hard. To her right, a line of palms. Running was solitude. *Watch out for the broken seashells. Reapply the sunblock when necessary. Consider the day ahead.*

When she got home she'd have to sort out the kids' breakfast, pack the bags ready for camp, get the children into the car, drive the mile to the drop-off.

Later she would meet friends for lunch at Tony's or Oasis. Then it would be the mad dash to the bus stop—the three-thirty pickup. Back home, dinner for the kids. Later, after the children were in bed, it would be dinner for her and Brett, a glass of wine—thank God! Then, into bed, and Brett probably...Well, she'd see. She laughed. Then she ran on, focusing on her rhythm, her pace, the ocean.

This day was so perfect—and Julie O'Connor so well hidden behind a cluster of three palm trees. Yep, Greta could not possibly notice the sloppy, sneering, smiling crazy lady.

CHAPTER 109

I SCREECHED OFF down Bexham Boulevard and back out onto New South Head Road. I knew Parsley Beach—it was in Vaucluse. Parsley Beach had a panoramic view. It had miles of soft, clean sand. And now it had Julie O'Connor.

Averaging ninety miles per hour, the faithful Mas took a little over two minutes to reach the turn-off. I saw another speed camera flash as I shot past. I swung a hard left off the main highway, onto a smaller road, followed the curves, descended a steep hill, and almost overshot the parking lot. I knew that the path down to the beach lay on the far side of the scrap of sandy ground. This morning, only one car was parked there—Greta's BMW 320i convertible.

I ran across the open space and down the first steps of the path that led through the reserve. I could hear the crashing of waves directly ahead. I stopped for a moment to yank off my shoes.

Then I slowed down. Julie O'Connor could be anywhere. I shoved away the awful thought that I might already be too late.

There was a bend in the path. I gripped the wooden handrail on one side as the descent became steep. Stopped, listened. Nothing but the sound of birds, waves, the breeze rustling the eucalyptus.

I glimpsed sand, a flash of blue water. The beach was less than a hundred feet ahead down the sloping, curving stairway.

A tight bend. I held the rail with both hands, eased down two steps, and there was Greta. She'd just reached the wooden pathway that led to the same wooden stairs I'd just walked down.

I was about to call to her, when I saw movement to her right. Julie O'Connor sprang from a cluster of weeds and high grass and palm trees.

"Greta!" I shouted.

She looked up, saw me, began to smile, and O'Connor was on her.

I felt my stomach flip, and for a second I froze.

Julie grabbed her around the neck, pulling her back. Greta stared at me, eyes wide, and screamed.

I took half a dozen steps toward them.

"*YOU BETTER STOP!*" Julie shouted.

I kept going.

"*STOP!* I've got a very, very big knife 'ere. And the tip of it is just touching this whore's spine."

Greta screamed again.

"Shut the fuck up!" Julie hissed in Greta's ear. Then Julie turned back to me.

"Let her go," I said.

Julie laughed. "Oh, yeah. I'd like to, but her and me have girl business to discuss. Don't we?" She twisted Greta's face round, her fingers digging into her cheeks.

I took another step forward. They were only about ten yards away now.

"STOP! I SAID STOP!"

I walked down two more steps.

"I TOLD YOU TO FUCKING STOP!"

Greta began shaking violently.

"Oh, look, she puked on her lovely little T-shirt," Julie said.

Greta's face had drained. She was panting, her eyes like black dishes.

Julie held up her knife. She smiled a hideous smile and waved the knife in the air. Drops of blood splattered from the knife onto Greta's white T-shirt.

"Just look. A little blood came to visit the puke on the shirt." She stopped talking for a moment. The mad smile on her face vanished.

"That was a little stab in the back. The next one's going in all the way," Julie said.

I stopped. Put my hands up. It was then that I caught a glimpse of movement behind Greta and O'Connor. My cousin Mark was waiting no more than ten steps behind Julie and Greta. Two officers were with him, guns drawn.

"Look, can we talk?" I said.

Julie laughed again, a nasty rasp.

"Why would I wanna talk? I have this bitch under my control. She's *mine*...She's mine. I can do what I want with her. Make her beg, make her squirm. She's a whore...right? She gives it up for Brett the Big Policeman. She gives it up and she gets her Chanel, her Prada, her holidays on Hamilton Island. Two kids, and her husband might screw around on the quiet, but it's a deal...right? What has this stupid bitch ever done for herself?"

"She's a human being, Julie."

CHAPTER 110

"THE KNIFE'S IN a bit further," Julie O'Connor said. She followed this statement with a witchlike cackle.

I could tell from the drowsy eyes and pale skin on Greta that Julie wasn't just bragging. Greta looked bad.

Julie looked down behind Greta's back.

"Oh, yeah...more blood. Lots more," she said. The crazy grin had returned to her face.

She stopped talking. But not for long.

"Oh, yeah, this bitch—"

Then Mark and his men rushed forward.

Greta fell to one side. She groaned softly as she fell. I saw Julie swing to her left, her knife slicing the air, nicking Mark's ear—a small wound, it seemed, but with a good amount of blood. Julie had a hateful look on her face as she ran off the path and back into the wooded area where the palm trees and weeds grew thick.

"You go up into the wooded area," Mark said to me, quietly. "I'll take the path and go in the other way."

Then he turned to his men. "Nichols—go back down to the beach and around. Taylor, stay with Mrs. Thorogood."

I could see that Greta wasn't badly hurt, so I ran up the steps. Mark's plan was a good one. Between us, we'd have the woman. I was sure of it.

Ten seconds later and I was at the top step, the parking lot ahead of me. I ran onto the sandy rectangle, skirted the edge, found the next path down to the beach, and headed onto it. I guessed Mark would be about thirty yards below on an adjacent path.

I took the steps down two at a time. Turned right, then left, another tight left. Drew up in the sand.

Mark was coming toward me along a sandy path. I caught a movement to my left. Julie charged through the bush and smacked into him, knocking him off balance. He stumbled to his left, pistol flying from his hand.

Julie was on him in a second, her right hand raised, the horrifying blade raised over Mark's face.

I didn't pause to think, just rushed forward and grabbed the woman by the shoulders. I was stunned by how powerful she was. Using all my strength, I managed to yank her away, but I was sent sprawling onto my back. She was incredibly agile and got to her feet ahead of me. I propelled myself upright, watched as she came for me. Mark began to pull up, but he was slow. Julie lunged at me, growling like an animal. I misjudged her thrust and felt a screech of pain rip through my abdomen.

I dropped to my knees and saw the point of the woman's knife coming toward my face. A moment later I heard the crack of a gun going off and felt a heavy weight slamming down on top of me.

CHAPTER 111

I SAW SOME sort of face on a man's body. The features on the face appeared and disappeared and then reappeared as if it were the face of a mannequin wearing and removing a series of masks. It was the face of my dead uncle, which morphed into the face of Brett, which then—I think—became my father and then my high-school tennis coach and then my cousin Mark. And then I waited. I waited for the next face.

But Mark's face did not disappear like the others. I waited. For whom? Who would be next? Jack Morgan? Johnny?

But the change never happened. It was Mark. It stayed Mark.

I could feel the coolness of cotton sheets. The room was filled with natural light, curtains pulled back across the window in the opposite wall.

Everything came to me slowly. But also very surely.

"You were very lucky," Mark said.

"I feel like I've been here before," I managed to say.

Mark smiled an unlikely warm smile.

"What's the damage?" I asked.

"Oh, perforated colon, slight nick to the spleen... The surgeon put you back together again. And that colostomy bag is only temporary. It comes off in two months."

"Great. A good news–bad news joke, only in reverse."

I lifted the sheet and saw a bunch of bloodied bandages across my abdomen.

"I got off light," I said cautiously.

"I got off lighter, Craig... Thanks to you. And you were unarmed."

"So, I'm either the brave one or the dumb one."

Mark grinned and looked down at his feet. Then he spoke.

"I don't think we're ready to be best friends or roommates or... Craig, to be honest... I'm worn out with this constant war. I may have fired the first shot. I may have been the asshole. But, God. It was all a long time ago. We've both lost..." He trailed off and looked into my face.

I sensed the numbing effect of painkillers.

"How long have I been out?"

He glanced at his watch. "Thirty-five, thirty-six hours."

I slowly pulled myself up in the bed.

"Sweet Jesus, this hurts," I said.

From the side of the bed, Mark handed me a long tube with a blue button attached.

"Press that little button. It'll pump you with some morphine."

I pressed. Within thirty seconds the pain diminished.

"Let's not talk ancient history, Mark. Tell me about what just happened. How'd it all end?"

"Julie O'Connor's under armed guard in intensive care."

"And Greta?"

"She's fine. In shock but unharmed. Nasty cut in her back. She was here earlier—but you were still out. You're her hero."

I produced a small laugh. "Ow! Christ. That morphine doesn't work on laughter."

"You know what they say. It only hurts when... Well, you know, Craig."

I lay back on the pillow and spoke.

"So, look... The O'Connor woman... she was just driven by pure jealousy, yeah?"

"More or less. Seems there was a little more to it than that. One of my guys found out something very interesting this morning. Three months ago, Julie O'Connor was the victim of a botched operation—a tuboplasty, they called it. It was to... unblock her fallopian tubes. Guess who the gynecologist was?"

"Cameron Granger... Of course."

"Your resident genius, Darlene, managed to get a lot of background stuff from the woman's scrapbook. Julie O'Connor was desperate to have children, and when the op went wrong, it went spectacularly wrong!"

"She became infertile?"

"Totally. Her life fell apart. She was already living on the breadline in Sandsville. Her boyfriend, Bruce Frimmel, left her. She killed him. It gave her the taste for doing it some more, I guess. And it was all made worse because of where she worked. In her scrapbook she refers to the Bellevue Hill women as 'whores.' She thought they were little more than prostitutes—leading lavish lives, thanks to rich husbands."

"Now we understand the ritual of the money inserted in the victims—a symbolic gesture."

"Not just money, Craig. *Fake money*...for what she saw as fake women, fake wives."

"Isn't it amazing, though?" I said. "The killer takes it out on other women. She didn't try to kill the person who caused all the trouble in the first place, Dr. Granger."

"We've both seen it before. O'Connor displaced the blame. That's why I said earlier it was exaggerated by the place she worked in. Deep down, repressed for years, she *was* envious of the women she saw each day in Bellevue Hill. Being messed up by Granger pushed her over the edge."

"We'll probably never know what the original spark could have been."

"Actually, we do. That Darlene really *is* a goddamn genius. She found a file on Julie O'Connor at St. Joseph's Psychiatric Hospital. Julie spent some time there almost ten years ago—she'd been living on the streets, raped, mugged. According to the reports, she claimed her mother had tortured her as a child. The authorities tried to check the story, but the woman, Sheila O'Connor, had moved abroad."

"The other ugly thing is that Cameron Granger got away with it."

"Don't be a downer, Craig. While you've been getting sewn up, the Sydney police have been working hard. Now that the truth is out, the hospital can't cover up for Dr. Granger anymore. We found two nurses and a resident who'll testify that he botched the operation."

I nodded, sighed heavily.

"Yeah, it's good news," Mark said.

I closed my eyes. I was ready to drift off. But first I opened my eyes and spoke.

"Yes, good news," I said. "Today I got a lot of good news."

CHAPTER 112

IT WAS THREE days after I was released from hospital.

I was driving Justine to the airport. I was moving along the same road I'd traveled three years ago when my family and I were headed for a vacation.

Now I was going to the airport again. Once again I had a beautiful woman sitting beside me. But there was no child in the backseat. And I was a very different person.

The airport was packed. Justine checked in, and I walked with her to the departure zone, the scanners and security guys just a few feet away.

"It's been...well, it's been 'eventful,'" I said.

"To say the least, Craig."

"You've been a great help. If you ever feel like a break from the L.A. office..."

"I might seriously consider that."

"Wish Jack my best, yeah?"

"I will."

She kissed me on the cheek, and I kissed the air next to her cheek. I watched her walk toward passport control. It was then that I called her name.

She stopped, turned, and walked back quickly toward me.

"There's one other thing I want you to tell Jack," I said.

She looked nervous, a little teary.

"What's that, Craig?"

"Tell him that he's the luckiest guy in the world."

She bit her lower lip. She blinked her eyes a few times. She shook her head up and down.

Then she turned and walked away.

CHAPTER 113

NO CAKE. NO balloons. No Welcome Back signs.

I had warned Darlene and Johnny to alert their colleagues at Private HQ that my coming back should be treated professionally and casually. Not that I wasn't happy to be back. It's just that I'm not a cake-and-balloons kind of guy. If you know *me*, then you know *that*.

I walked into the conference room at Private HQ. Well, come on. No balloons, but maybe there could have been more than a few grunts of "Morning, Craig" and "Hey, Craig." It was as if I'd never been away, never been wounded, never been— Then the entire room stood and applauded for fifteen seconds that felt to me like a half hour.

I surveyed the gathering—Johnny, Mary, Darlene, Cookie—the core of my work, the soul of my life.

"Thanks," I said rather weakly. "Not sure why I deserve it . . ."

"I think we all deserve a pat on the back, actually," Johnny said.

"You do. We all do. It's been one hell of a first week," I replied.

There was laughter and talk, and then I had to be the one to bring it back to business.

"So, how about an update? How's it all wound up?" I asked. "What about Ricky Holt?"

Johnny took that question.

"Seventeen stitches and a very rock 'n' roll scar. Mickey's fine. Spent a night in the hospital after his party, but no permanent harm done. He's rehearsing for a big tour. Out of gratitude, he's helping Holt settle his gambling debts. Katia is being deported."

"But what about the song you told me about? The one describing his own death. Why did he even write that?"

Johnny shrugged.

"I think it was purely an artistic gesture. He felt helpless, controlled by 'the suits.' He's a sensitive bloke, but that sensitivity must have slipped into paranoia. His phenomenal drug intake couldn't have helped!"

"And what about Hemi?"

"He's up and waddling."

We all laughed.

"He's mighty pissed, though—as you would imagine!" Johnny added.

"I heard you bumped into Al Loretto's boy, Jerry."

"Yeah, I did. He was helpful in making me realize what a mess Holt had gotten himself into."

I nodded. "What about the Ho family, Mary?"

"Dai is under observation at a psychiatric retreat in the suburbs. His father has booked him in for plastic surgery. The police here are liaising with the Hong Kong authorities. They're after the big boss, Fong Sum, but I'm pretty sure they're wasting their time."

"Untouchable?"

"For the moment. Ho is just relieved his son was saved. He now wants to have the case of his wife's murder reopened. He's convinced that twelve years ago a bent cop was in the pocket of the Sydney Triads and buried the evidence. He's sure the Triads killed Jiao. He wants to prove it *and* to identify those involved."

"Good luck to him!" I said, leaning back in my chair. Then I said, "Well, sounds like we've had a few positive results. Not bad for our first week!"

"And why shouldn't we have?" Darlene asked.

I smiled and said, "Yeah, you're right. Why shouldn't we have?"

"Oh, there are these, though," Johnny added, and pushed a small pile of papers toward me across the conference table.

I glanced at the top one. The words ROADS AND MARITIME SERVICES were printed in the top right corner.

"They're speeding tickets," Johnny said.

I lifted my eyes and saw that the entire team was grinning at me. Then I spoke.

"Looks like I might have to call in a favor."

Books by James Patterson

FEATURING ALEX CROSS

Cross My Heart
Alex Cross, Run
Merry Christmas, Alex Cross
Kill Alex Cross
Cross Fire
I, Alex Cross
Alex Cross's Trial (with Richard DiLallo)
Cross Country
Double Cross
Cross (also published as *Alex Cross*)
Mary, Mary
London Bridges
The Big Bad Wolf
Four Blind Mice
Violets Are Blue
Roses Are Red
Pop Goes the Weasel
Cat & Mouse
Jack & Jill
Kiss the Girls
Along Came a Spider

THE WOMEN'S MURDER CLUB

Unlucky 13 (with Maxine Paetro)
12th of Never (with Maxine Paetro)
11th Hour (with Maxine Paetro)
10th Anniversary (with Maxine Paetro)
The 9th Judgment (with Maxine Paetro)

The 8th Confession (with Maxine Paetro)
7th Heaven (with Maxine Paetro)
The 6th Target (with Maxine Paetro)
The 5th Horseman (with Maxine Paetro)
4th of July (with Maxine Paetro)
3rd Degree (with Andrew Gross)
2nd Chance (with Andrew Gross)
1st to Die

FEATURING MICHAEL BENNETT

Gone (with Michael Ledwidge)
I, Michael Bennett (with Michael Ledwidge)
Tick Tock (with Michael Ledwidge)
Worst Case (with Michael Ledwidge)
Run for Your Life (with Michael Ledwidge)
Step on a Crack (with Michael Ledwidge)

THE PRIVATE NOVELS

Private Down Under (with Michael White)
Private L.A. (with Mark Sullivan)
Private Berlin (with Mark Sullivan)
Private London (with Mark Pearson)
Private Games (with Mark Sullivan)
Private: #1 Suspect (with Maxine Paetro)
Private (with Maxine Paetro)

NYPD RED

NYPD Red 2 (with Marshall Karp)
NYPD Red (with Marshall Karp)

STANDALONE BOOKS

Invisible (with David Ellis)

First Love (with Emily Raymond, photographs by Sasha Illingworth)

Mistress (with David Ellis)

Second Honeymoon (with Howard Roughan)

Zoo (with Michael Ledwidge)

Guilty Wives (with David Ellis)

The Christmas Wedding (with Richard DiLallo)

Kill Me If You Can (with Marshall Karp)

Now You See Her (with Michael Ledwidge)

Toys (with Neil McMahon)

Don't Blink (with Howard Roughan)

The Postcard Killers (with Liza Marklund)

The Murder of King Tut (with Martin Dugard)

Swimsuit (with Maxine Paetro)

Against Medical Advice (with Hal Friedman)

Sail (with Howard Roughan)

Sundays at Tiffany's (with Gabrielle Charbonnet)

You've Been Warned (with Howard Roughan)

The Quickie (with Michael Ledwidge)

Judge & Jury (with Andrew Gross)

Beach Road (with Peter de Jonge)

Lifeguard (with Andrew Gross)

Honeymoon (with Howard Roughan)

Sam's Letters to Jennifer

The Lake House

The Jester (with Andrew Gross)

The Beach House (with Peter de Jonge)

Suzanne's Diary for Nicholas

Cradle and All
When the Wind Blows
Miracle on the 17th Green (with Peter de Jonge)
Hide & Seek
The Midnight Club
Black Friday (originally published as *Black Market*)
See How They Run (originally published as *The Jericho
    Commandment*)
Season of the Machete
The Thomas Berryman Number

FOR READERS OF ALL AGES

Homeroom Diaries (with Lisa Papademetriou, illustrated
    by Keino)
Middle School: Save Rafe! (with Chris Tebbetts,
    illustrated by Laura Park)
Middle School: Ultimate Showdown (with Julia Bergen, il-
    lustrated by Alec Longstretch)
I Even Funnier (with Chris Grabenstein, illustrated by
    Laura Park)
Confessions: The Private School Murders (with Maxine
    Paetro)
Treasure Hunters (with Chris Grabenstein and Mark
    Shulman, illustrated by Juliana Neufeld)
*Middle School: How I Survived Bullies, Broccoli, and Snake
    Hill* (with Chris Tebbetts, illustrated by Laura Park)
Middle School: My Brother Is a Big, Fat Liar (with Lisa
    Papademetriou, illustrated by Neil Swaab)
Witch & Wizard: The Kiss (with Jill Dembowski)
Maximum Ride: The Manga 6 (with NaRae Lee)

The Dangerous Days of Daniel X (with Michael
    Ledwidge)
The Final Warning: A Maximum Ride Novel
*Saving the World and Other Extreme Sports: A Maximum
    Ride Novel*
School's Out—Forever: A Maximum Ride Novel
Maximum Ride: The Angel Experiment
santaKid

For previews of upcoming books and more information
    about James Patterson, please visit JamesPatter-
    son.com or find him on Facebook or at your app
    store.

THE WORLD'S #1 BESTSELLING WRITER

JAMES PATTERSON has created more enduring fictional characters than any other novelist writing today. He is the author of the Alex Cross novels, the most popular detective series of the past twenty-five years. He also writes the bestselling Women's Murder Club novels, set in San Francisco, and the top-selling New York detective series of all time, featuring Detective Michael Bennett. James Patterson has had more *New York Times* bestsellers than any other writer, ever, according to *Guinness World Records*. Since his first novel won the Edgar Award in 1977, James Patterson's books have sold more than 300 million copies. For previews of his upcoming books and more information about the author, visit www.JamesPatterson.com.

DETECTIVE MICHAEL BENNETT
FINALLY RETURNS TO NEW YORK CITY —
AND TO THE MOST UNSETTLING, HORRIFIC
CASE OF HIS CAREER.

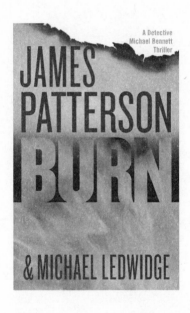

FOR AN EXCERPT, TURN THE PAGE.

LOS ANGELES, CALIFORNIA

THE WORK VAN was a new Mercedes, white and high roofed, with the bloodred words TURNKEY LOCKSMITH hand-painted on its side.

At a little before 7 a.m., it was winding through the Hollywood Hills northwest of LA, the steady drone of its diesel engine briefly rising in pitch as it turned onto the long climb of Kirkwood Drive in Laurel Canyon. Two hundred feet below the intersection of Kirkwood and Oak, the van coasted to a crackling stop on the gravel shoulder of the secluded road and shut off its engine. A minute passed, then two. No one got out.

As the bald Hispanic driver flipped down the visor to get the sun out of his eyes, he spotted a mule deer nosing out through the steep hillside's thick underbrush across the street.

Go for a lung shot, he thought as he imagined getting a bead on it with the new compound hunting bow his girlfriend had gotten him for his birthday. *Track the blood trail down between the infinity pools and twenty-person funkadelic hot tubs before lashing it to the van's front grille. See how that would go down with Frank Zappa and George Clooney and K. D. Lang and the rest of the Laurel Canyon faithful.*

He was feigning a bow draw when the elegant red deer suddenly noticed him and bolted. The driver sighed, leaned slightly to his right, and depressed the intercom button under the drink holder.

"How's this? Line of sight OK?" he said.

"Yes. Maintain here until the hand-off, then head for position two," intercommed back the sharp-featured, copper-haired woman sitting directly behind the driver in the sealed-off back of the high-tech surveillance van.

There was a dull mechanical hum as the woman flicked the joystick for the high-definition video camera concealed in the van's roof. On the console's flat screen in front of her, an off-white stucco bungalow a hundred and fifty feet up the canyon slowly came into view.

She panned the camera over the bungalow's short, steep driveway of bishop's hat paver stones, the broken terra-cotta roof tiles above its front door, the live oaks and lemon trees in its side yard. She'd been here several times before and knew the target house as well as her own at this point.

She was halfway through the tea-filled Tervis tumbler from her kit bag when a truck slowed in front of the target house. It was a new Ford Expedition SUV, glossy black with heavily tinted windows. After it reversed up the driveway almost butt-up against the garage, the passenger-side door opened and out stepped a lanky middle-aged white man in a gray business suit. He adjusted his Oakley sport sunglasses for a moment before he reached into the open door and retrieved what appeared to be a military-issue M-16.

Then, up on the porch above him, the bungalow's front door opened and Detective Michael Bennett came out of the house.

The woman almost spilled the tea in her lap as she quickly panned the camera left and zoomed in on Bennett and the crowd of people coming out behind him. His kids were in cartoon-character PJs, their tan and striking blond nanny, Mary Catherine, in a bathrobe, drying her hands with a dish towel. One of the Bennett boys—was Trent his name? Yes, Trent—immediately started climbing out over the stair's cast iron rail, until Mary Catherine pulled him back by his collar.

The cacophony of the family's calls and laughter rang in her earphone as she turned up the volume on the van's shotgun mike.

"*Arrivederci,*" Bennett said playfully to his rambunctious family as he went down the stairs. "*Sayonara, auf Wiedersehen.* And, oh, yeah. Later, guys."

The woman in the van watched silently as Bennett smiled and crossed his eyes and stuck his tongue out at his family. He was pushing forty, but still tall and trim and handsome in his dark-blue suit. Biting at her lower lip, she didn't stop focusing until his dimples and brown eyes slid out of the bottom of the frame into the SUV.

As the Ford rocketed out into the street, the copper-haired woman had already put down the joystick and was wheeling the captain's chair around toward the three men in bulky tactical gear sitting and sweating on the steel bench behind her.

If it hadn't been for the glistening snub-barreled Heckler & Koch machine guns in their laps, the large men could have been professional football players. Wide receivers in the huddle waiting for the quarterback to call the next play.

"To repeat one last time," she said calmly as the work van's engine suddenly roared to life and they lurched into the street. "Front door, side door, back door. When the doors pop, you will stay low until you are in position."

The poised woman quickly lifted her own subma-chine gun from the foam-lined hard case at her feet. Easily and expertly, she worked the H&K MP7's action, slamming the first HK 4.6x30mm cartridge into the gun's chamber with a loud snap.

"This isn't a drill, gentlemen," she said, looking up at the Bennett safe house growing rapidly now on the flat screen.

"Welcome to life and death."

THE WITNESS WAITING room adjacent to the second-floor federal courtroom where I was going to give my statement was a happy surprise after the fireworks show and my unexpected sidewalk rugby match. It had leather furniture and piped-in slow-dance Muzak and a rack of magazines next to the coffee machine.

For twenty minutes, I sat in it alone humming to Michael Bolton as Bob and his guys stood vigilantly in the hallway outside the locked door. The little stunt downstairs had fired them up beyond belief. Even with the tight courthouse security, they weren't taking any chances.

I'd just finished pouring myself a second cup of French vanilla coffee (which I probably didn't need, considering my already frazzled nerves) when the door unlocked and a middle-aged blond female court officer poked her friendly face inside and said it was time.

All eyes were on me as I followed the officer's blond ponytail into the bleached-wood-paneled courtroom. The line of orange-jumpsuited convicts sitting at the two defendants' tables peered at me curiously with "haven't I seen you someplace before" expressions as I made my way to a podium set up beside the witness box.

Alejandro Soto, the highest-ranking of the Tepito cartel members in attendance, seemed especially curious from where he sat, closest to the witness box. I recognized his gaunt, ugly features from the video of the Bronx motel where he had brought my friend Tara to rape and kill her.

I stared directly at Soto as the court clerk asked me to state my name for the record.

"My name is Bennett," I said, smiling at Soto. "*Detective* Michael Bennett."

"Bennett!" Soto yelled as he stood and started banging his shackled wrists on the table. "What is this? What is this?"

No wonder he was shocked. His organization was out to get me and suddenly, presto, here I was. *Be careful what you wish for,* I thought as two court officers shoved the skinny middle-aged scumbag back down into his seat.

The violent crack of Judge Kenneth Barnett's gavel at the commotion was a little painful in the low-ceilinged courtroom. Our side could set off some firecrackers, too, apparently. Tall and wide, Barnett had the build of a football player, bright-blue eyes, and a shock of gray hair slicked straight back.

"Detective Bennett," he said as I was about to take my prepared statement from my jacket pocket. "Before you begin, I would just like to gently remind you that the victim impact statement is not an occasion for you to address the defendants directly. It is a way for me, the sentencing judge, to understand what impact the crimes in this case have had on you and society and thereby determine what appropriate punishment to mete out to these convicted men. Do you understand?"

"Perfectly, Your Honor," I said.

Especially the punishment part, I thought, glancing at Soto again.

I took my written statement out of my pocket and flattened it against the podium as I brought the microphone closer to my mouth.

I FLAGGED DOWN a gypsy cab and headed home.

The whole way back up the 101 to Laurel Canyon, I listened to the Mexican driver behind the wheel play a type of music called *narcocorrido*. Having become familiar with it in my recent investigations into the cartels, I knew the traditional-sounding Mexican country music had gangster-rap-style lyrics about moving dope and taking out your enemies with AK-47s.

Though it had a nice, sad sort of rhythm, considering the fact that the story of my life had recently pretty much become a *narcocorrido,* I didn't think I'd be adding it to my iPod playlist anytime soon.

Finally standing in the street out in front of the safe house thirty minutes later, paying the driver, I heard a sudden shriek of rubber. Just south down the curving slope of Kirkwood, I stood and watched as a white Eurostyle work van fishtailed off the shoulder and barreled straight toward me.

No, was my weary thought as I watched it come. This couldn't be happening. The van shrieked again as it came around the closest curve and hit its brakes.

Forgetting the cabdriver, I palmed the stippled grip of my Glock and drew as I hit the driveway, ducked my head down, and ran up the steps of the house two at a time.

"Mary Catherine! Seamus!" I yelled as I pounded on the screen door with the pistol barrel.

My shocked-looking nanny, Mary Catherine, had just opened the front door when I heard the rattling metal roll of the van door opening at the bottom of the stairs.

"Mike, Mike! It's OK! Stand down! It's OK. It's me!" came a yell.

I turned. Down the stairs, a large bald guy with a gun was standing over my taxi driver, now lying facedown on the street. Also standing now in the open side doors of the white van was a woman. A very pretty woman in blue fatigues with brown—almost red—hair.

"Agent Parker. Long time no see. Are you out of your mind?" I screamed.

I should have known, I thought. It was a friend of mine. Emily Parker, special agent of the FBI. I guess I shouldn't have been surprised. Emily and I had taken down Perrine together less than a month before, and I knew she was still working in LA. I just didn't know *I* was her work.

I racked my weapon to make it safe as I came back down the stairs.

"I mean, Emily, you of all people should understand how paranoid I am these days about things like, I don't know, mysterious vans racing up on me. Is this some kind of practical joke? Why didn't you tell me you and the FBI were watching my house?"

"It was just a precaution for your court appearance today," she said as three drab-fatigue-clad FBI agents with large guns suddenly emerged from the foliage along the side of our house.

"Additional security was ordered," she said. "I kept it low key because you guys have been through enough. I didn't want to get you upset."

"In that case, I guess I'm not having a heart attack," I said.

"Listen, you should be the last one to talk about jokes, Mike," Emily said. "You know how many people are looking for you? Ditching the marshals after that verdict was beyond childish. We thought the bad guys got you. We've been worried sick."

"Ditched? I texted Joe. Besides, I'm a grown man, Parker," I said. "A grown man who needed some fresh air."

"During a gang riot?"

I shrugged.

"Taking my life back needs to start somewhere. I'm tired, Emily, of the death threats, all the worrying. I came out here because of Perrine, and now he's in the ground, and I'm done hiding. You and I both know the cartels are too busy killing each other for Perrine's turf to bother coming after me. Perrine was a monster. They don't get avenged, last time I checked. Judge Barnett has seen to that. What was it that BP oil spill CEO guy said? 'I want my life back.'"

I walked over and knelt down and finally paid my cabdriver, still facedown on the asphalt.

"What's the quote, Emily? 'Those who would sacrifice freedom for security deserve neither and will lose both'?"

"What's that other quote about a well-balanced Irishman?" Emily said, hopping from the van. "'They have a chip on both shoulders'?"

Then she surprised me for the second time in two minutes. She walked up and wrapped her arms around me and pressed her face hard against my neck.

"I'm going to miss you, Mike…working with you. Just working. Don't get the wrong idea," she whispered in my ear.

"Good-bye yourself, Parker. It was fun strictly and platonically working with you as well," I whispered back as she broke it up.

She hopped back into the fed van with the rest of the agents. As they pulled away, I looked up to see Mary Catherine standing at the top of the stairs by the iron railing of the porch.

I immediately gave her my brightest smile. The on-again, off-again relationship I had with Mary Catherine had most definitely become on-again during our close-quarters California exile. She'd actually had to kill a cartel hit woman to protect the kids. We'd talked about it, cried about it. I don't think I'd ever been closer to this incredible young woman. Or more attracted.

I thought her dander might be up a little at seeing me share a hug with Parker, who I'd once or twice almost had a romantic relationship with, but to my happy surprise, Mary Catherine's slim hand slid easily into mine as I got to the top of the stairs.

"Time to go home, Detective Bennett," Mary Catherine said in her musical brogue as she suddenly broke my grip and playfully pushed me toward the door.

Dear Reader,

When I sit down to write a book in the Private series, I'm full of ideas. I want to give the world's most exclusive detective agency the most exciting, mind-blowing cases imaginable.

Only a portion of those ideas end up in the final book. Some I decide against early on. Others might make it into the outline. Every now and then, I'll write a full case before deciding to let it go to give the rest a little more breathing room.

When I first began *Private Down Under,* the detectives were investigating four separate cases: the three you just read, along with some shady dealings at a brothel. Please turn through these last few pages to see what could have been one of Private Sydney's first cases.

MUCH AS WOMEN fascinate me, I am not at all interested in women's fashion. Not to sound like an ape...but my only fashion axiom is this: the less a woman is wearing, the better I like it. But for reasons I'd rather not analyze, I *am* interested in women's shoes.

So the moment the woman in the $900 black Christian Louboutin shoes—the ones with the red soles—walked into my office at Private, I knew something interesting would happen. This type of lady did not visit places like Private unless there was something serious on her mind.

Before she said a word, I'd profiled her. She looked a little too cool for the eastern suburbs. So my guess was Lower North Shore Yummy Mummy. She'd probably been a PR specialist or a lawyer back before those beautiful blond kids came along. I'd bet she was parking a BMW 5X. Husband? Two choices: bank CEO or stockbroker.

She walked quickly toward me. She smelled of Chanel No. 5 and confidence.

"Hi, my name is Pam Hewes." There was a definite New Zealand twang to her voice. "I need advice."

"Well, you've come to precisely the right place. Craig Gisto." I held out my hand. We shook, and I led her to my private conference room.

I pulled out a chair for her and walked around the table, sat down, my back to the window. I waited for her to tell me a story.

"Oh, God! I don't know where to begin!" She broke eye contact. "My husband…his name's Geoff…Geoff Hewes." She paused, as if I might have heard of Geoff Hewes.

I said that I didn't know the guy. I told her to keep talking.

"Well, Geoff didn't come home last night. There's no response to his cell or his office numbers. He didn't show up at home this morning. I went to his office in the CBD. No one's heard from him."

"I imagine this must be unusual or else you wouldn't be here."

"Well, yeah. Geoff works hard, and…he plays hard. I knew that about him before we were married. *Quid pro quo* and all that, but he's always kept some sort of balance—even if it was only for the sake of the kids. He has always come home each evening, and if there was some emergency and he has to go somewhere suddenly he *always* calls."

"And you haven't heard a word from him?"

"No."

"You haven't contacted the police?"

"No. I haven't."

"Why not?"

"Because...Well, I've got to be frank. I'm not a hundred percent sure that everything my husband does is absolutely legal."

"What does he *say* he does, Mrs. Hewes?"

I thought we were about to hit the "Please-call-me-Pam" level. And I was right.

"Please, call me Pam," she said. Then, "I'm not completely sure how to put him in a category. Geoff has his fingers in all sorts of pies. Always has some new business scheme. He lends money, he invests in businesses."

I looked her directly in the eye. "And you, Pam? What do you do?"

"I'm in real estate. I work at H and F Realty on the Lower North Shore."

"Okay, do you have any thoughts about Geoff? Any good guesses? Any possible leads? Are you familiar with your husband's associates or his friends?"

Pam shook her head and looked down at the carpet. "My husband has many associates—*many*—but when it comes to friends...well, I'd say you're talking to his only one."

"Anything else that might help?" I asked.

"Mr. Gisto, my husband plays his cards very close to his chest. Sure he tells me some things, but I'm sure of one thing: The information he gives me only comes from the very tip of the iceberg."

ONLY THIRTY-SIX HOURS before Pam Hewes visited Private, her husband, Geoff, was sitting in his favorite chair in his favorite pub, the Cloverleaf in Darlinghurst. He was drinking his favorite drink, Bombora Vodka with a splash of pineapple juice. Geoff Hewes was feeling quite pleased with himself.

That afternoon he'd won a couple of grand at the races. Then he squeezed about ten thousand more from the small businesses he was lending to in the western suburbs. Best of all, Geoff got news that the brothels he managed for Al Loretto, the biggest underworld name in Sydney, had increased their profits by almost 20 percent. It had been a good week.

He was about to take another sip of his drink when he felt a tap on the shoulder. He whirled round and was startled to see Al Loretto himself, and he was standing way too close. Another man Geoff half recognized was positioned behind him, arms folded.

"Hey, Al," Geoff said, doing a good job of disguising his surprise. "How you doing?"

Loretto didn't reply right away. He just stared down at Geoff and surveyed him with his hard black eyes. He then pulled up a chair and leaned forward. "Geoffrey," he said quietly. "Do I or do I not pay you well?"

"What do you mean, Al?"

"Simple question. Do I recompense you adequately for your services?" Obviously Al had been working on improving his speaking skills.

"Yeah, course you—"

He gripped Geoff's lapel and his companion took a step forward. "Then why are you being so disrespectful, Geoffrey?"

Loretto's wine-soaked breath quickly attacked Hewes's gag reflex as he kept talking. "You want to further capitalize on your employment position? Is that it, *amigo?*"

Geoff started to reply but stopped as Loretto tightened his grip.

"Geoffrey, how did you come to the conclusion that I would be happy for you to install cameras in my brothels?"

Geoff tried again to reply and again was cut short.

"Huh? Why did you do that? Didn't you imagine for a second that it was just a tad disrespectful, Geoffrey? Was there not a skerrick of doubt, not a moment when you thought you might *ask me first?*"

"I didn't think you would have a problem with it," Hewes said. "I thought —"

Loretto stood up. He was still holding Hewes by the lapels. So Hewes had little choice but to stand up also.

"I do *not* pay you to think, Geoffrey. Oh no. *I* do the thinking." Loretto began tapping his forehead.

"So, what do you . . . ?"

"What do I want you to do? I want you to fucking cease and fucking desist. I want you to take the fucking cameras out this afternoon and do what I pay you to do. Any more questions?"

Geoff looked at him blankly.

"I'll take that as a no," Loretto said. Then he pushed Geoff back into his chair. He then leaned over, picked up the almost full Bombora with pineapple juice, and poured it over Geoff's head.

Loretto and the muscled thug who had accompanied him left the bar. As soon as they were gone the waiter brought Geoff a large white dish towel. Geoff wiped his face and smoothed his wet hair.

Then Geoff smiled. The smile grew broader. Geoff knew that most men would be scared if they'd been spoken to the way Loretto had just spoken to him. But that little brain mechanism that let most men know when they were danger . . . well, Geoff was missing that brain device.

So he just kept on smiling. Then Geoff asked the waiter to please bring him another drink.

GEOFF HEWES HAD told himself years ago that he should never show that he was impressed by anything: beautiful women, hot cars, and especially rich men and their extraordinary houses. *Most* especially when those rich men in those extraordinary houses were the ones he did business with.

However, he could barely keep his eyes in their sockets whenever he was summoned to Al Loretto's palatial home in Point Piper.

A proper English butler led him to a vast glass conservatory at the back of the house. The room overlooked a fifty-meter pool surrounded by palm trees. Hewes knew that Ian Thorpe had trained for the Olympics in that pool. From each end, six-foot-long gold-plated dolphins spewed water, and a giant marble mermaid rose up on a plinth in the center of the pool.

Loretto was sitting in one of a pair of giant white wicker chairs at the far end of the glass-walled conservatory. He wore a silver-and-green silk robe and was reading the *Sydney Morning Herald*. The butler retreated, leaving Geoff standing a couple of yards from Loretto. Aside from the water-vomiting dolphins, the room was silent.

Loretto lowered the paper, saying nothing, forcing Geoff to speak first.

"You wanted a chat, Al?"

"Not happy, Geoffrey. *Really* not happy."

Geoff flicked a glance at the other wicker chair. Loretto saw the gesture and ignored it.

"May I?" Geoff asked and pointed to the seat.

"No, you may not."

"Okay," Geoff said. "What's up, Al?"

"'What's up, Al?'" Loretto mimicked in a whiny feminine voice. "I'll tell you what's fucking up, Geoffrey. You are lucky I'm even talking to you. I should have just had you popped in the fucking head." Loretto made the appropriate gesture, placing his fingers at his left temple.

Geoff knew what he was talking about: the cameras in the whorehouse. He'd known what this was about when he received the call from Al Loretto's assistant's assistant that afternoon. Hewes bet he could ride it successfully. As was often the case, Hewes had made the wrong bet.

Loretto was out of the chair, his nose a foot from Geoff's. "Don't fuck with me." He punctuated each word with a finger poke to Geoff's shoulder. By the third one, it hurt, but Hewes couldn't show it. "You didn't take the cameras out my brothels."

Geoff took a deep breath, feeling sweat bleed from his pores.

"I wanted to talk to you about that, Al..."

"There's nothing...got that? Nothing to talk about, Geoffrey. The salient point here is that I asked you very nicely, very patiently, to take the cameras out of the brothels and you did not acquiesce." Another finger poke.

Geoff pulled back, eyes blazing. He went to grab Al Loretto's hand and missed. The finger stabbed him in the neck.

"Fuck you!" Geoff said. Then he took a swing and found himself pinned to the ground by two hundred and fifty pounds of security. He had never even seen the guy appear.

A fist landed in Geoff's face. In a moment Geoff's nose was flattened and spewing blood. A second blow hit him in the right cheek. The connection was so hard that he could actually feel his teeth loosen. Then he was being pulled up to his feet, and Al Loretto was smiling at him.

"Geoffrey, Geoffrey...why are you doing this to yourself? Just when I thought we were becoming such good friends."

Blood streamed down from Geoff's nostrils, ran over his lips, dripped to the floor.

"Put this asshole in storage," Loretto hissed.

AL LORETTO'S GUYS had taken everything from Geoff Hewes's pockets—money, cell phone, car keys. They'd taken most of his clothes too. He was left wearing just a pair of black dress socks and green boxers with tiny blue dolphins on them. That's a pretty goofy-looking image, except Geoff Hewes wasn't laughing. He was a mass of pain and nausea and rage.

The ape who'd jumped on him must have smacked him over the head with something hard and heavy—maybe one of the hideous statues or planters or ashtrays that littered the solarium—and shoved him into a blacked-out room. When he came to, he could taste blood in his mouth.

Hewes pulled himself up, wincing and cursing. Then he felt incredibly sick and vomited copiously. When he touched his face, it was crusty with blood. His jaw was in agonizing pain. The room threw off the stench of garbage and feces and urine. Hewes suspected he wasn't the first guest to be assigned this room.

There was a small beam of light from a window high up, and Hewes could hear traffic far off. He made an educated guess that he was "in storage" in the basement of the bastard's huge house at Point Piper.

What the hell was Loretto doing? Was he trying to torture him before punching a bullet through his skull? That kind of move would be just like him: After all, why just kill someone when you can play with them first?

"Well you're not going to get me, you bastard!" Hewes yelled into the empty blackness.

GEOFF HEWES THOUGHT he might literally burst with hate and anger. He scratched at his chest. He pulled and twisted the flesh on his cheeks and his belly. When he could no longer bear the burning in his bladder or the gassy rumbling in his bowels, he stood and squatted in the corner and peed and defecated in the pail. He paced the six-foot-square basement cell in circles, in straight lines, corner to corner, against the walls, to and from the walls. The more he cursed the more the echoes of his curses infuriated him.

"That fucking asshole...that fucking bastard...that fucking Loretto!" he screamed.

He squinted up at the dark ceiling in the cell and imagined Loretto in his shiny clothes, sitting in his fat-ass wicker chair, smoking his Havanas, eating his disgusting red-sauce pasta.

Geoff was a genius compared to that dumbass wop. Geoff was a movie star compared to that ugly pile of shit. Geoff charmed the world around him. Loretto abused it with his thugs and his guns.

If Loretto believed he could control Geoff Hewes, well, then, Loretto was a bigger asshole than he thought. Want to control me, scumbag? Then shoot the fucking bullet through my fucking head.

Geoff sat on the floor of his cell. His feet and hands were covered with the filth of the floor. He ripped off his boxers and lay naked in the filth. He turned himself over. He banged his fists against the wretched floor. The smell made him gag. Yes, he might just burst.

He lay there. Yes, he thought. Loretto's plan had worked. What was it? Twenty-four hours? Forty-eight? He didn't know. It didn't matter. The plan had worked. Geoff Hewes was no longer a man. He was simply a naked animal.

Then he began to weep, the tears streaming down his face.

WAS THE HEWES house a mansion? A McMansion? A manor house? An estate? I sure wasn't qualified to decide. But whatever the correct name for this incredible piece of real estate at 20 Simeon Street in Neutral Bay, it was easy to imagine the closets full of Prada skirts and Armani jackets. There must have been a hundred versions of the red-soled $1,200 Laboutin shoes like the ones Pam Hewes wore the day she made her surprise visit to Private in pursuit of her missing husband.

A long stone path led through a neatly manicured garden to the front door. I spotted a black Porsche Cayenne in the drive. I'd been close when I'd guessed at a BMW 5X.

Pam met me at the door. She had on some sort of diaphanous caftan and Polynesian sandals. Her long blond hair was pulled back, and she was wearing very little makeup, if any. "Good to see you, Craig," she said. "Come on in."

We walked through the double-height entrance hall. A marble staircase swept up to the next floor. Passed a room on the right. Could have been a library. Two kids in school uniforms sat at a pair of laptops.

"They have to get on with homework as soon as they're home," she said lightly. "Or they'll never do it. We'll all be screaming and crying at one in the morning."

She led the way into a very large and very unlived-in living-room—polished wood floor, massive gray sofas, a couple of huge paintings. I recognized them as Kudditjis, ten to twenty grand apiece. Over the smaller fireplace hung one of Ed Baynard's kitchen bowl paintings.

"So, I'm assuming your husband is still AWOL?" I said sinking into one of the sofas. Pam sat on the facing sofa.

She nodded and looked at her clasped hands. "The bugger hasn't so much as called. I'm getting frightened now."

"And you definitely don't want the police involved?"

Now, I've got to say right here: if I thought the police should be involved I would not hesitate to call Brett and bring him up to date.

"No. I'm sure my husband's mostly legit. But I could be doing the worse thing for him if I told the police he was missing."

"Have you remembered anything more specific about his business ventures?"

"Not really, although one thing I do know—and I

don't know if this is important or not—Geoff does work a lot with Al Loretto."

"*The* Al Loretto?"

"Yeah, billionaire, investor, gangster, property developer, whatever..."

"What does your husband do with him?"

"What does he do when he isn't wiping his...? Oh, never mind," Pam replied, and then shook her head.

"Sorry. I'm just so bloody angry. I pray Geoff isn't dead in a Dumpster somewhere, but when I see him next..."

"Okay, Loretto is a start. But I can hardly turn up unannounced at a billionaire's home and start asking questions without a really good reason. If Geoff is acquainted with him, he must know lots of other *interesting* characters."

She nodded. "He does. Keith Newman for one—a retired lawyer—actually, he's a seedy little shyster, but from what I gather, Geoff does a lot of business with him."

"Okay, I know Keith. Not the worst person I've ever known. But certainly not the best. Maybe I'll pay him a visit."

I paused for a second.

Then I said, "I'll be straight with you, Pam. If your husband is mixing in those circles, he's up to his neck in things that are certainly *not* legit. You understand that, right?"

"Of course I understand it," Pam snapped. "Just because I look like a dumb bimbo doesn't mean I *am* a dumb bimbo."

"I never for a moment thought that you were."

I looked away, staring at one of the paintings.

Then I said, "I'm sorry. I just think we have to be really honest with one another. From what you've told me so far, I think your husband could be up to his eyeballs in shit."

THE ONLY THING I was sure of when I left Pam Hewes's house was this: Pam Hewes didn't know very much about the work life of Geoff Hewes. Either that or Pam was going to be totally closemouthed about it. And if that was the case I couldn't help her. I wouldn't help her.

I'd seen relationships like the Heweses' before. Usual story: an average guy who'd never grown up, fancied himself as a player, seen too many episodes of *The Sopranos*. Failed to realize that it was put together by writers and actors. The wife? She was usually the genuinely better half, the one with the straight career, or a "homemaker," bringing up the kids, worrying, trying to keep it all together. It transcended class.

Pam had told me you could usually find Keith Newman at a pub in Darlinghurst called the Cloverleaf. He held court there.

I Googled him on my iPhone. I could use a quick refresher course in Keith Newman. Over the years, Newman had worked for half a dozen prominent Sydney underworld figures. He was a good lawyer, saved the bacon of some key crime figures in the late seventies. Made a fortune in the eighties...sources unknown. He then invested it with some former clients whose business activities were what might be called dubious.

Newman's investments had paid off—he'd turned his nest egg into a golden hen and retired to a mansion on Chinaman's Beach on the Lower North Shore, a place known to Sydney-siders as Ka-ching Man's Beach.

The Cloverleaf was exactly the sort of dump a wealthy businessman with a yen for the "dark side" might frequent. It stank of beer, bad lighting, and slot machines that were most likely rigged.

I walked in and immediately spotted Keith sitting at the bar. It was still only five o'clock, early for most of the pub's clientele by the look of it. There were half a dozen guys in the room.

"Mr. Newman?" I said, pulling up a stool and glancing at the bartender. "Foster's please."

"And you are...?"

"Sorry, Craig Gisto." I extended a hand. Newman looked at it as if it might be infested with germs. Then he shook it.

"I know you, don't I, Mr. Gisto?" he said.

"As a matter of fact, we have met. Once when I was assisting in prosecuting the tax collection rackets for the longshoremen's union. And another time..."

Newman finished my sentence for me: "Another time when I was defending Leo McNulty when he was *falsely* accused of police bribery. I won that one."

"In a way, not really, though. Because McNulty was still on the street three months later, we were able to get him on a kiddie porn distribution charge. McNulty's still on holiday at Wellington Correctional."

Apparently Newman didn't care to discuss this case any further.

"And how might I help you, Mr. Gisto?" he said.

"I'm actually looking for Geoff Hewes. Heard he likes this pub."

"Why?"

"Why?"

"Yeah, Craig. Why do you wanna see this Geoff Hewes fellow?"

"I'd like to discuss a business prospectus with him," I said.

Newman looked around the room: the shrimpy little bartender with the red bulbous nose; the underage kid in the jeans and Afro at one end of the bar; the muscle-bound goon at the other end. Then Newman leaned in close to me.

"I'm afraid I can't help you. I don't know anyone named Geoff Hewes."

"That's too bad for me. I understand that Hewes has some fine connections to some of the city's most enthusiastic investors. I was hoping for an introduction. Say, to people like...Al Loretto."

Newman shrugged. His eyes widened.

"Al Loretto, huh? Now there's another name I'm not familiar with," he said.

"Everyone knows Al Loretto," I said, fighting hard to keep the conversation at a bantering we're-just-two-friendly-guys-bullshitting level.

Newman's jaw tightened. "Like I said, I'm not familiar with this Art Loretto."

I nodded. "Al. His name is Al. It's not Art."

"Either one. I'm not familiar with either Al or Art. Are they brothers?"

"You know what, Keith? You and I should have been born when they still had vaudeville," I said. "We'd have made a mint. We'd be funny as shit."

Just then a song came on the jukebox. The Moody Blues, "Nights in White Satin." I've always hated it. A fat-ass goon at the bar, a black kid who looked like Urkel trying to look like Jay Z, and a bartender so drunk he had mastered only one sentence: "Waddle ya 'av?" All this and the Moody Blues. When I stepped through the door of the Golden Wheel, did I step back to the seventies also?

Finally I said, "You ever go up to Wellington and visit Leo McNulty for a few hours?" I asked.

"McNulty? I don't know anyone calls himself McNulty," Newman said.

"We were talking about Leo McNulty about five minutes ago, about how you got him off the cop bribery rap. We were just discussing him."

"Not me," Newman said. "You can't keep confusing the wops and the micks and the captains and the privates. What I'm trying to tell you, but you refuse to get it. I don't know anybody. I don't know my mother, my aunt Mary, the rabbi at my temple. I know who I'm told to know. And you, Craig, you'd better play by these rules...or leave the game completely."

The bartender stumbled toward us. He asked Newman if he needed a refill on his brandy Alexander.

"Yes. That'd be just the taste I'd like to taste again," Newman said, and he gave the bartender a slight thumbs-up sign. Immediately the bartender asked me if I needed a refill.

I never got a chance to answer. Keith Newman answered for me.

"Mr. Gisto's got to run. Just put his Foster's on my tab. So he can leave."

"Thanks anyway, but no," I said. "I'm not leaving. I really would like another beer."

"Please don't, Mr, Gisto. Do what you're told."

Newman's face was turning pinkish-red. I looked squarely at the bartender and said, "I'm very thirsty, my man."

Keith lowered himself from the barstool. He was a whole lot shorter than I'd have guessed. Not that anyone would ever ask me to guess. Keith flicked his head toward the right.

Within, I'd say, a tenth of a second, a guy was standing next to us. At first I couldn't quite work out where he'd sprung from. Then I realized that it was the huge thug sitting at the end of the bar.

"Hey, Borg," Newman said, quietly. "Could you escort this gentleman from the premises, please?"

The goon grabbed my arm.

"Did I offend you in some way?" I asked.

"Yeah, buddy, you did," Keith Newman snapped. "I wouldn't bother putting up a fight. We call my big friend here Borg... 'Resistance is futile.'"